The Grace Writers

Heather Morse Alexander

The Grace Writers
Copyright © 2025
By Heather Morse Alexander

Published by St. Helens Press
Toledo, Washington
www.sthelenspress.com

ISBN 978-1-963467-07-9 print
ISBN 978-1-963467-09-3 ebook

Library of Congress Control Number:

Cover design by Kathy Campbell

Publisher's note: This is a work of fiction. Names, characters, organizations, places, events, and incidents are used fictitiously or products of the author's imagination. Any resemblance to persons living or dead is coincidental.

Subjects: Novel / Contemporary Fiction / Christian Fiction

Dedication

To Donna Morse,
the woman who
has encouraged me to write
throughout my life.
Love you, Mom.

"Make straight paths for your feet

so that what is lame may not be put out of joint

but rather be healed."

Hebrews 12:13 (ESV)

Chapter 1

CLAIRE BALDWIN WATCHED the sheet tacked over the open window flutter softly in the dark of the unfamiliar room. The fresh air attempted to banish the stale smell of a house steeped in years of vacancy, to no avail.

She listened to the rhythm of her husband's breathing.

As always, Will slept with ease.

Claire dropped her gaze to the window seat, imagining how pretty it would be with a fresh coat of paint and a soft cushion. She loved the bungalow's vintage moldings, heart pine floors, and paned windows. The nooks and crannies reminded her of the quirky home they'd left in suburban Colorado. This was the only house for sale in town with three bedrooms and a basement—albeit unfinished—enough room for her grown children to visit all at once. Thankfully, its weathered charm was exactly what Claire wanted.

She closed her eyes and took in a long, deep breath—beginning her nightly game of hide-and-seek with slumber.

Where are you, sleep?

The game began innocently enough—her mind rehashing the events of the day and the laundry list of tasks to complete. Then, if sleep didn't come soon enough, Claire ventured into deeper, darker thoughts. Tonight, they pounced quickly.

It was only a year ago that Will had roused her from a deep sleep, his strong, commanding voice stripped of strength. She could still feel the punch of realization that he bore bad news.

Tears filled her eyes as memories assaulted her in the dark of the strange room.

Her husband was the first police officer to arrive on the scene. He recognized the bumper sticker immediately: *Proud Grandparents of a U.S. Army Soldier*, untarnished—the only part of the car not crumpled like a discarded receipt.

Her parents' car.

They were hit head-on—killed instantly.

A drunk driver.

Claire rolled to her side—her pillow wet with tears. She sniffed quietly, trying not to wake Will again with her sorrow.

She mourned the little things—her mom's laugh and her dad's optimism. She missed watching their banter with the kids, and conversation, the ability to pick up the phone and talk, or run across the street to share a cup of coffee. She missed that the most.

The void, vast and deep, boiled at the edges.

Then, as always, grief turned to anger. That one detail—the drunk driver was a deacon at their church, a pillar of righteousness. Claire squeezed her eyes shut—as much an attempt to stop the tears as to stifle her rage.

The playlist of comments from people at church filled her mind:

"He said he wasn't drunk. Are you saying he's a liar?"

"He is devastated by what happened."

"Thank God the charges were dropped. He's suffered so much already!"

And the pièce de résistance, "Forgive him, Claire. God works all things for His good."

Claire's mind swirled with the admonitions of people she thought were friends.

She reached blindly to the bedside table. No tissues. She hadn't unpacked them yet. She wiped her tears with the sheet and sniffed again.

"You okay?" Will's drowsy voice echoed in the near-empty room.

"Yeah, I'm fine." Claire had told that lie so many times that it flowed from her lips as if true.

"Love you." Will rolled over, and it wasn't long before his breathing took on the heaviness of sleep.

"I love you, too." Claire whispered her declaration to Will, her parents, and her faraway kids.

෴

Claire opened one eye and focused on the mottled ceiling. *Where am I?*

She rubbed the sleep from her eyes and remembered. Her arm touched the covers beside her. *Where's Will?*

Her husband backed through the bedroom door, gripping two steaming mugs of coffee.

"You're awake." He maneuvered around a stack of boxes, set the mugs on the bedside table, and drew her into his arms.

As she breathed in Will's scent, comfort washed over her. The bedroom was unfamiliar, but Will was constant. Claire squeezed him tighter. "How many boxes did you have to open to find the coffee maker?"

Claire heard him smile. He always let air escape from his nose when he smiled. "Six."

Her mouth turned up in a grin despite the churning in her gut. She leaned back to look in his eyes. "When do you go to work?"

"Nine o'clock. You'll be okay, right?"

"I have plenty to do—I'll be fine."

"That's my girl." Will handed her a mug. "Wish me luck. I'm going to search for the cereal and bowls."

Claire threw her legs over the side of the bed. She stretched on her way to the window and pushed aside the breeze-blown sheet. A beam of sunlight peeked through the branches of an oak, and the grass sparkled with dew.

Her mind wandered to a moment just a few days ago. She and Kate stood in the dorm parking lot. Claire hugged her far too long, breathing in the scent of her daughter's hair, her cool ear against her cheek. Her baby didn't pull away.

"I love you, Mom. Thanks for everything."

Pain seared Claire's heart as she loosened her embrace.

"I love you, too, sweetie." One last kiss on the cheek, and Kate walked away, her ponytail bobbing to and fro just as it had when she left for kindergarten.

Claire missed her kids and daily motherhood, but she yearned for so much more—peace of mind and relief from the hurt she nourished as a prized possession.

Would she like it here in Walters Bluff? Was it a good idea to move? Yes. It had to be. When Will's old friend asked him to apply for this position, Claire encouraged him to do so. She wanted to escape the weight of constant reminders, pity, and judgment. Will was ready for a slower pace. Yes, it was a good move at precisely the right time.

But this was an enormous change.

Tears filled her eyes. Through the blur, a goldfinch jumped from branch to branch. One more jump, and it flew away—much like her kids, her parents, her faith in the church … and in the God she thought she knew.

The ocean of grief has a wicked undertow, but *this* morning, Claire wrestled herself from its grip. She dried her tears. Today was the first day of a new life.

Chapter 2

GUY WITHERSPOON MADE one final rip with the table saw. He removed his earmuffs and examined the board's edge—time for a new blade. His stomach growled as the door flew open.

"Breakfast is ready," Bertie called.

"Perfect timing." Guy followed her to the kitchen, and they sat together, eating their morning oatmeal. He read the newspaper while Bertie gazed out the window as she always did, watching birds at the feeder.

Guy peered over the paper at his wife, her silver hair pulled into a low, soft knot, and the white eyelet apron spotted with evidence of years in the kitchen. Her mouth turned up in a smile.

Bertie *always* smiled. It was one of the things he loved most about her.

"Let's walk downtown." Guy folded the paper. "I need a new blade for my saw."

"How's the cradle coming? I can't wait to see Olivia rock her dolls in it. I've almost finished the quilt."

Guy loved how her eyes sparkled when she talked about the grandkids.

"It's coming along. And I'm carving the chess pieces for Matt. It'll all be done in time for Christmas. Good thing I still have a couple of months."

"You always get it done. I have faith in you."

"God bless you, Bertie."

"Maybe we could pick something up from Goodies on the way home and meet the new neighbors." Bertie's voice sang with excitement as she cleared the table.

"Good idea."

Guy slipped on his coat and whispered a little prayer, asking God to bring people to his path who might need a blessing. A few minutes later, he and Bertie strolled out the door, arm in arm.

"God bless you!" Guy waved to Amos Kicklighter as he scuffled down his broken cement path to fetch the paper.

Amos waved his hand as if to dismiss the blessing. His robe fell open, revealing red plaid boxers and a worn T-shirt. "Dag nabbit," he mumbled, yanking it closed.

Guy squeezed Bertie's hand as she stifled a giggle.

A gentle wind rustled yellow and orange leaves on oak and maple trees. He glanced down at his wife. Her eyes watched the school bus on the corner of Sweet Pea and Main. A line of children climbed aboard—the cacophony of laughter and conversation wafting through the cool air.

"I love autumn," Bertie said.

They waited for the bus to pass and turned to walk down Main Street.

"You know what, Bert? A thought just occurred to me. It's fritter season."

"Oh, for heaven's sake, you're right."

Guy's hand was pulled forward as her pace quickened.

Chief Miller emerged from The Daily Brew with a steaming cup.

"Good morning, Chief. God bless you." Guy held the door open as the police chief pushed through.

"Thank you, Guy." He hugged Bertie. "I'm excited for retirement but sad to leave my friends. Gotta move closer to the grandkids." He smiled. "You know, of all the things I'm going to miss about Walters Bluff, I'll miss your blessings the most."

"We'll miss you, too." Guy squeezed Chief Miller's free hand in both of his. "Word has it your replacement moved in next door to us."

"Will Baldwin's a good man. I worked with him years ago." The chief sipped his coffee. "Walters Bluff is lucky to have him."

࿐

On the way to the kitchen, Claire heard a knock at the door. She opened it to find a tall, slender man in a wool jacket holding a bakery box and a newspaper. A plump woman stood beside him—a smile forcing her blue eyes into happy little half-moons.

"Welcome to the neighborhood. I'm Guy Witherspoon, and this is my better half, Bertie."

"I'm Claire Baldwin." She stood in the doorway.

Will appeared from the bedroom, straightening his duty belt. "And I'm Will. Come on in." He reached around Claire and shook Guy's outstretched hand.

They stepped back, making room in the entryway.

"God bless you both," Guy said. "We live in the blue house next door."

Bertie squeezed Claire's arm. "We're just so happy to have new neighbors."

"The new police chief should be up on all the important news." He handed Will the thin *Durham County Herald*.

"Thank you." Will examined the front page.

"Published every Tuesday and Friday."

Bertie nudged her husband. "Give them the fritters." She leaned toward Claire. "Goodies Bakery has the best apple fritters."

Guy extended the box to Claire. His infectious smile reminded her of her father. His brown eyes sparkled, and friendly wrinkles formed on either side of them.

"Welcome to Walters Bluff," Bertie gushed as if speaking on behalf of the whole town. "I'd like to invite you to our church, First Community—the big white church smack in the center of town."

Her enthusiasm was attractive, but Claire bristled. *No way.*

"Thanks for the invitation. I was going to ask about churches in the area," Will said.

Claire's head jerked to look at her husband. His comment spoke volumes.

He was ready.

I'm not.

"Folks here are very welcoming, you'll see." Bertie patted her arm as if sensing her discomfort. "We'll get out of your hair. Enjoy the fritters." She took Guy's hand as he opened the door.

"If you need anything, you know where to find us." They stepped into the crisp autumn sunshine.

"What a glorious morning," Bertie declared as they maneuvered down the porch steps.

Claire watched them walk down the sidewalk. She closed the door. "They seem very nice."

"We should go," Will said.

"Where?" Claire's mind raced. *No. Not happening.*

"You know what I'm talking about. First Community. We should go." Will's voice was firm.

Claire looked into her husband's eyes. They were determined and weary. It had been nearly a year since they'd darkened the door of the church Claire had attended since she was a girl. The hurt was too great—too raw.

He took her hand in his. "We need to go back. It's time." As Will's jaw clenched, she knew he wasn't budging.

≈

Claire spent the morning unpacking boxes and putting away dishes, pots, and pans. Four boxes blocked the hallway, each filled with items that didn't fit into her new, cozy kitchen. She poured another cup of coffee and picked up the newspaper.

The Dear Wanda column caught her eye.

> *Dear Wanda,*
> *How do I ask a girl to the hayride at the Autumn Festival? What do I do if she says no?*
> *Signed, Scared.*

> *Dear Scared,*
> *Mr. Henderson asked me to go to the hayride fifty-four years ago, and I said yes. There are no guarantees, but how will you know if you don't ask? Every girl likes to be invited, but if she says no, square your shoulders and tell her to have a lovely day. It won't kill you to be rejected, and you'll be proud of yourself for trying. The next time will be a tiny bit easier. Good luck, young man.*

Claire smiled. She'd moved to Podunk, Nowhere, far from the anguish and memories of home.

She peered into the boxes of stuff she could no longer keep. In a way, it was a cleansing, a purging of junk they thought they needed. Like church. She'd washed herself clean of them, and Will wanted to drag her right back into the muck. Claire sighed as she grabbed another box, knelt on the living room floor, and ran a blade through a line of tape. The cardboard flaps popped open, and a handmade box met her gaze.

Claire's heart beat in her ears as she lifted it to the coffee table.

On her thirteenth birthday, her father presented her with the carved walnut box. The top featured her name carved amid a tangle of vines and flowers.

She lifted the lid.

Inside, in his tidy print, he'd written, "Happy 13th birthday, Punkin. I love you. Dad."

A tear fell to the letter sitting atop the pile of keepsakes— her name and address printed neatly on the front. Claire examined it. The flap remained sealed, the envelope as crisp as the day it arrived.

She tucked it back into the box, shut the lid, and fastened the latch.

Chapter 3

CLAIRE CLOSED HER JOURNAL—angst about visiting the First Community Church filled two pages. She thought about ripping them from her notebook and throwing the pages in the trash, but she left them for now. How many times had she wadded up and tossed her thoughts in the trash? Too many to count. It was cathartic to release her feelings on paper, but she dared not let anyone read her rage-filled rants.

She reluctantly chose a dress and straightened it around her waist. Claire sifted through her checklist. Did it make her look fat? Was it too tight, wrinkled, or short? Then, the real question revealed itself. What will *this* church be like?

How did I let Will talk me into this?

Imagining the worst was easy with betrayal as fresh as the autumn air.

Claire pulled on her coat and clutched Will's hand as they descended the porch steps. Sunshine warmed her face and calmed her spirit. They strode down Sweet Pea Street and turned onto Main, arriving at the First Community Church of Walters Bluff, smack in the middle of town, just as Bertie had described. The reader board on the lawn announced: *Our church is like fudge—sweet with a few nuts.* Claire grinned, despite her pounding heart, as they walked through the small parking lot and up the steps to the tall, carved doors held open by weathered bricks.

As they crossed the threshold, the aroma of old books, coffee, and pine cleaner mixed into a familiar scent—Grandma's house and judgment, love, and angst.

Church.

"Welcome to First Community." An older woman with dyed blonde hair and a smear of coral lipstick hurried over to them. "You must be new in town. I'm Joan Appleton. My husband is the pastor here at First Community."

"You came!" Bertie spotted them across the foyer. "Joan, this is Will and Claire Baldwin. Will is the new police chief."

"Thank you for coming. After the service, I'll introduce you to Karl—Pastor Karl." Joan winked and shuffled away.

Bertie led them to the sanctuary—a grand room with large windows. Panes of stained glass cast squares of colorful light over the congregation. Wide-planked wooden floors squeaked as Bertie ushered them to a pew in the center of the sanctuary.

A tiny woman scooted into the row behind them and tapped Claire on the shoulder. "I'm Millie Mitchum. We're just so happy to have you with us this morning." Her friendly brown eyes sparkled in the light of the grand room.

"It's a pleasure to meet you. I'm Claire." She smiled at the woman.

A tall man led the singing, one hand holding a hymnal, the other swinging back and forth as if the congregation were a choir. The pianist leaned backward and forward as she played, dramatically lifting her hands from the keys. A woman nearby sang off-key—confidently, loudly—her voice holding notes too long, then rushing to catch up.

Claire didn't sing. Instead, she listened to the words of a hymn her father had loved so much.

He leadeth me, O blessèd thought.
O words with heav'nly comfort fraught!
Whate'er I do, where'er I be
Still 'tis God's hand that leadeth me.

He leadeth me? Did God lead me to this small town—to this pew today? She swallowed hard. *Did he lead my parents to their deaths a year ago?* Claire surveyed the congregation. Souls standing erect, clutching hymnbooks, voices raised in song. Church used to be a comfortable place—home even. *Who are these people? They smile and sing, closing their eyes in reverence, but deep down, what are they really like?* Claire's eyes landed on the hymnal—the piano's trills an accompaniment to her thoughts.

Lord I would clasp thy hand in mine,
Nor ever murmur, nor repine;
Content whatever lot I see
Still 'tis my God that leadeth me.

Content whatever lot I see? Hardly. How will I ever find contentment again? The words repeated in Claire's mind as music played.

So much angst churned in her heart as the piano faded and the tall man opened a folder.

"I see we have visitors this morning." He nodded in their direction. "Let's show them a hearty First Community welcome, shall we?"

"Welcome." Several congregants raised their voices.

"Glad you're here." Others exclaimed.

Claire felt her face flush. *Am I embarrassed or relieved? Both.*

As he continued with announcements, Millie tapped Claire's shoulder again. "The Ladies Auxiliary meeting is a great way to get acquainted," she whispered.

"Good to know."

Another announcement and another tap. "The Livingstons are missionaries to India. That's why we're having a curry church supper. Doesn't matter what you bring. Just slap some curry in it."

The announcements droned on. She felt another tap.

"The Grace Writers is so much fun. If you like to write, it's the only place to be on a Tuesday morning."

"Interesting. Thank you, Millie." She mulled the idea of attending a writing group as the pastor began his sermon. Claire began journaling after her parents died. At first, she wrote her favorite memories of them, then sorrowful essays filled with questions and words of anger—at the deacon, at the church that protected him, and ultimately at God.

Claire's interest was piqued. *What do they write about? Can I write something worth reading?* She ruminated on her questions and the possibility of writing—for fun. Her mind wandered until the service ended. She and Will meandered to the foyer, pausing for greetings from parishioners.

Joan introduced them to Pastor Karl. As Will and the pastor talked, Joan grabbed a woman's arm as she hustled by. "Josephine, this is Claire Baldwin."

The older woman appeared irritated by the diversion. Her lips formed a thin, straight line.

Claire smiled and held out her hand. "Nice to meet you."

Josephine made a fuss of moving her large Bible from one arm to the other. She quickly gave Claire's hand a limp shake and then made another fuss of moving the Bible back to its original position. She looked Claire over and whispered to Joan, "Are we done here?"

"Yes, I just wanted you two to meet," Joan said.

"Fine, did you see Wyatt Bingham whiz through here like a shot? I need to find his mother. Have you seen her?" Josephine's gaze scanned the people passing by.

"No, but don't worry. Wyatt isn't hurting anyone."

"He's not hurting anyone until someone gets hurt." Josephine scurried away, eyes darting.

Joan sighed. "Church ladies."

How refreshing.

After a few more introductions, Claire's face ached from smiling.

Will held her hand as they strode between the tall church doors and down Main Street toward the diner. "That was friendly," he said.

"Yes, they all seem very nice, but …."

"Give them a chance."

"Ugh. I just …"

"It's hard for me, too, but I miss having a church family. I know, deep down, you do, too. Try to let your guard down a little." His hand squeezed hers.

The morning reminded her how much she *had* loved belonging to a church for all those decades, before everything changed. *How can I simply move on?* A wave of grief threatened—pain over the loss of her parents, her church, and the belief that God's people were inherently good.

A bell jingled as Claire and Will pushed open the diner's door. They scooted through the crowded tables to the counter and found two empty stools. A pretty waitress dropped a menu in front of them as she flew past on her way to the kitchen. Claire wound her arm through Will's, and they examined it.

"Who're you?"

Claire leaned forward, looking to the other side of her husband to see who possessed the gravelly voice. She saw a bomber jacket covered with pins—in it, a man with deep lines around piercing blue-gray eyes. He had an unkempt beard, and his hair, graying at the temples, was pulled into a thin ponytail at the base of his head. The stale stench of alcohol stung Claire's nose.

A drunk. She took a deep breath.

Will offered his hand. "I'm Will, and this is Claire. And you are…?"

"Harley Bushkin the third," he growled. "New in town?"

"Yes, the new police chief."

"Good to meet ya. I own the bar on Main."

Of course.

"What'll ya have?" The waitress reappeared, pen poised on her ticket book. "The mac and cheese is dry, but the pie's good—blackberry today."

"Jeannie'll never steer ya wrong," Harley added.

"Pie sounds good. I'll have mine à la mode." Claire set aside the menu and looked around the diner. Maybe they could move to an empty table away from this guy.

"I'll have a hot fudge sundae, heavy on the hot fudge—and an extra cherry." Will winked at Claire.

"Be right back." Jeannie ripped the ticket from the book and disappeared through a swinging door.

Harley hunched over a cup of coffee topped with a curl of steam. A wad of empty sugar packets littered the counter next to him. "Skip lunch and go straight for dessert. I like the way you folks think."

"Stressed is desserts spelled upside-down." A rotund waitress topped off Harley's coffee as she ran a towel across the counter in front of Will and Claire.

"Backward." Harley chuckled. "Dottie's a walking cliché if she can get 'em right."

"Backward, upside-down, what difference does it make?" Dottie snorted as she headed to another table to top off the coffee.

Harley smiled and took a swig from the steaming cup.

"You're a biker, I presume," Will said. "Your name and the pins give it away."

"Nope. I'm a Cadillac guy—love the old Caddies. I don't own a bike." Harley chuckled. "Folks give me the pins when they stop to wet their whistles."

Why is Will talking to this guy? Claire noticed Jeannie removing empty plates from a table by the door as a family gathered their things to go.

"How long have you owned the bar?" Will asked.

"Twenty-four years, but my great-great-granddaddy opened it over a hundred years ago."

Claire shifted in her seat. *I wonder if he overserves deacons who get drunk and kill people.*

She glanced at the table again. The family lingered. *Come on, leave already.*

Harley sat up a little straighter. "I'm proud of the place, although I thought I'd go into law enforcement as a kid." He sighed. "The bar's our legacy. Couldn't let the family down."

"Sounds like you made a success of it," Will said.

Claire took another look around the diner, silently pleading for someone to vacate a table.

"Sure enough." Harley rolled off the stool. "Nice to meet you folks. Cops always have good stories to tell, and I love to hear 'em. You know where to find me."

"Oh, I've got stories." Will chuckled, stood, and shook the gruff man's hand. "Pleasure to meet you."

"Pleasure's mine. Later, Jeannie." Harley nodded to Claire and waved to Dottie as she carried a plate to another patron.

As he ambled his way to the door, Harley greeted each person he passed.

"He's a teddy bear. You'd never know it lookin' at 'im," Jeannie said.

Claire bit her lip. *A drunk is a drunk.*

Chapter 4

CLAIRE LIFTED A STACK of books and arranged them on a shelf. *Hmmm. Where are the rest?*

"How's it going in here?" Will leaned against the door as he buttoned his uniform shirt.

"Are there any more boxes of books in the garage?" Claire asked.

"I don't think so. I brought everything into the house." Will tucked his shirt into his pants. "I'm missing stuff, too. I'll bet we left some of our things with the antiques in storage."

"Great. We'll never find them." Claire sighed.

Will scratched his chin. "You know, we need to clear out that storage unit eventually … you *could* still go forward with your plans to open a shop.

"How?"

"There's that vacant storefront downtown." Will's blue eyes fixed on hers.

He's serious.

"My *mom* and I were going to open the antique shop."
Claire's eyes filled. "How could I do it alone?"

"You could. I know you could." He moved toward her.
"You've been stuck in limbo. I want to see that light in your eyes
again." His strong arms pulled her into a hug.

Claire leaned into his embrace.

"It's been a hard year. I believe your mom *and* your dad
would want you to proceed with your plans. You have
everything you need to do it."

"Except my mom."

"I know it seems impossible, but I'll always support whatever
you do and help however I can." He kissed her head. "I think
moving ahead with your plans would be cathartic somehow."

"I love you." Claire brushed a tear from her cheek.

Will squeezed her tight and released her. "Love you too." He
lifted his service belt around his waist, lined up the Velcro, and
pressed it in place. "I have to go."

Claire followed him to the door and kissed him goodbye.

Her mind swirled with thoughts of the boxes and furniture
stacked in the enormous storage unit. The plan was to open a
shop, and they were about to sign a lease when …. How could
she deal with it all now? Her head ached at the thought.

Can I open an antique shop? She plopped on the sofa. *I wish
I could call Mom.* Claire played out the conversation in her
mind. *She'd tell me to go for it.*

I wish I could talk to her about going to that church. What
would her mom think of Josephine? She chuckled. Her mind
moved to Harley—an alcoholic, no doubt.

Claire swallowed hard, but white-hot anger snuck in.
Bitterness is a warm fire for the cold anguish of grief. Brooding
on the wrong done to her and her parents was somehow
satisfying. *Dad always said giving and forgiveness determines the*

quality of our lives and receiving it, our destination in death. But it doesn't matter. No one's apologized. And God doesn't seem to care.
She drew in a deep breath. Her mother would tell her to stay busy—bake something. She meandered to the kitchen and opened the old metal recipe box. Her mother's handwriting comforted her as she picked through the cards. She found the brownie recipe, looked it over, and tucked it back. She didn't need it. She'd been making the same brownies for decades. The secret was a splash of vanilla.

As they baked, a fudgy aroma filled the house. Claire emptied a few more boxes of linens and craft supplies, adding another box to the giveaway pile. The doorbell rang just as the timer chimed. She quickly pulled the brownies from the oven, set them on the stove, and hustled to the door.

She'd barely cracked it open when a foil casserole dish was thrust through with a chorus of voices singing, "Welcome to Walters Bluff!"

Two smiling women stood on the porch.

A short, chubby lady stepped forward. Her dark skin was highlighted by beautiful silver-streaked ebony hair smoothed into a tidy, tight bun. "I'm Ella Mae Walker." She placed her hand on her generous bosom and leaned forward with concern. "We planned to be here sooner."

"My fault." A tall woman with impossibly red hair raised her hand. "It was just a little fire, thank the Lord. The only casualty was my favorite potholder."

"This happens all the time," Ella Mae whispered.

"Oh, my." Claire didn't know what else to say.

"I'm Rita Reyburn." The tall woman spoke. "We represent the Ladies Auxiliary at the First Community Church. It's wonderful that your husband accepted the call to be our new police chief."

"Where's the kitchen?" Ella Mae's eyes scanned the house.

"This way." Claire led them through the living and dining rooms. "Pardon the mess. I'm still unpacking."

"What's that smell?" Ella Mae lifted her nose.

"Oh, I just took brownies out of the oven."

"A heavenly aroma." Rita closed her eyes and inhaled a long, drawn-out sniff while setting a grocery bag on the counter.

"They might need a touch of vanilla." Ella Mae set a casserole on the counter and removed a canvas bag from her arm. She winked at Claire. "I know brownies."

"Hush, Ella Mae." Rita smiled apologetically. "Let's see here. We brought apple cider from Adelaide Orchard, homemade pickles, jam, and a couple of casseroles, so you won't have to worry about cooking dinner while you settle in." She patted the bottom of a grocery bag.

"I baked you a loaf of my award-winning lemon pound cake." Ella Mae beamed.

"Thank you." Claire tucked a curl behind her ear.

"You're more than welcome," Rita said. "We love spoiling folks. I was just saying, I think it's been a year since someone new moved to town. Didn't I say that, Ella Mae?"

"Yes, you sure did."

Claire looked at Ella Mae. "Wait, did you say my brownies need vanilla?"

"Oh, I have a nose for baked goods. Just my opinion." She placed a paper lace doily on the counter before setting her pound cake, wrapped in cellophane, atop it.

"Ella Mae bakes the *best* brownies," Rita said, looking around the kitchen. "I've always wondered what this house was like inside."

"I make the best baked goods, period." Ella Mae chuckled. "That *sounds* conceited, but it's what everyone says, so ... not my words."

Claire chuckled.

Ella Mae glanced over, unsmiling.

"Well, I'm sure looking forward to trying that cake," she said. "I'll bet it's amazing."

"It is. I can attest." Rita had her hand on Ella Mae's shoulder as if attempting to direct the woman to bite her tongue.

Claire watched as they opened the refrigerator and deposited the casseroles inside. Rita put a note on the fridge, attaching it with a First Community Church magnet. "If you have questions or need help finding services in town, call the number on the magnet," she offered.

Claire straightened her shirt. "Thank you for your hospitality. I'm sorry Will isn't here. He's working today."

"And we're thankful for his dedication," Rita said. "Do you have children?"

"Three. All grown. Our youngest just started college."

"Well, what a perfect time to move. A brand-new start with an empty nest." Rita seemed so sure.

"Yes." Claire agreed but wondered if it were true. The loss of her parents, her kids grown, and moving from the only place she'd ever lived—it was more than she'd anticipated. As she tried to quell the emotions overwhelming her. Rita waved Ella Mae toward the front door.

"And we're off! My phone number's on the slip of paper on your fridge. Have Will call if he needs help with the heavy lifting. My Hank loves to work."

Claire watched their eyes scan the house as they headed out the front door.

"One more thing before we go." Rita reached into her pocket and handed Claire an envelope. "An invitation to the Grace Writers—Tuesday mornings at nine. I do hope you'll join us."

"Millie invited me too. What does everyone write? Fiction or Nonfiction?"

"Whatever you want. Our prompt is to write a poem, but I know for a fact that Josephine isn't going to write one, and I don't think I am either. It's a suggestion."

"Thank you—for everything. I'll think about it."

The two ladies shuffled out the door into the breezy autumn afternoon.

Claire shut it behind them.

What were their names again? Oh yes, Ella Mae and Rita. Her face broke into a smile. "My brownies need vanilla?" The smile disappeared. "Who does she think she is? We just met." Claire wandered to the lemon pound cake, removing the wrapping. She sliced a corner from the end. "We'll see who needs vanilla." The morsel of cake melted in her mouth. Perfectly tart, buttery, and delicious. "Maybe my brownies *do* need more vanilla."

She opened Rita's invitation.

> *You're invited to The Grace Writers.*
> *Tuesday mornings at 9 a.m. in the Fellowship Room,*
> *First Community Church.*
> *The Grace Writers was formed to inspire women of*
> *faith to write their stories. Whether you journal, blog, or*
> *dream of writing the Great American Novel, you can join*
> *us for inspiration and encouragement (and Ella Mae's*
> *treats).*
> *Hope to see you there!*
> *Rita Reyburn, Fearless Leader*

Claire smiled. This might be a fun group if Rita and Ella Mae were any indication. Maybe she'd go once and test it out.

She returned to the ever-beckoning boxes, recalling a shoebox of old photos. People she didn't know. Maybe she could write some of their stories—make up a fun family history for herself. The thought of writing renewed her vigor to unpack and create an inspiring space in one of the spare bedrooms. As she sorted the contents of so many boxes, her mind wandered to Sunday morning at church. Despite her angst, there was also a familiarity, like church felt when she was a child, before the harsh reality had tainted her. People *always* disappoint.

She flattened another empty box and added it to the growing pile of cardboard. The next carton was marked *Mom and Dad's stuff*. Claire drew in a breath as if it would protect her from yet another swell of emotion. She pulled at the tape and opened the flaps. A bulging shoebox sat on top of a pile of framed photos.

There it is.

Claire looked inside to find a mess of black-and-white snapshots. A smile formed as she sifted through the photos: families enjoying a picnic, a birthday party, beach days, and a funeral. Individuals standing on porches, in front of houses, cars, and fields—the stuff of American life from days gone by.

Enchanted by the pictures, she didn't immediately jump up when the doorbell rang. After the second ring, she raced to answer. She found Bertie standing on the porch. "Come in."

"I just popped by to tell you it was so good to see you at church. I hope you'll see fit to come back. We're just a bunch of sinners who love Jesus." Bertie smiled.

"Yes, well ....."

"I know you've been through big changes moving to this little piece of heaven, but I hope you feel welcome."

"We do. Thank you.

"Well, we're happy you're here. And I'm excited to see what you do with the house."

"It'll be fun to spruce up the place. The wallpaper's coming down as soon as I'm done unpacking."

"Well, I'm keeping you from it," Bertie said. "You know where to find me if you need a break."

"I do." Claire smiled.

Bertie turned to leave. "Oh, and I almost forgot, our husbands were discussing woodworking. Will wants to learn a few things, and Guy loves to teach. He wondered if this Saturday morning would work. And if so, you come too, and we'll visit."

"That'll work just fine."

Bertie walked out the door. "I'll let Guy know."

Claire returned to the living room. If she didn't set aside the photos, she'd spend the whole evening gazing at them. She picked at a curled seam of faded wallpaper. It peeled off easily.

She called each of her kids as she worked, opening boxes, finding homes for the contents, and peeling paper from the walls. Their voices filled the room as she moved about— laughter offering a bit of comfort in this strange, new place.

It wasn't long before she had unpacked most of the boxes and stripped away much of the wallpaper. She finished just as Will appeared through the door. He removed his hat and smoothed his graying hair.

Claire kissed his cheek, then ran to the kitchen to slice the lemon pound cake. "Ella Mae and Rita from the church stopped by. Come and taste this cake." Claire offered Will a bite as he hung up his jacket.

Will grunted with delight. "This is so …"

"Divine. It just melts in your mouth." Claire nibbled a bite, savoring the delicacy.

"I think First Community could be our new church home." The words sounded so easy, tumbling off her husband's tongue. "Solid preaching, friendly people, what more could we ask for?"

Claire's face grew hot, and her heart pounded. "Just like that?"

"What are our choices? The Catholic church, a Lutheran church, and a Foursquare church meeting in a house. I think First Community is a good fit."

Claire looked at her husband. His eyes seemed to plead with her to give it another chance. The people she'd met so far were kind. But it was a significant risk to let them in.

"What if they're ...." She searched for the word. *Fake. Phony. Judgmental.*

"Disappointing? They will be. So what?"

"So what?" Claire looked at the handsome man, licking sticky lemon cake from his fingers. *Do you have a clue what I'm feeling?*

"We can stay stuck in our old church, which is what we would be doing if we gave up, right?" He didn't wait for her to answer. "Or we can move forward and ...."

"Risk being hurt again."

"Yes. It's a risk, Claire." He pulled her into his embrace. "I'm willing to take that risk, but I want you to be with me, and I'll be with you. Just as we've supported each other through everything."

He wants this—needs it. I wish I wanted to go, but I just don't. She looked into her husband's eyes. How could she say no when he wanted what was supposed to be good? "Okay. I'll take the risk with you."

Lord, I can't take any more disappointment.

It was her first prayer in a long time.

Chapter 5

THE MORNING SUN filtered through the oak tree in the backyard, drawing Claire's eye to a battered window box overflowing with moss. She stepped outside for a closer look.

On her way, she plucked weeds. Spent lavender, dahlias, hydrangeas, and other plants sopped up sunlight. Claire's heart leaped at the variety of flora in the overgrown yard. Spring would be like Christmas as the garden bloomed to life, unveiling hidden gifts. Were there tulip bulbs in those flower beds? Time would tell, and she could hardly wait.

She meandered to the window box.

Tucked between a dandelion and a clump of brown leaves, she spied an abandoned nest of twigs, grass, feathers, and strands of multicolored thread—a work of art. Claire gently lifted it from the box and brought the nest inside, setting it on the windowsill by her desk. She opened her notebook as a poem flowed from her heart onto the page.

Where did that come from? Her eyes moved to the envelope Rita had given her. The writing group. *And now I have a poem to share.*

Her heart pounded.

She would attend the Grace Writers meeting despite the worry that she was inviting trouble.

∂

Claire kissed Will as he stopped to thumb through a stack of mail. "You're home early."

"Law enforcement in a small town is non-stop one day and a whole lot of nothing the next," he declared. He disappeared into the bedroom to change his clothes.

"Hey, I baked an apple cake for the neighbor in the yellow house. We still haven't met him."

Will reappeared. "Sounds good. Want to go now?"

"Sure, let's pop over."

They walked hand in hand to a drooping picket fence circling a lawn dotted with yellow dandelions and white spheres of puff. They entered the yard through the opening left by a broken gate and maneuvered up the fractured cement walkway to the front door. Will rang the doorbell. It didn't work, so he knocked.

A disheveled man peeked through a curtain drawn tight in the window beside the door.

"Did you see that?" Claire whispered.

The deadbolt clicked, and the door cracked open.

"Whaddya want?" The man's eyebrows, like two caterpillars, furrowed against the bridge of his bulbous nose.

"I'm Will Baldwin, and this is my wife, Claire. We moved in next door."

"We brought you an apple cake." Claire lifted the plate.

"Oh. Just wait right there a sec." The door shut. Claire heard footsteps and then silence. A couple of minutes ticked by before the door opened again. "Had to put on my britches. Didn't 'spect no visitors."

"We just wanted to say hello and introduce ourselves."

"Amos Kicklighter, here." He sniffed the cake. "Smells all right. These apples from the tree out back there?"

"Yes. I think they're Jonagold. They're delicious." Claire tried to sound cheerful.

"Yeah, 'bout that tree. Some of them branches are over th' fence line there, and the apples made a mess in m'yard. I was wond'rin if you'd trim 'em back so's I don't have t' clean up a mess next year."

"Sure thing, Amos. I'll get on that this weekend. You're welcome to pick them if you'd like." Will smiled.

Claire noticed her husband stood a bit taller.

"Nah, I'd just a' soon eat apples in a cake than raw."

"I like the way you think," Will said. "Enjoy the cake—it's nice to meet you."

Amos shut the door without another word.

≈

Claire grabbed a notebook, pen, and the poem she'd written, gathered her courage, and strode out the door, taking in the beauty of the red and gold leaves. Her phone vibrated in her jacket pocket—a text from her son.

Michael: Mom, is it okay if I bring Annie home for Christmas?
Claire: Of course. We'd love to meet her. She must be pretty special.
Michael: ☺

Claire smiled and tucked her phone into her pocket. Was Annie as wonderful as Michael described? He certainly seemed happy and settled.

Maybe she's the one.

Claire breathed in the fragrance of autumn—smoky and sweet—as she wandered down Main Street. She thought about Kate, Emma, and Michael.

Motherhood was reduced to texts and phone calls now—many phone calls. Her heart longed to see them—to spend time with them. She could hardly wait for Thanksgiving when Kate would come home to their *new* home. In the meantime, she would try to settle into her life in Walters Bluff.

She continued toward the large white church, each step a bit slower than the one before. *What am I doing?* Claire paused at the carved wooden doors.

This is a mistake.

Despite her hesitation, she pulled the door open and stepped across the threshold.

A low hum of voices wafted from a set of double doors at the back of the foyer. It was friendly banter—like a homing beacon to her heart. Although the aroma of coffee drew her forward, her steps grew hesitant as she approached.

A few gray-haired church ladies stood in the cavernous room, chattering about the upcoming children's program. *Classic.* Claire positioned her foot for a pivot and quick retreat.

I shouldn't have come.

"Oh, look, a visitor!" Ella Mae approached, hands reaching for her.

What is she going to do? Hug me?

That's precisely what she did. The plump woman with a bright smile and happy eyes drew Claire into a squishy hug.

"Welcome to the Grace Writers. I'm Ella Mae, in case you forgot."

"So good to see you again."

"Come on in. All the ladies are here." Ella Mae pointed to the table. "Have a scone. They're the best in Walters Bluff."

With her shock of red hair, Rita hurried to Claire, taking her hand. "We have the best treats, it's true. We're so glad you decided to join us today."

There is no turning back, no escape.

The ladies standing at the table chose their seats, and Claire followed Rita to an empty chair, fumbling to remove her jacket.

Rita pointed to each woman as she introduced them. "This is Josephine, Ramona, Millie, and you met Ella Mae, oh, and that's Joan."

Claire settled into her seat. Rita sat beside her while Ella Mae fiddled with the platter of scones and napkins. The ladies greeted her and continued talking amongst themselves.

Rita raised her voice above the din. "Ladies, we should begin. Since we have a new writer with us today, we'll go around the table, introduce ourselves, and share what we like to write. And, just for fun, let's share one thing that the others may *not* know about us. Claire, you begin since you're the newbie." Rita's bracelets jingled as she straightened her notebook. She winked at Claire as if to impart courage.

Claire's heart pounded, and her face warmed. "I'm Claire. I'm married to Will. We just moved to Walters Bluff, and it's quite a change for us." She tucked a curl behind her ear. "Our kids are grown, and our nest is empty."

"Welcome." The chorus of voices echoed through the large room.

"Her husband is the new chief of police. Claire, what do you do?"

Claire hesitated. "Well, I've been a mom for the last twenty-six years, and now I'm deciding what to do next."

"Hallelujah for that." Rita sounded so confident. "I'm glad you joined us today. Do you write? If so, what do you like to write?"

"I write in my journal, but I want to write fiction." Claire hesitated. She looked around the circle of women. *Are they glad*

I'm here, or am I an intruder? "And I have a few family stories I'd like to write."

"Family stories are the best," Millie said, licking crumbs from her fingers. "I can't tell half of mine—too many skeletons in the closet."

"We've all got skeletons," Ella Mae groaned.

"Hmmmph." Josephine dabbed her mouth with a napkin and shifted in her seat.

Was she the litmus for the entire group? Perpetually irritated and holier than thou—just the type of person Claire wanted to avoid.

"We'd love to hear your stories." Rita smiled. "Millie, your turn."

"Okay, I'm Millie, but you know that." The petite woman adjusted her glasses. Her brown eyes sparkled. "And I own Stuff and Things, a second-hand store. It's a block that way." She pointed to the right.

"It's the other way," Josephine said, pointing left.

"Oh, yes, I think you're right. I'm so discombobulated in this big room." Millie patted Josephine's hand. "Anyways, I keep a journal, too, and I like writing fiction. I don't have anything too interesting to say about myself. Let's see …." Her finger tapped her chin. "Well, I'm a collector. I like old things and have a growing collection of Walters Bluff memorabilia. I don't know what to do with it all, but …."

"I have some things to add to that collection," Rita said.

"You know where to bring it." Millie looked to her right, where Josephine sat with her hands folded on the table. "Your turn."

Josephine wore her gray hair short and tidy. The high neck of her blouse spoke to her demeanor: buttoned up. "I met Claire already, but in case you forgot, my name is Josephine Pritchert.

I take notes during church and write summaries of the sermons." She didn't smile and sat with perfect posture in the metal folding chair. "The rest of you may not know that in thirty years, I've never missed a single Sunday at church."

"Wow, Jo, that's impressive," said Ramona.

"Yes, it is. Church attendance is essential." She turned her body as if to signal she was done.

"I'm Ramona. I'm the librarian at the Walters Bluff library, and I'm writing a book about the history of Walters Bluff. We have some interesting characters here, I'll tell you."

Claire noticed a smudge of mascara under her eye; she'd missed the second button on her blouse.

"Right now, I'm editing the many stories I've collected about Walters Bluff—including interviews with many special people around town." She took a sip of coffee—it dripped down her shirt. "One thing that most of you don't know is that I stay up way past midnight every night, writing and reading." Ramona pulled on her collar, making it stand up on one side, not the other.

"You don't say." Josephine folded her arms.

"I haven't had a good night's sleep since I started my book." She put her hand on Josephine's. "This sweet lady has worked with me at the library for years, and she's taken on a greater workload lately to help me. You forgot to mention that, Jo."

"If we're telling every single thing, I work two days a week at Greenwald's Floral too." The grouchy woman narrowed her eyes, appearing even more annoyed.

"Your turn, Joan," Ramona said.

"I had the pleasure of meeting Claire on Sunday, too. Let's see, I like to write stories about our time here in this church." Joan's friendly eyes sparkled as she spoke, as did her bleached-blonde hair. "Karl has pastored First Community for twenty-one years, and I'm just trying to document what God has taught me since we moved here. Oh goodness, what a blessing it's been."

"We all know you're the pastor's wife. What's something we don't know about you?" asked Millie.

"Oh, gracious, let me think. I'm an open book. You all know everything about me." Joan looked at the ceiling and chuckled. "Hmmm, well, okay. There is something, but you can't repeat it outside this room because Karl will strangle me."

The ladies nodded, assuring each other of utter secrecy.

"Karl's nickname for me is Sweet Cheeks." She slapped the table. "I mean it. That doesn't leave this room."

As Claire joined in the giggles erupting around the room, she saw Josephine roll her eyes.

"Not a word." Joan fanned herself.

"My turn. As you know, I'm Rita, and I write poetry, and sometimes I write Bible studies and—brace yourselves—I have six toes on one foot."

The ladies gasped in unison.

"Six?" Millie asked, her brown eyes wide.

"Yes, one extra, just in case I need a spare." Her bracelets jingled as she scratched her nose. "Now you know why I avoid the strappy little sandals."

Claire chuckled. *These women are a lot of fun.*

"I did not need to know that." Ella Mae wiped her hands on a napkin. "I'm Ella Mae, and I'm writing our family stories too—so the kids don't forget about us." She smoothed her glossy black hair. "Oh, and I've met Elvis."

"What?" The circle of ladies leaned forward.

"The king of rock and roll? *That* Elvis?" Millie's eyebrows lifted in wonder.

"Yes, but it's a long story, and we need to get on with the meeting, so ...."

"I want to hear the story," Joan said.

Claire smiled as the ladies clamored for more.

"Do we have time?" Ella Mae looked at Rita.

She nodded with enthusiasm.

"Well, all right, if you insist. When the kids were little, George took me on a picnic at the reservoir." Ella Mae rocked back and forth as she began the story.

"Claire, that's where the kids go to park," Rita interrupted. "Sorry, Ella Mae, carry on."

"So, there we were, and George picked a purple-tinted daisy and put it in my hair. It was an unusually romantic gesture coming from my George, so I wanted to remember it forever. When we got home, I pressed the daisy into a novel. A few months later, we took a trip to Memphis without the kids. I packed the book because I'd finally have time to read. We stayed at a nice little motor inn, and George splurged for a room facing the pool—it even had a heart-shaped bathtub." Ella Mae looked at Josephine and winked.

The grouchy woman crossed her arms.

"So, I was reading by the pool when something flew out from the pages on a gust of wind. I saw my beautiful daisy scooting across the grass. I remembered the lovely picnic at the reservoir, and I thought to myself, *I can't lose that daisy,* so I chased it."

"When did you meet Elvis?" asked Joan.

"Be patient. A gust of wind blew the daisy up and over the side of a Cadillac convertible parked on the street. I immediately thought, *Oh, how fortunate. I'll just open the door and grab the daisy.* But how wrong I was. I tried the door, and it was locked. Tell me, does it make sense to lock a convertible with the top down? Does it?"

Claire looked around the circle of ladies. They shook their heads, leaning forward in rapt attention.

Josephine yawned.

"I looked around for the owner, and there didn't seem to be anyone nearby, so I took matters into my own hands. I could see the daisy lying on the little hump on the floor of the back seat. It was too far for me to reach, so I had to climb up and over the door and stretch my five-foot-one-inch self to reach the thing without losing my balance."

"Couldn't George reach it for you? Where was George?" Rita's arms flailed with excitement as she asked the question.

"He'd gone to buy us some barbecue." Ella Mae sighed. "So, I hoisted myself up, and I had to balance because, as you can see, my bosom is bigger than my bum, and if I didn't plan it just right, I'd fall right in. Unfortunately, I put too much oomph into the push and landed face-first on the floorboard of that convertible."

The room erupted in gasps and giggles, and Ella Mae began giggling herself.

"Oh, my, I was stuck and stunned. The rough carpet scratched my forehead, and I can only imagine what I looked like—feet in the air, face on the floor."

"For pity's sake." Josephine scowled.

"But that isn't the half of it. I couldn't holler because my face was smashed, so I tried to wiggle my arms under me to push myself up." Ella Mae cleared her throat. "Then I heard someone say, *'Ma'am, can I help you?'*

"I thought to myself as I stared at the tan carpeting—*I know that voice.* So, I took a moment to think—*who is that?* Then I got my second wind and pushed hard enough to turn my head to see who was there, and wouldn't you know, it was Mr. Elvis Presley himself!" Ella Mae's brown face glowed with joy as she spoke.

A collective gasp resounded in the room. Claire's hand flew to her gaping mouth.

"Well, then I was so flustered, I started kicking wildly—anything to turn myself right side up." She paused for a sip of coffee. "I accidentally kicked away his hand as he tried to help me. By the time I turned around and sat in the back seat of the car, he was laughing so hard, he snorted. The king of rock and roll snorted like a pig. Well, that made *me* laugh." Ella Mae stopped to chuckle, her chins jiggling.

"Elvis and I, we laughed and snorted, and then he leaned against the car and pulled up the lock—*he pulled up the lock!* I could have done that in the first place. I didn't even *think* of that. He opened the door and said, *'Here you go, ma'am,'* and I stepped out of the car."

The room filled with *oh my goodnesses, oh my lands,* and *oh my stars.*

Josephine clutched her sweater at the neck.

Ella Mae continued. "I straightened my shirt and apologized for kicking him." She sighed. "Ladies, he was more than gracious. He asked why I was upside down in the back of his convertible, and I told him about George and our anniversary and the picnic at the reservoir and the daisy."

"You didn't," Rita clucked.

"Of course I did. He loved the story. Elvis Presley reached into the car, retrieved the daisy, and handed it to me with a dramatic bow." Ella Mae swirled her hand in grand fashion.

"What happened then?" Millie reached across the table as if to pull more information from her.

"Well, he said, *'Hold on to that daisy, little lady.'* His lip turned up like when he sang Hound Dog, and I felt faint. Then he said, *'George is a very lucky man.'* And he jumped into his convertible and drove away." She folded her hands on the table and smiled with pride.

The ladies repeated, "Wow," one after the other.

"And that's the story of how I met Elvis." Ella Mae took a bite of her scone.

Josephine looked at her watch. "We'd better start."

"Ella Mae, you should write about that," Rita said between chuckles. "It's a great story."

"Oh, I'll add it to the list." Ella Mae jotted the suggestion in her notebook.

Josephine cleared her throat loudly, and Millie was the first to read.

Claire's heart beat faster. Could she read her poem to the group? Millie's was fascinating. Her own poem seemed juvenile by comparison.

Then, it was her turn.

"Do you have anything to share today?" Rita asked.

I could say no. Avoid the embarrassment altogether.

"Yes." *Why did I say that?* Claire's hands shook. "It's just a little poem I wrote the other day as I thought about my youngest going to college."

"We'd love to hear it," Rita said.

All the ladies nodded in agreement.

Claire put on her reading glasses.

Here goes nothing.

> The Empty Nest.
> A busy nest so full of life.
> Tiny eggs to guard from strife.
> Little hatchlings beg for food.
> Mother bird cares for her brood.
> Flying in and flying out.
> Back and forth she darts about.
> Always caring, constant, true.
> Loving is what mothers do.

'Til the fledglings leave the nest.
Mother bird gives them her best.
Now, the nest is vacant, calm.
Silence is a restful balm.
Soon the mother starts to see,
All that she can do and be.

When Claire finished, relief swept over her. She felt like she'd jumped off a cliff and landed on a soft cloud.

"Oh, I like that."

"Me too."

"Thank you. I don't usually write poetry." Claire's face warmed.

"It's lovely. I think we all relate to those sentiments," Rita said.

No one said, 'That was stupid.' But why would they say that out loud?

Rita moved on. "Joan, did you write this week? Do you want to share?"

And so it went, around the circle of women. They admired each other's style and commented on the use of words and subject matter. Ramona wanted critique, and the ladies jotted down suggestions as she read. Everyone shared except Rita, who hadn't had time to write.

A tiny bit of angst slipped from her heart.

"Ladies, the prompt for this week is to write a story about your favorite aunt, and if you don't have an aunt, or didn't like your aunt, make up a story." Rita giggled. "Whatever you want to write is fine."

Claire smiled. She'd write about the photograph of a woman with a big purse.

Chapter 6

CLAIRE TOOK HER LAST SIP of coffee and grabbed her coat.

"Let's go," Will said.

It looked as if God had spilled a jar of glitter on the world. Frost sparkled in the morning sun. Claire admired the twinkling spider webs as they strolled to Main Street.

Sweet cinnamon and apple wafted from the little bakery, beckoning the citizens of Walters Bluff to the doors. They joined the line for Goodies' prized fritters and carried a warm box to Guy and Bertie's house.

As they rounded the corner to Sweet Pea Street, they saw Guy in the distance walking a dog.

"God bless you!" Guy let go of the leash, and the cocker spaniel bolted toward them, tail wagging so hard she ran a zigzag.

"This is Daffy. She's a lover, this one."

"You're such a good girl." Claire scratched her ears as Daffy grunted in delight.

"Let's go on up to the house. Bertie's got the coffee on."

Warmth enveloped them as they stepped through the door into the red and white kitchen. The linoleum was scrubbed clean, and the old metal cabinets sparkled. Bertie poured coffee. "Good morning. Make yourselves at home."

"We brought fritters," Claire announced.

Bertie's smile brightened. "They're our favorite. You spoil us."

They sat around the Formica table, discussing how cold it was and how the Shady Pines Retirement Home had lost a couple of trees in the last storm. It was as if she were talking to her parents. They had spent Saturday mornings around their kitchen table, talking about the neighborhood happenings … before the accident. As she listened, Claire realized her heart was at ease, as if at home.

When the fritters were gone, the men excused themselves to the garage.

"Let's visit." Bertie took Claire's hand and led her into a large blue living room. The creamy white sofa was littered with blue ruffled throw pillows.

"Guy's so happy Will wants to learn woodworking. He loves to share his passion. None of our boys were interested. They're car guys, all five of them."

"It's so kind of him to take the time. Will admires Guy very much."

"The feeling's mutual. You picked a good one, Claire." Bertie sipped her coffee. "How do you like it here so far?"

"It's a lovely town. And I attended the Grace Writers meeting at church last Tuesday."

"Then you've met Ramona Wickham. She's writing a book, you know."

"Yes, she said she interviewed many special people."

"Ramona interviewed Guy and me. I don't know why she thought us book-worthy." Bertie shifted her weight on the couch. Her blue checked blouse perfectly matched her eyes, not to mention the room. "The grandson of Walter Wickham lives in Shady Pines—that's Ramona's grandfather. He's a hundred and two years old—the only person left in town with a vague recollection of Walter."

"Who's Walter?" Aside from the name of this town, Claire had never heard of the man.

"Oh my, you haven't heard of Walter Wickham." Bertie sat up straighter and leaned in. "He's the founder of Walters Bluff. He saved this town from becoming a den of iniquity. Goodness gracious, if he hadn't stepped up, well, I don't know."

"Walters Bluff? A den of iniquity?" Claire couldn't imagine it.

"Guy is a relative of Walter Wickham, too—a distant relative. Let's see, Walter's granddaughter married one of Guy's great-uncles or some such. I honestly can't keep track of that sort of thing." Bertie sipped her coffee. "Tell me about your family."

"Well, Michael is a captain in the Army, Emma is a teacher, and Kate just started college." Claire tried not to boast as Bertie asked questions about each one. But pride seeped into every word.

"Claire, they sound like wonderful people, and isn't that what we hope for as mothers?" Bertie sighed.

"Yes, I'm grateful." Her heart burst in her chest with love for her children. She loved to talk about them.

"And what about you, dear? Do you have brothers and sisters?"

"No. I'm an only child." Claire hesitated. "I don't have any family left."

"Oh, heavens." Bertie leaned forward. "What happened to your parents? If you don't mind me asking."

The ache of tears startled Claire. Could she talk about her loss with Bertie?

"They died a year ago … killed by a drunk driver." A tear slipped down her cheek.

"Heavens." Bertie moved next to her. She held her hand as Claire tried to pull herself from a wave of emotion.

"It's been very difficult." Hearing her own voice, Claire, once again, realized how much she'd lost.

"If I can be so bold … I sense you are a woman of faith." Bertie leaned forward.

"Yes, I am …" Claire stopped herself. "I was."

"How has your faith weathered this tragedy, dear?" Bertie squeezed her hand.

Claire let a humorless chuckle escape her lips. "*My* faith? I don't know, I feel like God dropped the ball, and my faith in people … in God's people—" Claire's voice left her.

"I'm sorry. We can be … well, we can be awful."

Bertie's words surprised Claire, wrapping her in an embrace of understanding. "Yes." Another tear escaped. "I used to love my church … I loved *going* to church—my whole life."

Silence hovered between them.

Bertie sighed. "And now you don't. You seemed uncomfortable with my invitation."

"Yes. I'm not ready." Claire drew in a breath. *I'm dumping it all.* "The drunk driver who killed my parents was a deacon at our church. The evidence was mishandled, charges were dropped, and then he lied to everyone about being drunk."

"Mercy."

"People I had known my whole life turned their backs on me and supported him. He was the man of God, above reproach. I was viewed as an angry, unforgiving, bitter woman. But Will was at the scene and witnessed what happened. We *know* the truth."

"Oh, my."

"I don't—" She hesitated. "I don't trust church people."

"I can certainly understand why." The older woman huffed.

Claire was at a loss for words. She had prepared herself for a rebuke—a reminder that no one is without sin or that God tells us to forgive seventy times seven and all of that.

Bertie took in a breath. "Claire, if I may be so bold once again. I've been furious with God's people, too. Oh, gracious, I've been mad at God, if I'm honest."

"*You* have?"

"I lost a baby—our only girl. Sweet Sarah." Bertie clutched Claire's hand a bit tighter. "I had the five boys, and then our little girl snuck into our lives unexpectedly. We were thrilled. I knew in my heart that God blessed us with a daughter. The day came, and labor started. Guy and I went to the hospital, filled with joy." Bertie took in a deep breath and let it out. "She was stillborn—gone for a couple of days. I thought she'd just run out of room when I didn't feel movement."

"Oh, Bertie, I'm so sorry."

"I was hopping mad—what a cruel joke. God played a 'gotcha' on me, and I wouldn't forgive Him."

Claire nodded.

"People told me it was a *blessing* to have lost her in the womb because I didn't attach to her." The older woman's eyes glistened. "Gracious, I was so attached to my precious girl."

Claire swiped a tear.

"I told God exactly what I thought of Him—how cruel He was, how unfair, how mean." Bertie chuckled. "Claire, I told Him He had no idea what it felt like to lose a child. The God who sent His Son to die for my sins didn't understand my pain? Oh, boy ...."

"But you forgave Him?"

Bertie's kindness shone in her soft smile. "I realized I had nothing to forgive. He is God. He *does* work for the good of those who love Him—and I'm not quoting Romans 8:28 *at* you. Boy, oh boy, that verse probably made me the maddest when my grief was raw."

Claire bristled. That verse was hurled like a dart by people who wouldn't hear the truth.

"One night, I sat at the dinner table and watched Guy and the boys devour the dinner I'd spent so much time preparing. I love my family, but I began to feel sorry for myself." She shifted her weight on the sofa. "Right then, a veil lifted. That's the only way I can describe it. I saw my precious boys and my Guy. What blessings. How could I hold a loss against God when He'd given me so much?" She brushed a tear. "I still grieved our daughter—still do today. But I've grown in gratitude for what I *have*. At that moment, I remembered a verse I'd memorized long ago: Who has ever given to God that God should repay him?"

Bertie was silent for a moment, staring at her hands. "And I realized He owes me nothing, yet He gives me countless blessings." She sighed and looked into Claire's eyes. "Perspective. It takes time to get there."

"I feel as if God just lets His followers do whatever they want. That He doesn't care who they hurt."

"He does. He does let us do whatever we want. I do, that's for darn sure." Bertie shook her head. "I wish I didn't hurt people, but until I see the pearly gates, that's the battle. I try to love people well, but I fail far too often."

Claire looked into Bertie's eyes. They were sincere … caring.

"It takes time. It's all fresh and raw, and you're in the middle of a big change. Talk to God about it. Ask Him to help you." Bertie wrapped her arms around her.

"I'll try." Claire felt the comfort of a mother's embrace. She squeezed Bertie tight. "Thank you for sharing your story with me."

"I hope I didn't assume anything. I just heard your pain and felt we shared a common wound." The older woman dabbed at her nose with a tissue pulled from a blue crochet-covered tissue holder.

She understands.

Claire's heart lifted a bit. The ache faded. The wave receded. Relief flowed in.

They continued talking over the whirr of saws and the screech of drills. A while later, they heard the door to the garage creak open. The two men bantered about what Will might attempt to make next. As they turned the corner into the living room, Guy announced, "Will built a beauty, Claire."

Claire looked to the hallway as her husband appeared, holding a beautifully mounted board framed in walnut, a look of pride on his face. He stopped and positioned it against the wall.

The doorjamb from their old house, covered with lines, measurements, names, and dates. The history of her children's growth was propped on their neighbor's living room wall. "You framed it? It's beautiful. How is it here?"

Will smiled. "I pulled it out of the garage the other day while you were grocery shopping."

"I love it. I love that you did this." Claire kissed Will and then approached the tall, slender man who reminded her so much of her father. She hugged Guy.

"Will's a quick study. He'll be whipping out all kinds of projects in no time." Guy slapped Will's back. "Let me know when you want to start the next one."

"Next week, if it works with your schedule." Will lifted the board and held it.

"I'm retired, Will. I don't have a schedule." Guy laughed. "When *you* retire, your wife will be glad you have a hobby to keep you out of her hair."

Bertie leaned toward Claire. "It's the gospel truth."

Claire and Will thanked the older couple for a lovely morning and headed home.

Will stopped in the living room, holding the precious piece of art. "Where do you want it?"

"By the fireplace. I love it more than you know."

He planted a kiss on her head. "I'm going to shower and wash the sawdust out of my hair." He turned and strode down the hall.

Claire gazed at the growth chart—her mind returning to the day they left the house, the only *home* their family had ever known.

The knot in her stomach had tightened as the moving truck backed out of the driveway and drove out of sight.

"Are you ready to go?" Kate wheeled a suitcase toward the front door.

"Are *you* ready to go?" Claire swallowed hard to combat the urge to burst into childish sobs.

"Almost." Her daughter hesitated. "I want to look at my room one more time."

As Will loaded odds and ends into his truck, Claire wandered the house, reminiscing. Her fingers touched each line of the growth chart penciled on the doorjamb in the kitchen. Christmas mornings, Easter egg hunts, countless family dinners, and birthday parties—the memories flooded in. She'd paced this hall, bouncing colicky babies, collecting her thoughts before handing down a punishment, and waiting for teenagers to come home after a date. How could she leave this home?

But the change had to happen.

She couldn't spend the rest of her life in a town inhabited by so much sorrow. She couldn't run into former church friends at the grocery store, bearing their sorrowful looks of pity and judgment. "Have you gone to a grief counselor? Perhaps our pastor can help you." As if they could understand an iota of her pain. As if they knew her heart. As if she had no right to grief and anger.

So, that day, in a burst of resolve, she'd marched to Will's truck, grabbed a crowbar, and pried the growth chart out of the door frame.

"What are you doing?" Kate asked, her face frantic.

"I'm not leaving this." The board popped loose on one side.

"Whoa, what's going on here?" A scowl covered Will's face, then it melted away.

He helped her finish the job.

Claire held the board, tears filling her eyes. "Whoever bought our house will just paint over it."

"I'll call the realtor—and hire someone to fix this." Will hugged her, then loaded the piece of their family history into his truck.

Claire once again touched the beautifully framed relic. Every six months, they recorded the kids' heights: spring forward, fall back, measure the kids, and change the batteries in the smoke detectors. The sorrow of missing her children, parents, and even her church overwhelmed her heart. Thoughts of how her life *should* have unfolded swirled in her mind.

Claire could not let sorrow have the upper hand forever.

"Lord, help me."

Chapter 7

CLAIRE GLANCED THROUGH the photos. People she didn't know. Relatives? Friends of her parents? Strangers? No clue. But each image held a story. It was time to write them. Her parents didn't have siblings, and neither did Claire. She'd always wanted a big extended family. Now that her kids were far away and her parents … gone, she'd adopt the people in the photos. A smile broke her pensive gaze as the image of the plump woman holding a large purse peeked out from the pile.

"You're just who I was looking for." She turned the photograph over. Nothing was written on the back. *Why don't people write identifiers on photos for future generations?* "You'll be Aunt Ermyl with the big purse full of anything anyone ever needs." A giggle caught her off guard. This was going to be fun.

Will peeked into the room. "You ready for that shelf?"

"Yes." Claire moved a box away from the wall.

As Will measured, drilled, and hung the shelf, she pulled framed family pictures from the box.

She looked around the room. This spare bedroom had become her little sanctuary, a place to write stories and read books. She hadn't had a quiet, creative space of her own since becoming a mother.

The empty nest proved to be a good thing indeed.

"Perfectly level," Will announced. "You've been working so hard. Let's go out to dinner."

"We both have." Claire smiled. "But I'll get out of making dinner anytime."

"Where do you want to go?"

Claire chuckled. "Where do I want to go? Are you offering to drive to Walkersville?"

"Hey, there's the bakery, the hamburger joint at the edge of town, hot dogs and nachos at the gas station, or the diner. It's a legitimate question." Will chuckled. "So, the diner then?"

They strode hand in hand—hoods on, heads bent into the wind. Claire didn't mind the weather. She rarely drove her car anymore unless she left Walters Bluff. No reason to. She could walk everywhere. Even today, as the cold rain nipped her face, she relished the sweet aroma of autumn.

The door to the diner jingled as they pushed it open, a sound that made Claire's heart happy as Dottie waved them to the counter. She suddenly felt like a local. Claire smiled. *I am a local.*

"Harley, good to see you," Will said, taking the stool beside him.

"We meet again—and again." Harley chuckled and sipped his coffee.

Claire listened while the two men talked about the teenager who ruined the courthouse lawn by doing donuts in his mother's station wagon. They bantered about the new radios the department issued to officers and the plan for traffic at the

Autumn Festival. Claire watched Will's easy conversation with the gruff guy they sat beside whenever they came to the diner. *Harley must not cook at all.*

His gravelly laugh rang out as Will told him an amusing story of a traffic stop from years before. Harley roared again at the end of the story, hitting the bar with his large hand. Then she noticed he wore a gold band on his right ring finger. It appeared to be a wedding band. Her mind wandered to what the ring could mean. Probably nothing. He must be a bachelor. Or maybe his wife left him? But then she heard his tone change. His voice grew soft, and he stumbled to find words.

"Yes, a daughter, Rebecca."

Claire's mind cleared, and she leaned forward to listen.

"How old?" Will asked.

"Twenty-four."

"So, she's all grown up." Will's voice expressed understanding.

"Yup. All grown up." Harley's pensive tone and sad eyes, locked on his cup of coffee, spoke volumes.

What happened to his wife? His daughter? Claire wanted to know but couldn't think of a casual way to ask. She remained silent.

"How often do you see her?" Will asked one of the questions on Claire's tongue.

Harley let out a sigh.

"Didn't mean to dig. Come by the station this weekend. Oscar's spit-shining one of our rigs to display at the Autumn Festival."

"He mentioned that. I'll wander by Friday afternoon—before the rush."

"We'll look for you." Will's upbeat tone diminished any residual awkwardness.

"Good to see you folks. The bartender's holdin' down the fort, so I'd better go back." He rolled off the stool and stood, looking from Claire to Will, letting a chuckle rumble. "See you two next Thursday for dinner then?"

Will answered quickly. "Of course you will."

Claire offered a smile. The man was nice enough, but ....

❧

The morning sun streamed through the shop windows, illuminating shelves of second-hand curiosities. Stuff and Things might be a second-hand store, but Millie kept the shop spotless and neatly stocked. She was proud of the place, and it showed.

She shifted items on the shelves, rearranging displays of vintage porcelain teacups, stacks of old leather books, and blue mason jars. Millie deposited the money in the register and wandered back to the office. She started a pot of coffee and opened the paper.

> *Dear Wanda,*
> *My husband criticizes everything I do. He doesn't like the way I wash the dishes, and he doesn't like the way I fold his underwear and socks. I used to work in a department store, so I fold them beautifully if I do say so myself. I don't know how to please him. Please help!*
> *Tired of trying.*

> *Dear Tired of trying,*
> *Men are curious creatures, aren't they? Mr. Henderson used to complain about the way I folded towels. I tried to fold them his way, but they didn't stack as neatly in the linen closet, so I did what any wife would*

*do: I did it my way. He fussed about it until I left a pile
of towels on his recliner for him to fold when he came
home from work. He asked, "What is this?" I told him
he was free to fold them any way his heart desired and
kissed him on the cheek. He looked at me as if I'd lost
my mind. "I don't want to fold towels," he said. "I want
to watch football." So I graciously offered to fold them. I
did it my way and put them away. He never fussed about
the towels again. The key: be sweet. You'll catch more flies
with honey than vinegar.*

"Humph. Men are a lot of trouble." Millie set aside the
paper.

She wasn't a fan of romance. Her passion was in old things,
used items, cast-offs, and the unwanted, like her rescue cat,
Fussy.

Millie opened her desk drawer, spying her old engagement
and wedding rings in a little dish beside the paper clips. She
stuck her pinky in the circles, lifting them out of the drawer.
The tiny diamond sparkled in the morning light shining
through a small window.

Millie sighed. Once upon a time, she believed in romance.
Shortly before graduating from high school, Barry stole her
heart and innocence.

But he didn't stick around when she miscarried his baby right
after their wedding—the reason he'd proposed in the first place.

As Millie picked up the pieces of her broken and hardened
heart, she didn't trust her ability to know a good man when she
saw one.

Yard and estate sales were her therapy, and Millie
accumulated piles of treasure. She opened Stuff and Things as
a way to keep buying so she could nose through the trappings

of lives well lived. Back then, it was an effort to discover a way to make hers worth living, too.

She examined the rings hanging on her pinky finger. It might be time to put them into the jewelry case. She could get a little money for them. Millie stared at them for a moment and then let them drop off her finger into the drawer.

Why do I keep them?

It had been twenty-five years. Barry and his third wife lived two doors down with three delinquent teenagers. She was long over him.

I can't make another mistake.

The rings were a reminder.

Don't trust. Don't let go.

The creak of the door jarred Millie's attention.

☙

The large glass door opened to reveal a mecca of second-hand goods rivaling that of a big-city flea market. A gray cat with white paws wound her body around Claire's ankles.

"Welcome to Stuff and Things. How can I help?" A familiar voice echoed from the back of the store.

Claire turned to see a tiny woman in a blue cardigan making her way to greet her. "Millie!"

"Claire! I wondered when you'd find your way here. How did you like the Grace Writers meeting?" Two pigtails at the base of her head gave her the look of a teenager—the gray in her hair and the laugh lines around her big brown eyes were the only signs she wasn't.

"I liked it." Claire bent to scratch the purring cat's head.

"That's Fussy. Her name suits her. She doesn't like everybody, but she seems to have taken a shine to you."

Claire smiled. "I'm honored. I was wondering—do you take donations?"

"Yes, I do. I'd be happy to take 'em. Ten cents of every dollar goes to the Shady Pines Retirement Home. They're real nice folks down there."

"I have several boxes in the car. We moved into a smaller house," Claire said.

"The old Honeycutt place on Sweet Pea Street. It's a beaut. Doesn't it have a full basement?"

"Yes, but it's unfinished—on the to-do list."

Small towns—everyone knows everything, including where I live, apparently.

"That house was vacant for a couple of years. Harley looked after the place. Old man Honeycutt was his mother's stepbrother."

Interesting. "He did a good job. I've been redecorating, and the house seems to be in good shape." Claire's eyes scanned the shop. Rows of shelves were filled with knickknacks, kitchen goods, books, and antiquities. Racks of clothing occupied the back wall. "You have a nice store, Millie."

"Too much stuff and so many things." She giggled as she glanced through the mail by the cash register.

"I'll run to the car and bring in my donations."

"That'd be fine, just fine. Put them here behind the counter. I'll make some space."

Claire pushed through the door and nearly ran into Harley. "Oops, I'm sorry."

"Hey, Claire." He held open the door.

"I'll be right back. I have donations to bring in." Claire popped her trunk.

Two large hands reached beside her for a box.

"Oh, thank you."

Claire and Harley made two trips to the car, stacking the boxes next to the counter.

"How do you two know each other?" Millie asked.

"We met at the diner, and I keep seeing her and Will there. I think they're stalking me." Harley chuckled.

"He and Will talk shop. We look forward to seeing you." Claire said the words without thinking. She smiled at the man. Did she look forward to having dinner with the man who smelled of stale alcohol? But the guy who owned the bar *was* a nice man. That reality surprised her.

"Will's a good guy. I like bending his ear." Something caught Harley's eye. "What's that?"

"What's what?" Millie turned her head to where he was looking.

"Where did you find that photo?" Harley pointed to the wall full of framed photos next to the register.

"I found that one when I cleaned the Honeycutts' old place. I suppose we should start calling it the Baldwin place, though." Millie winked at Claire.

"That's me right there." He pointed at a little boy standing outside the diner with an older gentleman, circa the early 1970s. "That's my Caddy—used to belong to old man Honeycutt. You've got quite a collection here, Mill."

"I thought that boy looked familiar. Here, you should have it." She reached for the photo on the wall.

"Nah, keep it. It's a good view of the diner. I'll just throw it in a drawer. What other history have you uncovered?"

"I have old dishes from the dinner house that used to be next to Goodies Bakery, pictures of downtown back in the day, signs from the old Wash Tub, and even a few old menus from the diner." Millie's hands pointed to locations on Main Street as she spoke. "I found court records when I cleaned out Judge Whitaker's place—now that's an interesting read. I wish we had a museum or somewhere to display this stuff, but there just isn't any place. So, I assembled this little display here."

"Hmmmph." Harley scratched his head.

Claire examined the photos. "No museum? What a shame. So much history right here in this little shop."

"I've got some of my great-great-granddaddy's stuff on the walls of the bar, too." Harley furrowed his brow. "Well, I'm off to find a kettle. Nice collection, Millie." He headed down the housewares aisle.

"I don't think I have any kettles," Millie called after him.

After a quick once-over, Harley returned to the counter. "I guess the General Store's gonna get my business then."

"Thanks for givin' me a look-see."

"You're always my first stop, Mill. Have a nice afternoon, ladies." He pushed through the door.

Millie smiled at him. Her gaze lingered as he ambled across the street.

Claire leaned toward Millie. "Have you and Harley ever dated?"

"Harley and me? Nah. He's a good friend, but I don't mess with drinkers." She paused and then added, "I was married once, never again."

Claire wasn't sure how to respond, so she just nodded.

"I went to school with Harley. He was a few years ahead of me. He was married, too. Did you know that?" She didn't wait for Claire to answer. "His wife left him on account of the drinking. Danielle was a good woman, but I didn't know her well. She was from Walkersville, on the other side of the county."

Claire soaked in the information.

"They had a daughter, Rebecca. Cute little thing—but word around town was they left him. It was probably eighteen or twenty years ago now—right after the Autumn Festival. Not sure of the details. Harley never talks about it, and I haven't asked."

"Oh, that's just …."

"Sad, that's what it is." Millie rummaged through a box. "You donated some good stuff."

"I'm glad you think so. I'm happy to be rid of it." Claire didn't want the conversation to end there, but apparently, it was over. She removed her keys from her pocket.

Millie looked up from the boxes. "Will you come to the Grace Writers next week?"

"Yes. I think I will."

Chapter 8

WITH WILL'S ENCOURAGEMENT, Claire decided to stroll downtown to peek in the windows of the vacant storefront. Just dreaming. Just curious. The idea of opening an antique shop sounded good. *But can I do it alone?*

She descended her porch steps, deep in thought.

"God bless you, Claire." Guy waved as he filled the bird feeder. Daffy sat at his feet, no doubt resting after their morning walk.

Claire waved. "Good morning, Guy." She rushed over to hug the sweet man before heading down Sweet Pea Street toward Main.

As she wandered by Amos Kicklighter's house, she noticed him smoking a cigarette on his front porch in his bathrobe.

Should I say hello? Why not?

"Good morning, Amos." Claire forced a smile and waved. She watched as he lifted his hand, extinguished the cigarette on the porch post, and ducked into the house.

Claire chuckled and pressed on. She dug her hands deeper into her pockets. Birds scavenged through the fallen leaves beneath naked trees, shivering in a gentle wind. A garbage truck rumbled by, the brakes squealing as it stopped to pick up rubbish. Dogs barked, and the smoke of burning leaves wafted through the air as she moseyed downtown.

She passed the Daily Brew, the General Store, Goodies Bakery, and the hardware store. She stopped at a crosswalk and looked left. A neon sign blinked in the window of a shop halfway down the block on Butternut Street—Greenwald's Floral—right next to the vacant storefront.

She approached the door, padlocked shut—a faded "For Sale" sign in the window. *How long has it been on the market?* She peeked into the windows of the small space—a former travel agency. An old desk was shoved against a wall near the window. Claire cupped her hands around her eyes, straining to see through the dirt. A torn airline poster hung by one thumbtack on a wall. Another lay on the floor. The sun shone bright through the window, illuminating a layer of dust covering the entire space. On the back wall, she spied two open doors. One hung by a single hinge—behind it a sink—likely a bathroom. The other was a small closet. She sighed.

It's not big enough for a proper antique shop. She and her mother had dreamed of a spacious, friendly space where folks could reminisce and share stories while searching for treasures. This was not that dream.

Disappointment weighed on Claire's heart. She had allowed the idea of opening the store to churn over the past few weeks. Had it taken root? The fear of doing it alone, though, filled her with doubt.

Someone exited Greenwald's Floral carrying a bouquet of roses. Claire smiled. Her mind drifted to her mother's flower garden. A colorful explosion of flowers in an antique pitcher or crock adorned her mom's dining table all summer long. She turned from the empty storefront and stepped to the flower shop door.

A handwritten sign in the window caught her eye.

FOR SALE. Inquire within.

She pushed open the door, breathing in spicy carnations, fresh roses, and sweet lilies—blooms of every sort perfectly blended—her favorite perfume.

"Claire."

The sound of her name caused her to jump.

Josephine carried an arrangement to the counter, her eyes staring and her lips a straight line across her softly wrinkled face.

"Hello, Josephine. I didn't know you worked here."

"I mentioned it when we introduced ourselves at the Grace Writers meeting. You must not have listened."

Claire was flummoxed. *Yes, I must have missed it.*

Thankfully, the door to the workroom opened, and a pretty woman with auburn hair and a friendly smile entered the shop. "She meant to ask how she can help you, didn't you, Jo?" She swung her arm around the older woman's shoulders and pulled her into a stiff side hug.

The once straight line of Josephine's lips turned down to a frown. "How can I help?"

"Oh, I'm just looking and …." Claire spied a line of buckets filled with colorful blooms wrapped in brown paper. "I need a bouquet."

"You've come to the right place," the younger woman chirped. Then she turned to Josephine. "Would you mind sweeping up the workroom before you leave?"

The older woman turned and disappeared through the swinging door.

"I'm sorry about that," the young lady whispered. "She's a wonderful florist and a sweet person once you get to know her, but she makes a snippy first impression."

Claire smiled. "I've met her a few times at church."

"Well then, a snippy second and third impression as well."

Claire giggled.

"Welcome to Greenwald's Floral. I'm Fern." The woman's smile brightened the room like a field of sunflowers. "I live on the other side of Guy and Bertie, but I haven't had a moment to come over and introduce myself."

"We're neighbors? I'm Claire."

"I'm glad to meet you finally. I have four-year-old twins, so that sort of explains it all, right?"

"I noticed your sign outside. You're selling the shop?"

"Well, Laurel and I ... she's my sister ... we just ...." Fern's gaze dropped to the floor. "I put that sign out this morning, and ... we don't want to sell it. It's our family business. We've just struggled for so long. I mean ... people don't buy flowers as often as they used to."

"I understand."

"We're in a pickle." Fern clutched her hands together.

"I'm off to the library," Josephine announced.

"Thank you, Jo." Fern smiled at her, and Josephine's mouth turned up on one side. The older woman donned a rain jacket and hurried out the door. Before it could slap shut, it swung open again.

"Oscar wants to know how many wreaths we want this year. Oh, I'm sorry ...." A petite woman with strawberry blonde curls glanced between Claire and Fern.

"Laurel, this is Claire. Claire, my sister Laurel." Fern waved her hands as she introduced them.

"It's nice to meet you." Laurel smiled." She turned to Fern. "What about the wreaths? How many do you think?"

Fern hesitated. "I mean, it's hard to say, we weren't sure we'd be open after Thanksgiving."

"Don't say that, Ferny." Laurel frowned. "Besides, we sold out of wreaths on Thanksgiving weekend last year, so … let's try to stay open. December is always profitable."

"I don't know." Fern sighed.

The shop door swung open, and Millie bounded in.

"For sale? What's that sign all about?" The tiny woman threw her arms wide as she asked the question.

"We can't keep losing money," Fern said.

Millie frowned. "Hmmmmm …." She tapped her chin. "There's got to be a way to make this work."

"Well, if you think of a way, we're open to ideas," Laurel said.

"I'm full of 'em." Millie lifted her finger. "Here's one: A partnership, maybe? But don't look at me."

"That's a good idea, but … who?"

Claire was examining the bouquets. *Partnership?* Claire's mind flew to the vacant space next door, to the storage unit filled with antiquities, and a question formed. *Could this be an opportunity?* A smile bloomed on her face.

"Claire?" Millie touched her arm.

She pulled a bouquet of daisies from a bucket. "A partnership is a great idea." She drew in a cleansing breath. "I'd like to buy these, please."

The Grace Writers filed in, and Claire found a seat beside Joan. The room hummed with conversation.

The lively banter stopped when Ella Mae presented her date bars.

"This is Aunt Twylla's recipe. George's Aunt Twylla. She taught me everything I know about anything in the kitchen.

Honest to oatmeal, the first time I met her, she was in such a baking frenzy that she hollered, '*If you're in my kitchen, you'd better be stirring something in a bowl!*' I wrote about her, so I'll shut up. Enjoy the date bars compliments of dear departed Aunt Twylla."

"I hate dates with a holy passion," Millie said, wrinkling her nose. Despite her declaration, she placed a bar onto a napkin and picked at it until it disappeared.

Claire savored the flaky crust. Then curiosity overwhelmed her. "What's the trick to this crust, Ella Mae?"

Every lady stopped chewing and looked back and forth between Claire and Ella Mae.

"Darlin' if I told you that, I wouldn't be the best cook in Durham County, now, would I?" Ella Mae's brown eyes squinted.

Claire smiled. *Is that a challenge?* "I suppose not." *Challenge accepted.*

"So," Rita said, "the prompt was to write about your favorite aunt. But of course, anything you write is just fine. Millie, do you want to start?"

Millie shared a story about her mother's sister. Claire was impressed with her descriptions and use of similes. *I've always struggled with similes.* Joan wrote a poem about being an aunt. It didn't rhyme, but it flowed like a song, and her words were lovely. *I need to expand my vocabulary.* Josephine read her summary of the Sunday sermon. *Was I even there? Why do I not remember that sermon?* She appreciated the grumpy woman's take on what Pastor Karl had gleaned from the Word. Claire had yet to fully engage in one of his sermons. *Maybe it's time to pay closer attention.* Ella Mae wrote about her Aunt Twylla—a sweet woman who loved to bless people with good food. It explained much about the competitive woman, determined to be the best. Aunt Twylla had set high standards and was, herself, exceptional.

Claire was the last to share. "This is about Aunt Ermyl. I brought a photo of her." She produced a photograph of a woman sitting on porch steps holding an enormous purse.

"She's cute," said Millie. "Is her handbag in the story?"

"If you'd be quiet and let her read, we'd know, wouldn't we?" Josephine snapped.

Claire hesitated.

What will they think of my story? They might think it's silly. Maybe it's only interesting to me. Too late now. She took a deep breath.

Aunt Ermyl's mantra was: It's better to have what you don't need than need what you don't have. This was handy when packing for a picnic or road trip, but Ermyl took it to another level.

She carried everything anyone could want for any occasion in her incredible purse. Need a cough drop? She had menthol, cherry, and licorice-flavored lozenges. Her purse contained aspirin, a hot water bottle, and bunion pads in different sizes—sunglasses (unisex, of course) and sunscreen. Wind in your hair? She kept a can of Aquanet at the ready. Aunt Ermyl had safety pins, bobby pins, writing pens of every color, candies of all kinds, and chewing gum. If an emergency occurred and she wasn't in attendance, someone inevitably declared, "I wish Ermyl were here."

One Sunday, the church held a picnic. The young people built a bonfire and gathered sticks for roasting marshmallows. Aunt Ermyl provided the matches and newspaper, tucked into her bag, just in case.

The fire roared, and the fun began. Teenage boys started throwing a football, and Harvey McBride, wanting to prove his youth to his new gal, Fannie, joined the fun. He ran to the other side of the fire to catch a pass and leaped in the air as the ball flew into his grip. He landed hard but immediately jumped up.

"I'm okay," he said, hands in the air.

Fannie called, "Harve, be careful."

The next pass came, and Harvey ran under the branches of a tree to do a one-handed grab. One of the branches brushed him in the head and bent back as he ran by, hooking his hair—or rather, hooking his hair*piece* in its web of twigs. His momentum propelled him forward, but the branch snapped back, flinging his hair into the fire.

There was a collective gasp. The fire crackled as it consumed the toupee.

Harvey stood motionless under the branches of the tree.

Aunt Ermyl didn't miss a beat. She lifted herself off the bench and scurried around the fire—one hand searched in her purse as the other struggled to carry its weight. She huffed and puffed as she shuffled to the tree. Everyone watched, wondering what on earth Ermyl had in her bag with which to rescue Harvey. Her hand emerged from her purse, holding what looked like a small orange cat. No one could see clearly since the branches blocked their view.

Murmuring ensued, and the onlookers heard, "Just put it on. No one will notice."

A few seconds later, Aunt Ermyl emerged from the branches. She looked around the circle of people and pointed as if to say, *'Be nice.'* She scurried back to her seat.

Harvey stepped from beneath the tree. There was a shocked silence, followed by applause. On top of his head was an auburn toupee. He usually sported a dark brown hairpiece, but he *had* red hair—before it all fell out. The new toupee looked quite natural on him.

Fannie loved it instantly. "Harve, you look so handsome." She shimmied through the onlookers to give him a little peck on the cheek.

He blushed, and the crowd continued roasting and talking.

Aunt Ermyl smiled, pleased with herself. Then, the barrage of questions began. "Why on earth would you have a toupee in your bag?" and "Where did you get it?" and "How long has *that* been in there?"

"I got it at the thrift store many years ago. You never know what you'll need." Ermyl patted her purse and declared, "It's better to have what you don't need than need what you don't have.

Claire closed her notebook to the sound of giggles, and even Josephine had a smile on her face.

"Is that true?" asked Joan, "Did she really keep a toupee in her purse?

"It's fiction," Claire said. "I found this picture in a box of my parents' things. I think she's family, but I'm not sure."

"That's a cute story, Claire," said Millie.

"My mother had a purse full of odd stuff, but I don't think she ever had a toupee in there." Ramona chuckled. "She did have the tail of a raccoon, though. It fell off my brother's hat."

Claire smiled. A weight lifted. These ladies were encouraging and fun.

Rita stood and cleared her throat. "I loved all your stories this week. Our next prompt is: Write about a favorite recipe."

Ella Mae smirked. "I've got this in the bag."

Chapter 9

CLAIRE ARRANGED A MEETING at the flower shop to present an idea to Fern and Laurel.

She and Will had talked late into the night—many nights—since her first visit. They'd brainstormed ideas and crunched numbers, and in the end, her inheritance would more than cover the costs.

Will the sisters be willing to explore my idea?

A block from the flower shop, the door to Harley's was propped open with a brick. She quickened her pace to pass by it, but an urge to peek inside overwhelmed her. A blaze burned in a grand fireplace on the far wall—permeating the room, the scent of burning pine mixed with the sweet smell of ale. A man sat on a stool, his arms resting on the smooth wood bar.

Harley was nowhere in sight.

Claire stepped inside, her eyes wandering around the large room. The walls were covered with photos and history, just as he'd described.

I'm not sure what I expected, but it wasn't this.

"Look what the cat drug in."

Harley's drumbeat chuckle brought a smile to Claire's lips.

"I saw the door open and thought I'd pop in to say 'Hi.'"

"Hi yourself." He smiled. "Let me show you around." Harley waved to a far wall and moved in that direction.

Claire followed, noting the spotless, worn wood floor and the intricately carved leaves along the bar's edge. *This is by far the cleanest, most lovely bar I've ever been in.*

"This here is my great-great-grandaddy. Harley Bushkin the first." He pointed to a framed sepia cabinet card. The man was a slightly thinner version of Harley with thicker, darker hair. His eyes smiled, although his mouth barely turned up on one side. He appeared proud.

"You look a lot like him."

"This here's the first dollar he earned in the bar." Harley pointed to a framed silver dollar.

Claire moved to the photo beside it—a similar depiction of his grandfather and a woman.

"That's my great-great-grandma, Lillian. Isn't she a looker?" He threw his head back and laughed.

The woman had a prominent nose veering to the right of her deep-set eyes. No, she wasn't a looker. It appeared she had taken a blow to the face at some point. "What happened to her?"

"A horse kicked her. Guess they didn't know how to fix a busted-up nose back then."

"Poor thing." Claire chuckled.

They wandered around the room—Harley sharing stories about each photo and artifact. She noted the passion with which he spoke about the bar's history. She soaked in the information. The man was loyal to his legacy in Walters Bluff—to this bar and to his family.

One last picture showed a younger Harley standing on Main Street, the bar in the background, a pretty young woman and a little girl beside him.

"Oh, is this you?" Claire pointed.

Harley reached for the photo and took it off the wall.

"*Was* me ... a long time ago." He trudged away with the photo in his hand, set it behind the bar, and then returned to her.

Claire didn't know what to say. Her heart filled with compassion as she made her way to the door. *He's a man with regrets.* "Thanks for the tour. It's like a museum—and that old bar is just beautiful." She pointed, noticing their reflection in the grand mirror. Harley smiled—the same slight smile his great-great-grandfather wore in the first photo—with a touch of sadness.

"I'm glad you stopped by. See you tomorrow at the diner?"

"Yes, we'll be there." Claire turned and walked out, pondering the bar and the unlikely man softening the edges of her heart.

༄

Claire pushed through the door of Greenwald's Floral. She breathed in the scent of flowers. Like soldiers in formation, bouquets filled buckets along the wall.

"Who are you?" A little boy stood inside the door, looking her over.

Claire couldn't help but smile when she saw his blue eyes, nose dotted with freckles, and a mop of strawberry blonde curls. "I'm Claire. Who are you?"

"Sage."

A girl about the same age appeared through the workroom door. She had the same periwinkle eyes and freckles, but her hair was longer and held back by a shimmering tiara.

"That's Marigold," he announced, pointing. Fern followed the girl. "Kids, this is Mrs. Baldwin. She moved into the white house next to Nana and Papa Witherspoon." Fern tousled Sage's hair. "Auntie Laurel, Mrs. Baldwin, and I are going to have a meeting."

"What are *we* going to do?" Marigold twirled, running into Sage as she did.

"Hey!" Sage pushed her. "Can we play a game?"

"Yes. And Meg will be here to play with you, too."

The kids took off for the workroom.

Laurel appeared with a teenage girl.

"Sorry, I'm late." She wiggled out of her jacket. "Where are the kids?"

"In the workroom." Fern turned to the girl. "Thanks for babysitting on short notice."

"Sure thing." The girl popped her gum and disappeared through the swinging door.

"Let's sit," she said, waving to a table and chairs in the corner of the shop.

"Thank you for meeting with me." Claire sat and pulled a notebook from her purse.

Fern drew in a breath. "Before we begin, I need to share something. We are in an even more precarious place than before." Fern looked at Laurel. The two clasped each other's hands on the tabletop. "My husband left ... well, I kicked him out. That's why the kids are here."

"Oh, Fern ...." Claire wasn't sure what to say.

"He's a cheater. I had a feeling he wasn't faithful. But my plate was full, and I didn't want to deal with the reality of what that meant. I should have prepared myself better, but with the kids and a business ...." She drew a deep breath. "Yesterday, I filed for divorce. He didn't come home from work on Friday and announced he's moving to Walk…." Her voice caught in a sob.

"I'm so sorry." Claire stood and approached Fern, hugging her.

"You'll be all right, Ferny." Laurel brushed tears from her eyes and looked at Claire. "Our mom is coming to help for a few months."

"I know … everything will work out. It always does, right?" Fern dabbed at her eyes.

"That makes what we're talking about even more urgent then, doesn't it?" Claire returned to her chair and opened her notebook. "Maybe talking this out will offer you some comfort … one less thing to worry about."

"What's your idea? I'll admit, when you asked to meet with us, I talked to Bertie and Millie about you and researched you … as much as possible. And … I'm sorry about your parents."

The sentiment startled Claire. "Oh, thank you. You did do your research."

Fern turned from sorrowful to serious. "This is my livelihood … and Laurel's … and our family business for over thirty years."

"I respect that." Claire breathed a silent prayer. Would the sisters like her idea as much as she did? "Well, when I first met you, I was actually peeking in the windows next door to see if that empty space would be large enough for an antique shop. It wasn't."

"Unless you want a hole in the wall," Fern interjected.

"I want a large, welcoming place where people can shop and visit." Claire swung her arms wide.

"I love that," Laurel said.

"I am offering to buy the flower shop, and I'll buy the empty office space next door to create one large shop. I talked with a realtor, and she pulled comparables to give me rough numbers." She tried to read Fern and Laurel's expressions as they watched her.

"I would like to create an antique and flower shop. We could be partners and work out the particulars together. It would be one unified shop." Claire cleared her throat. "I mean, this isn't actually my idea. Millie came into the shop when I visited last week, and a partnership was her grand idea. It sparked this vision in me."

Fern and Laurel looked at each other. *What are they thinking?* Their eye contact was intense, and Laurel's eyes welled as Fern clutched her hand.

Claire looked at the sisters. "I realize it's a big change, and we don't know each other well." *They must hate the idea.*

"I love the idea. We love the idea," Fern said.

"You haven't even talked about it yet." Claire looked from sister to sister. They were smiling—at her and each other.

"We do need to take the time to see if we can work well together," Fern said.

"Yes," Claire agreed.

"We've always wanted to do that very thing, but the shop didn't make enough money, and there wasn't enough space." Laurel once again swiped at tears.

"It's been a rough five years since our dad died." Fern drew in a deep breath. "I feel like God has sent you to help us."

"I think it's the other way around." Claire smiled. "The greatest hindrance to opening an antique shop was doing it alone. Having partners … well, it would be a gift."

The women talked and brainstormed, sharing their stories and ideas.

"Let's have dinner at my house later this week. Bring your kids, Fern—and Laurel, bring Oscar."

"That sounds wonderful. In the meantime, we will talk with each other and our mom. She sold the shop to us, but her input is still important." Fern clutched her sister's hand.

Laurel smiled. "I'm excited."

Claire walked home filled with gratitude. Her mother's dream—no, their mutual dream—may become a reality.

꙳

Claire heard Will's car pull into the driveway. She finished the last sentence of her story and closed her laptop.

His footsteps echoed in the hallway as he peeked into the room. "I'm glad you're still up. Harley was drunk and disorderly at his bar tonight—gave Buster Simpson a bloody lip." His voice faded as he disappeared into the kitchen.

Claire jumped up and followed him. "Aren't they friends?"

"The booze got the best of him." Will was matter-of-fact. "Makes people do stupid stuff."

"Did you arrest him?"

"Buster didn't want to press charges. We took Harley up to his apartment to sleep it off. He was lucky this time, but he's *got* to get a handle on his drinking. It doesn't help that he's always in that bar."

Claire thought about the gruff guy. Her husband always gravitated to him at the diner.

Why?

He said it was because Harley seemed to want a better life beyond the bar, but he was the chosen descendant—the one to keep the legacy alive. It was his duty to run the family business, or so he thought. Claire had softened a bit toward him recently despite her initial reservations.

But this news gave her pause. "It'll be awkward the next time we go to the diner. Maybe we should give him space."

"Nah, he knows I was doing my job. He was embarrassed, but we'll talk it through." Will sat on the couch and ran his hands through his graying hair. "It's nice working in a small town. I can make a difference rather than just mess up someone's day." He stared out the window into the darkness. "I like that."

Claire frowned. As much as she'd grown to tolerate Harley, she couldn't sympathize with the situation he'd created. He *should* feel awful. It *should* be awkward. What if he'd driven his tank of a Cadillac while he was drunk? He could've—"

Claire shivered.

A blade of sunlight cut through Harley Bushkin's recurring dream. He's sitting in a church—indecipherable mumblings filling his ears.

Confusion.

Why do I keep dreaming that? I haven't been to church since the third grade.

He rubbed his eyes and fully awoke to the stark realization— it was twenty years ago today. His head pounded with the dregs of last night's intoxication.

He lumbered to the kitchen. A note rested on the table.

Call me when you wake up.

Buster

Harley tried to recall what had happened the night before. Had he drained a bottle of bourbon—or was it that good bottle of Irish whisky he'd been saving for a special occasion? He hoped not. He didn't remember tasting the liquid, only consuming it.

What a waste that would be.

He ran his hand through his thinning hair. His knuckle stung. He glanced down.

What the—?

Dried blood indicated he'd taken a swing at something … someone.

Now that he thought about it, how did he get here, in his apartment? Last he remembered, he was pouring ….

It was the Irish Whisky.

Harley heaved a sigh and opened the door. He descended the stairs, strode through the office, past the restrooms, and into the bar.

Photos and artifacts covered the walls—a framed silver dollar, a torn paper with his great-great-grandfather's name printed in charcoal, and a few pieces of carved wood. He retrieved a feather duster from behind the bar, swiping it over the memorabilia. One photo caught his eye. The caption read: *Harley Bushkin, 1886.* His ancestor looked proud, ambitious. Harley didn't feel either. *Where did it all go wrong?*

He strolled the perimeter of the room, taking in the history. A photo of his daddy and mama stopped him cold. They smiled, but he knew better. They'd been gone since he was a kid.

One after the other, they drank themselves to death.

Will I meet the same fate?

He moved behind the great carved bar, a mirror reflecting light from the high windows across the room. He took a good, long look at his reflection. Haggard, tired. He felt control slipping away again.

Have I ever had control of my life?

Surely, he could manage one little thing—his drinking. He rubbed his eyes. Oh, yes, and today marked twenty years. A familiar sadness washed over him.

He recalled the letter to Dear Wanda precisely two decades ago.

Dear Wanda,
How does a man get his wife to come home after she ups and leaves?

Her response was cold but honest.

He takes a long look in the mirror and asks hard questions. Am I worthy of her? Am I doing my best?

Would I leave me if I were her? Then you change what you must and ask her to give you another chance.

Harley tried to stop drinking, but at the time, it was easier to let the two most important people in his life slip away—Danielle and sweet little Rebecca.

He looked into his blue-gray eyes, bloodshot and weary. The thought of what may have happened last night made him angry, fed up with that tired old man in the mirror.

A knock echoed through the quiet room.

Harley trudged across the worn wood floor and opened the door. Buster stood outside.

"C'mon in." Harley stepped aside.

Buster's lip was puffed and red. "You okay this morning?"

"Fine, fine." He looked down at his bloodied knuckles and back at his friend's lip. "Did I do that?"

"You did." Buster stood just inside the door.

"I'm sorry. I don't remember much of last night."

"You swung at me like a scorned girl on prom night." Buster offered a smile.

Harley tried to grin. His heavy heart wouldn't allow it.

"Water under the bridge." Harley's friend looked away and added, "You've been drinkin' more'n usual, buddy. That's what started the ruckus. I wouldn't let you have another shot."

"It's twenty years today," Harley confessed. "I guess I just—."

"Gotcha." Buster stared at the floor.

"So I'm turnin' over a new leaf. I've never hurt nobody before." Harley stood up straighter. "I'm cuttin' back."

"Look, Harley, you might just need to quit. Give it up altogether. I'd help you. Dad-gum, I'd call you on the carpet."

"I don't doubt it. But how's a guy supposed to quit when he owns a bar?"

"It can be done. I used to be here pert near every day." Buster's words sliced Harley's excuse to ribbons.

Maybe I can quit. "You really think so?"

"I know so." Buster put his hand on Harley's shoulder. "You want to come with me to AA this week?"

Harley looked at his feet. *I've wasted so much time.* He thought of Danielle and sweet Rebecca. *Why? Why didn't I stop drinking twenty years ago?* "Yeah. I'll go."

Buster squeezed his shoulder before letting his hand drop to his side. "I'll pick you up at six on Tuesday."

"Thanks. You're a good man. A good friend." Harley scratched his beard.

"I'm on my way to church, but I wanted to make sure you're okay. You want to come along?"

"You know I don't like church. But, sorry 'bout the lip."

"You're better'n that. I know it 'n so do you."

Maybe I am. Harley looked into his friend's eyes, filled with concern. "Thanks for the reminder."

࿔

Claire gathered the dead vines and raked up the withered plants in the garden.

"Yer hedge is choking my camellia over here." A voice grumbled from behind the laurel separating her yard from Amos Kicklighter's.

Claire stood up and peered around it. "Oh, hi, Amos. I can cut it back for you."

"Nah, it's man's work. I just wanted you to know." He scratched his armpit. "The Honeycutts planted all kinds of stuff on the fence. Don't know why. Just bugs the tar outta me. I'm always havin' ta trim it back."

Claire didn't know what to say. "Well, if you ever need help trimming the hedge, let Will know. He's a whiz with a hedge trimmer."

Amos grunted and trudged back into his house. He returned a short time later.

"Here's your plate. The apple cake was good. Linda put more cinnamon in hers. Her cake was better 'n what you made. I ate it, though." He handed Claire the plate, weeks-old crumbs dotting its surface.

Claire had counted the plate a loss. "Oh, thank you. Good to know. I'll make a note in the recipe. Is Linda your wife?"

"Was."

"Oh, I'm sorry."

"What fer?"

"Well, did she pass away or ..." *How on earth did I get painted into this corner?*

"Yeah, she's dead, but she died after the divorce. We were married twenty-two years, and she left because she said I was a chauffered pig."

Huh? A moment of uncomfortable silence passed as Amos stared at Claire, his nose wrinkled into a scowl.

"Oh, a chau—oh." Claire looked down at her feet—trying desperately not to smile.

Amos turned on his heels and shuffled back into the house.

Claire let a chuckle escape. Amos was a piece of work—unpleasant, but not altogether repulsive. Didn't she always laugh after an encounter with him?

She finished weeding the garden, pulling the compost bin around the house, through the gate to the driveway. It felt good to complete a job she'd put off far too long. It was almost Thanksgiving, after all.

"God bless you, Claire," Guy called to her as he opened Bertie's car door.

Guy and Bertie had worked themselves into her heart. Love and comfort—that's what she felt when she was with them. And they lived next door, just like her parents had before. She stopped herself from letting her mind open a Pandora's box of grief, and instead, the blessing of it all filled her heart.

"Where are you two headed?" Claire smiled at the sweet couple as they situated themselves in the car.

"Serving lunch at Shady Pines." Bertie waved through the rolled-down window of their old Ford Galaxy.

"Have fun." Claire waved as the car drove away. She smiled to herself and sighed. Hadn't Bertie told her it would take time to gain perspective? To see the blessings? Maybe she was making progress.

❧

Claire's eyes scanned the diner for Harley.

"There he is," Will said, pointing.

"Hey." The man always sounded as if he had gravel in his throat.

"You're dressed up tonight." Will shook his hand.

Jeannie arrived at the table with napkins and glasses of ice water. "The soup is split pea." She lowered her voice. "I wouldn't eat it if it were the last thing on earth, and I was half-starved." She cleared her throat and continued. "The special is Salisbury Steak, and it's very good, but I recommend the Chicken Pot Pie. It's to die for."

Dottie stopped, her arm full of dirty plates. "You warned them about the soup, right?"

"I did." Jeannie giggled.

"The new cook isn't cuttin' the mayo." Dottie winked as she headed for the kitchen.

"Mustard," Harley said. "It's cut the mustard." He chuckled.

"Chicken Pot Pie for me," Claire announced.

Will agreed. "Make that two."

"I'll have the same," Harley said.

Jeannie scribbled their choices onto a pad and strode to the counter.

"Why are you all dressed up?" Will asked.

Claire noticed Harley's beard was trimmed.

"Oh, just turnin' over a new leaf, I suppose. My aunt used to make me dress up for dinner, so I thought I'd start there." He wore a plaid cotton shirt and dark slacks.

"Were you raised by your aunt?" Claire wanted to know more about the man.

"Yeah, my folks died when I was a kid. The alcohol got 'em. Makes one think, you know?"

"That it does," Will said.

"You look nice, Harley. Your aunt would be proud." Claire watched his mouth turn up in a grin.

"That means a lot." Harley appeared pensive as he looked at his hands, folded on the table. "I went to an AA meeting with Buster. I gave up drinkin'. It's time."

"Harley, that's good news," Will said. "Good, good news."

Claire reached over and put her hand on Harley's. "I'm so happy for you."

"Thank you." He smiled.

Jeannie arrived with the food and an extra basket of rolls. "For my favorite customers, but you didn't hear that from me," she said.

Harley dug into his Chicken Pot Pie, holding his fork like a dagger. The man in his forties looked like a kid eating his dinner. Claire felt a motherly tug at her heart. She tried to squash it, but it only grew. Harley was who everyone said he was—a teddy bear.

"Got a new cruiser yesterday. You're welcome to come down to the station and check it out when you can. Oscar's working the kinks out of the radio, so it's not on the road yet. She's a beaut." Will and Harley began a discussion about all things law enforcement. Harley loved talking about guns, cars, engine performance, and equipment. Claire listened to them talk. Will's enthusiasm about his job gave her pause. She felt the same joy in talking about her role as a mother. But now she was starting a business. The uncertainty of beginning a new venture overwhelmed her, but then she remembered she was not in it alone. She was so thankful for Fern and Laurel and the friends they had become to her. Solid plans were forming. It was exciting.

Harley pulled Claire from her wandering thoughts. "Are you curious, Claire?"

"What? I'm sorry, I was daydreaming."

"I told Harley about my woodworking with Guy. He asked what I was making, but I can't say—you know, the holidays are coming." Will grinned at her.

"I'll admit, I am curious."

"Guy's a good man," Harley said with conviction.

"He is, and a great woodworker, too." Will took a sip of water. "By the way, I wanted to mention something, Harley …."

Claire smiled as she watched the two men talk. They were becoming friends. How ironic—the chief of police and a town drunk—former drunk.

But he was trying to do better. Claire looked at the man with the slicked-back hair—a troubled soul, yearning for change.

She wanted to believe it with all her heart. But just the other night, he got drunk and busted his friend's lip. Claire knew all too well it could have been so much worse.

～

Claire settled into a chair next to Millie. The hum of conversation was a symphony of friendship. The harmony washed over her as she contemplated reading another of her stories. Not only was she writing them, but sharing them seemed to give them, and her, new life.

"Who wants to be first?" Rita posed the question as she nibbled on a scone. She turned to Ella Mae. "What kind of scones are these?"

"Jerjer," she replied, covering her mouth with a napkin.

"Ginger." Josephine scowled at Ella Mae. "Don't talk with your mouth full."

Ella Mae swallowed the bite and rolled her eyes, "Yes, ginger—lemon ginger, to be exact."

"I use lemon zest in mine. Do you use juice or zest?" Claire asked the question while examining a scone.

"Uh-oh." Millie giggled.

"I'll never tell, but you just did." Ella Mae winked.

"Oops, I did, didn't I?" Claire chuckled. She hadn't meant to start anything, but it gave her a little thrill to think she had.

"They're delicious, as always," Rita declared. "The prompt was to write about a favorite recipe. Who wants to start?" She looked around the circle of ladies.

"I will," Millie volunteered. She read a story about her mother's macaroni and cheese. When she finished, Rita claimed that *her* mother had baked the best macaroni and cheese.

"You're wrong. I make the very best—hands down," Ella Mae declared.

"I'll grant you that," Millie agreed. "Honestly, you've got a gift."

"Practically goes without saying." Ella Mae glanced at Claire.

She smiled. "I have a #1 Mac and Cheese trophy." She looked at Ella Mae, who had just taken a large bite of her scone. "My kids gave it to me last Thanksgiving."

"That's cute," Ella Mae mumbled.

"Let's begin," Rita interjected.

Each essay proved food's connection to comfort, memory, and love. As expected, Ella Mae wrote about her favorite recipe, giving no hints about the ingredients. Joan surprised the group when she produced a plate of Cathedral Window cookies after sharing about the treats her kids still expected at Christmastime. The ladies gobbled them up, and Claire watched with wonder as Josephine ate more than her usual self-imposed limit of one.

"Your turn, Claire," Rita said. "I hope you didn't bring a sample to go with your story. We'll have to roll out of here if you did."

"No, no samples." Claire opened her notebook and began to read.

> Great Aunt Martha was the queen of pies. She won blue ribbons in every pie category at the county fair, except one—custard.
>
> One summer, she traveled to Iowa to visit her sister, Faye. While there, she helped her bake pies for the church picnic. The pies won rave reviews, but chatter among the picnickers compared hers to the ones baked by Miss Eunice Pickering—and many were concerned with her whereabouts.
>
> There was a collective sigh of relief when a blue Plymouth Deluxe Coupe skidded to a halt next to the picnic table holding the pies. Eunice opened the car's trunk to reveal her stash of award-winners, including the most notable of all, coconut custard. She arranged them on the table, moving Martha's half-eaten pies to the side. Her coconut custard was met with a swirling mass of bodies reaching and grabbing for the smallest slice.

Martha was intrigued.

Faye approached her as she watched the hubbub retreat. "I was able to snag a sliver of the coconut custard," she whispered.

Martha's mouth opened to receive a coveted morsel. It crossed her lips and melted on the spot—coconut, vanilla, a hint of butter, and the sweetest cream danced on her tongue. The texture was divine, the flavors balanced throughout—the crust flaky and flawless. Martha *had* to have the recipe.

She could practically feel the silky blue ribbon between her fingers.

Faye introduced Martha to Eunice. They chatted about flower arranging, cocker spaniels, and pies. Unfortunately, Eunice did not offer the recipe.

As the picnic ended, Martha visited the ladies' room, where she overheard a conversation between Eunice and the pastor's wife.

"I'll be visiting the shut-ins Tuesday morning. May I stop by to discuss the plans for the ladies' luncheon?" Eunice asked.

"That would be lovely. What time do you think you'll be by?"

"If I leave at nine, I could do my visiting and be at your house by eleven." Eunice paused. "How does that sound?"

"I'll see you then."

Martha sat silently in the bathroom stall, underthings about her ankles, pondering an idea.

Tuesday morning dawned bright and sunny, and Martha strolled into the garden. Her niece, Rose, ran after her to help choose blooms for a lovely bouquet.

"Auntie Martha, is that for Mama?" Rose asked.

"Um, no, I'm going to deliver them to Miss Eunice." Aunt Martha felt the tiniest twinge of guilt, but she brushed it aside.

"Can I come with you?" Rose pulled on Aunt Martha's hand. "Please?"

"I'm sorry, not this time. I won't be long." The twinge reappeared, but she pushed it away and hurried down the lane to Eunice's front door.

She knocked.

Nothing.

Perfect.

Martha shuffled around to the back door, which was unlocked as is typical in a small town. She entered the kitchen, placed the flowers in an empty jar by the sink, and filled it with water. Her eyes scanned the surfaces for anything resembling a recipe box. On the counter, right next to the mixer, was a metal box stuffed with cards and papers. Martha flipped through the tabbed dividers. Main dishes, vegetables, breads, cookies, cakes, pies—bingo!

The very first card was coconut custard.

She removed a small notebook and pen from her brassiere and began to copy the recipe, double-checking the measurements and taking great care to copy the notes Eunice wrote in the margins: *'I use half and half* 'next to the whole milk ingredient. *'Extra-large eggs'* by the egg line.

Martha chuckled.

It was just too easy.

She tucked the notebook back into her bosom, but as she turned to leave, a mouse scurried across the polished linoleum floor.

Martha let out a yelp as she scrambled onto a chair. Unfortunately, the chair tipped, sending her tumbling. On the way down, she knocked over the flowers and a plate of freshly baked muffins sitting nearby. Martha landed flat on her back in the middle of broken glass, spilled water, and smashed muffins. The whole mess was sprinkled with colorful, delicate petals.

Deafening silence swallowed the room.

She lay there, paralyzed with fear, as her eyes scanned all around her.

It appeared the mouse had left the building, and who could blame it? She pushed herself up, but as she did, Martha heard the door creak open.

Had Rose followed her?

Eunice appeared around the corner and jumped at the sight of Martha sprawled in the middle of her kitchen. The notebook, flung from Martha's bosom in the fall, lay beside her, conveniently open to the hastily written recipe.

Eunice grunted as she picked up the notebook.

Rose appeared in the doorway and ran to Aunt Martha to help her up.

"I told you I wouldn't be long." Aunt Martha whispered.

She brushed herself off, asked for a broom, and swept up the mess.

Eunice watched, notebook clutched in her hand.

When the kitchen was clean, Martha took Rose's hand, turned to Eunice, and asked, "May I please have my notebook?"

"You know, you could have asked me for the recipe. I would have given it to you."

Eunice's smug expression was too much for Martha to bear. She held out her hand.

With a slap, the notebook landed in her palm. Her face beet red, Martha mumbled, "I'm sorry."

No one said anything about the incident until the following Thanksgiving when Martha presented a coconut custard pie.

Little Rose innocently asked, "Is this the pie you stole from Miss Eunice when you crashed in her kitchen?"

Aunt Martha begrudgingly told the tale, and the pie was re-named Humble Pie (although Rose always called it Tumble Pie), and it went down in family history as the most loved and scandalous pie of all time."

Claire giggled as she closed her notebook and looked up.

Ella Mae snorted. "Don't you ladies get any ideas about *my* recipes."

"Oooooh my." Joan dabbed at the corners of her eyes, still chuckling, "Aunt Martha was quite a character."

"I like her." Millie giggled as she stuffed her notebook into her tote bag.

Josephine grunted. "That's ungodly. The idea that she would do something so sneaky."

"Oh, Josephine, you're no fun," Millie sighed. "Is it a true story?"

"Yes, Rose was my mother," Claire said softly, as if sneaking her into the conversation.

"Was?" Millie asked. "Has your mom passed to glory?"

The question surprised her but without the usual slap. "Yes, glory." Claire's mouth turned up on one side. What a tender way to ask a difficult question.

"I love the story." Rita patted Claire's hand and opened her notebook. "Let's see, what shall our next prompt be? Oh, I know. Let's write about motherhood."

Chapter 10

PASTOR KARL'S STRONG VOICE belted the sermon as Claire's mind wandered, yet again. She looked to her left. Bertie listened intently, her hand in Guy's. Millie sat to her right, doodling in the margins of her Bible—flowers and geometric shapes. Will was working today. Without his comforting presence, fear tiptoed in—the realization of where she was gave her pause.

What if Bertie, Guy, and Millie are like the people I thought I knew at my other church? She felt a punch in her gut. *But they're not. No, they can't be, can they?* The thought of him—the deacon—made her stomach churn. She had known him for much longer than she knew these people who had become so dear, so quickly.

She drew in a breath.

Pastor Karl's voice rang in her ears: "Forgive as the Lord forgave you."

Claire looked up. *Forgive the deacon?* She shivered.

Her greatest fear was that the deacon *was* sorry—that she'd *have* to forgive him. Because she *would* have to, right? And although bitterness was a bed of nails, it soothed something inside her—a longing to do justice for her mom and dad.

And she wouldn't forsake her parents' memory by letting the deacon off the hook.

Over a year had passed—no apology.

Or was there?

The letter in the carved box—no, she'd never open it.

And she'd never forgive the church, for that matter, for accusing her of doing the greater wrong—attempting to expose the truth while navigating the grief of the loss of her parents, killed by the drunk deacon on that awful autumn night.

☙

Claire filled a plate with turkey, stuffing, mashed potatoes and gravy, her family's favorite broccoli casserole, cranberry sauce, and homemade rolls. She and Will headed next door to Amos Kicklighter's weathered front porch.

Claire rang the doorbell.

Amos peered through the window. She heard footsteps, and the door creaked open a sliver.

"Whatcha want?"

"Happy Thanksgiving!" Claire held up the plate.

"We brought you dinner. I'm sorry you weren't feeling up to joining us," Will said.

The door opened wide, and Claire handed the plate to the disheveled, unsmiling man. "I hope you enjoy it."

"Looks all right." Amos sniffed the plate. "Smells good."

"Claire made the rolls. They're delicious," Will boasted.

"Well, I hope you're enjoying the break from the rain." Claire smiled at the grouch.

Amos's downturned mouth, void of lips, mirrored the angle of his hunched shoulders. "Less noise in the kitchen."

"Noise in the kitchen?" Claire squinted, not understanding. *The man makes no sense.*

"Dad-burn pinging." He nearly shouted his response. "Makes Pete madder'n a hornet."

Will scratched his chin. "I'm sorry, I don't understand."

"The drips hit the dadgum bucket, and Pete starts in with the howling."

"Who's Pete?" Claire tried to see around the man standing in the doorway.

"My cat." His hands clutched the plate of food—the porcelain the same color as the grip of his dry fingers.

"Oh, I didn't realize you had a cat," Will said. "Is your roof leaking?"

"Didn't I just say that?" Amos's thick caterpillar eyebrows shot up in mock surprise. "Only when it rains."

"I've fixed a leaky roof before. Do you want me to come over and look at it tomorrow?"

Her husband's knee-jerk response surprised Claire. She imagined Will climbing on the roof while Amos hurled insulting remarks from the security of solid ground.

"Suit yourself."

Suit yourself? Claire watched as Amos turned, crossed the threshold, and shut the door with a slap.

Will chuckled. "He's a character."

"Are you going to fix his roof? What if it's a major leak?"

"I'll ask Guy to help me. He'll know how to get the job done." Will took Claire's hand as they strolled home. "And he loves Amos."

Claire sighed. "Guy loves everyone."

Will smiled. "Ain't that the truth?"

❧

Claire's phone pinged a text as she walked to the church for the Grace Writers meeting.

> Mom, thanks again for the fun Thanksgiving! I can see why you love Guy and Bertie so much. Love you! Kate

It had been a small but good Thanksgiving dinner, culminating in dessert with Guy and Bertie and two of their boys and their families. The games and banter that ensued reminded her of their family Thanksgivings of years past. It was a refreshing, comforting, and joy-filled day.

She shoved her phone and hands deeper into her pockets and quickened her steps. The air had turned from crisp to bone-chilling overnight.

Claire arrived at the church to find the ladies in a bit of a tizzy.

Ella Mae hustled into the room a little late.

"Oh, for pity's sake, what are those?" Millie's eyes followed Ella Mae as she approached the table.

"White Chocolate Cranberry Dreams," Ella Mae boasted. She ran a knife through the bars draped with red and white speckled frosting.

Millie fanned herself with her notebook. "Hurry up, lady, we're comin' off a Thanksgiving sugar high. We need a fix."

The ladies began grabbing when Ella Mae placed the large platter on the table. They'd barely had a chance to taste them before the compliments flowed.

"You've outdone yourself this time," Joan said.

"Will you just this once share your recipe?" Millie asked, nose wrinkled.

"You look pitiful. Don't beg. She won't share it." Josephine licked her fingers. She slid her hand to the platter again and took another cookie. Her blue eyes danced as she lifted it to her thin lips.

Ella Mae has these women wrapped around her finger.

"My mom used to make these," Claire said.

Why is it so fun to poke her?

"Not these. I invented them." Ella Mae's eyes flashed.

"Oh, then something similar." Claire took another bite. A bit of satisfying guilt nudged her. "They're just like my mom's."

Rita interrupted the feisty banter. "So, this week, the prompt was to write about motherhood. Claire, do you want to start?"

"Sure." Claire cleared her throat.

When my son was five years old and losing his baby teeth, I looked forward to being his tooth fairy like my mom had done for me. My mother wrapped coins in pink, stretchy crepe paper and, while I slept, exchanged the pretty package for my tooth. I never caught her, and she never forgot.

Michael lost his first tooth, and I performed right on cue—success. Two lost teeth later, I fell asleep on the job, waking the next morning with a start.

I jumped up and ran to his room.

"Mom, what are you doing?" he asked.

"Oh, I'm just checking to see if the tooth fairy came," I said.

He stuck his arms under the pillow. "Yes, she did. Look."

It was a close call, but my cover wasn't blown.

The next time the tooth fairy was called to duty, I snuck in a little too soon, and his eyes popped open as I searched under the pillow for the tooth box.

A few more teeth and a few close calls later, I resigned myself to being a sub-par tooth fairy. How could I be so bad at something so simple? I hoped he didn't know my secret, but my hopes were dashed one spring day.

After school, Michael ran in the door, excited to tell me a story.

On the playground, another student bragged about his mother's important job, and all the other kids joined in.

"Mom, guess what? Sara's mom is a nurse, Mark's mom is a hair cutter, and Jessica's mom is a teacher." Michael beamed as he rattled off his list.

As a stay-at-home mom, I wondered what he told his friends about my job.

"What did you say I do?" I asked.

Without hesitating, he said, "You're the tooth fairy." He was elated to have unloaded the secret he'd kept for quite some time.

Upon further questioning, I realized he didn't think I was just *his* tooth fairy, but he had assumed I was the tooth fairy for every child in the world. His classmates were impressed.

After I stopped laughing, I told him the truth. "Yes, I am the tooth fairy." He'd caught me.

Truth be told, through months of failure, I had grown to dread the words, "Mom, I lost a tooth." I associated it with another opportunity to drop the ball. Try as I might, I couldn't get my act together at the end of a long day. It was one of many ways I thought I didn't measure up to other moms.

When my son told me his story, I was blessed. I realized my son naturally thought the best of me. Instead of being disappointed that I was a lousy tooth fairy, he had thought I was an even more excellent one—the tooth fairy to the world.

As I mothered my kids to adulthood, many opportunities arose for guilt and comparison. When frustration reared its ugly head, I remembered I was the tooth fairy. And although I fail, I am just right for *my* kids.

Claire closed her notebook.

"Oh, Claire, that's such a sweet story." Joan giggled. "I was caught being the tooth fairy when my son was seven, and I had to pay him triple the normal tooth rate so he wouldn't rat me out to his little brother."

"What a tangled web." Josephine sighed.

Millie patted Josephine's hand. "Oh, Jo, it's all in fun."

"Lying is not *fun*." The older woman raised one eyebrow.

Everyone shared their stories, and Josephine, breaking from her usual sermon summary, wrote a lovely tribute to her childless Aunt Olivetta, who raised her from the age of eight.

Claire noted Josephine's tenderness when she read. Perhaps she wasn't as steely as she appeared.

"This week, let's write about a gift," Rita announced.

Claire remembered a photo that fit the prompt. Her stories began as fiction, but they were beginning to document memories she didn't want to forget. Stories her mother used to tell, and stories of her experiences, had wiggled their way into her mind and onto the page. Preserved, saved forever, never to be forgotten—her grief a bit easier to bear.

Chapter 11

CLAIRE PICKED UP THE PHOTO of a woman she didn't know. She held a gift—her eyes filled with excitement. Claire gazed at the blank computer screen. What was the story going to be?

Her eyes moved from the screen to the window. Soft rain pattered against the pane, blurring her view.

The yard was still. No birds fluttered about.

In the stillness—the quiet of the house and the gentle dripping drizzle—Claire's mind wandered to Harley's tour of the bar. Pride and angst mixed into a man whose heart was bigger than his vice. The spotless floor, the gleaming bar, the hand-carved vines. It was beautiful.

Claire didn't know how to feel. How can she have compassion for one drunk and utter disdain for another?

Did the deacon feel sorrow for her loss? Did *he* wish better for *himself*?

The carved box, perched on a shelf, caught her eye. She opened it and looked at the letter. The name on the return address: Richard Simpson. The deacon. Did the envelope hold his sorrow? Was she ready to read it? After more than a year of angst and the move to Walters Bluff, could she read the sorrowful words of a man who paid no price other than a suspended license and a few fines? Was he waiting for her reply? A twinge of guilt plucked her heart, then the memories flooded in.

I'm not ready.

The pain was still too sharp. Someday, she'd read his letter. Maybe she'd even forgive him. Not today. She pushed thoughts of Richard from her mind. Today, she wanted to think of the antique shop, the box of photos, and a visit from Bertie.

The doorbell halted her train of thought.

Bertie stood on the porch with a bag from Goodies Bakery.

"Come in, my goodness. It feels like winter out there."

"Thank you, dear. It's cold, but I wouldn't have it any other way during the holidays." Bertie took off her coat and rain boots.

They settled on the sofa with coffee and fritters. Claire held the warm mug. "Will has spent so much time in your garage with Guy. I wonder what they're making. He won't tell me."

"Guy loves Will. I think they laugh more than they work, but you didn't hear that from me." Bertie smiled. "He misses having the boys around. Will is so much like our sons—he's been adopted, in case you didn't know—such a blessing to Guy."

"The feeling's mutual. You know, Will's never had a father figure to look up to."

"He doesn't have a dad?"

"He does, but he's not …." *How do I describe Will's father?* "Well, he's not fatherly."

"I'm sorry to hear that. Is he still living?"

"I think so. We don't communicate with his family. They're gamblers. When we do hear from them, they ask for money. We don't give it, and then they disappear for a few years."

"If only they knew what they've missed. Kate is such a dear. I can only imagine how sweet the other kids are." Bertie's eyes grew misty.

"I try not to think about it. And that made losing my parents so much more …."

"Mercy." Bertie put her hand on her heart. "Have you and God hashed it out? I know it's a burden."

"I've been mulling it with Him a lot more lately."

Bertie patted her knee. "He's always at work. He hears our hearts even when we don't utter a word."

Claire told Bertie about Fern, Laurel, and the new shop. "We're so excited to get started."

"See?" Bertie sipped her coffee. "He cares about the details. I'm so thankful you have partners to do this with you. They are dear girls. I've known them since they were little."

Claire gazed at the sweet woman sitting next to her. She looked forward to every visit.

Mom would have loved Bertie.

Guy and Bertie's essence had seeped into the void, filling it to the brim. The two women finished the coffee and fritters, chatting like old friends—or perhaps as a mother and daughter.

Will knocked on Amos Kicklighter's front door. He waited quite a while. Amos didn't like unexpected visitors—no, he didn't like visitors, period.

"Whatcha want?" Amos asked the question through a crack in the door.

"I came by to look at your roof before it starts to rain again next week. Maybe I can fix the leak or at least cover it with plastic until you can get a professional on the job."

"You have to come in my house?"

"Well, that would help. I can look at the roof first if you prefer. You said the water was coming into the kitchen?"

"Yeah."

"Where is the kitchen in relation to your roof?"

Amos pointed. "That corner over yonder. You cain't be coming in my house."

"What about the attic?"

"Attic's full."

"Full?"

"I'm a collector."

"I see. Well, that's fine. Do you mind if I look at the outside anyway? Maybe we can stop the leak."

"We?" Amos' eyebrows lifted.

"Guy and me."

"Suit yourself."

Will brought over a ladder and climbed onto the roof. He saw the build-up of branches and leaves on the corner of the house, no doubt a result of the last two storms. He cleared away the debris and saw the damage. He could fix it with a couple of extra hands. He climbed down and knocked on the back door.

"Go around."

Will barely heard the muffled voice. He walked to the front door. Amos was waiting when he arrived.

"You find it?" The crotchety man scowled.

"I did."

"Hey, Will. God bless you, Amos. I hear there's some work to be done." Guy lumbered carefully down the broken cement path.

Amos scratched his armpit as he scowled at the men on his porch.

"While we patch your roof, you might want to check the attic in case the water damaged anything," Guy said.

"Nah." Amos shook his head. "It's only been leaking a couple o' weeks. Everything'll dry out fine."

"I have spare shingles left from building our shed." Guy smiled at the grump wedged in the door. "They might not match, but it's on the back of the house, so it won't show. Does that sound okay?"

"Suit yourself. You gonna clean up after yourselves like the people on the TV commercial do, or am I gonna have stuff all over my back porch?"

Despite the sarcasm, Will saw gratitude in his eyes.

"We'll clean up the mess." Will chuckled. "Don't worry."

"Shouldn't take but a couple of hours, and we'll be out of your way." Guy winked at Will.

"Good." Amos shut the door.

The two men detoured to Guy's shed and gathered the materials in a wheelbarrow.

"Amos has always been odd. He keeps to himself most of the time." Guy grabbed another hammer and roofing nails, adding them to the pile.

"He's funny. I kind of like him. He bugs Claire to no end, though."

"Bertie, too. I think he's not too keen on womenfolk."

The two men laughed and set to work.

Despite Guy's age, Will struggled to keep up with him. He enjoyed working with the man. Carpentry, fixing a roof—it didn't matter what they did. He loved spending time with Guy. He missed Claire's father fiercely but thanked the Lord for moving them next to such a fatherly man.

❧

Claire arrived at Greenwald's Floral carrying a plate of chocolate cupcakes.

Josephine greeted her with a scowl.

"Did you hear the news?" Claire chirped.

"Did *you* hear the news?" Josephine snapped.

"What news are you talking about?"

"Bill Wiggins ordered these flowers for Marta Fowler. Not appropriate, in my opinion."

"Why not?"

"It has the appearance of mischief."

"Wasn't there a prayer request for Marta? She had surgery the other day." Claire marveled at the heights the older woman could jump to conclusions.

"Hmmmph." Josephine shook her head and continued arranging. "Just looks a little suspicious if you ask me."

Claire changed the subject. "Have you always lived in Walters Bluff?"

"No. Why?"

"I just want to know you better."

"Hmph. I used to live in Dubuque."

"What brought you here?"

"My parents died." Josephine snipped a bunch of baby's breath.

Claire's heart softened a bit to the mysterious, judgmental woman. They had something in common. "I'm so sorry. When did they pass?"

"I was a girl."

"That's why your aunt raised you? I remember you shared about her at the Grace Writers."

"What is this, twenty questions?"

"No, I don't mean to pry. You don't have to answer."

"Yes, Aunt Olivetta. What about *your* parents? You're not the only one who gets to interrogate."

"Oh, well …." Claire hesitated. "They were killed by a drunk driver just over a year ago."

"Oh." Josephine turned away and adjusted the greenery. "I'm sorry."

"I'm glad they were with me as long as they were. I'm trying to focus on being grateful for what I *had*—and what I *have*."

"That's good."

"Not that I'm succeeding, but Bertie's helped me a lot. She's a dear soul."

"Yes, she is." The older woman cleared her throat.

Silence hung between them for a moment.

"So, what's *your* big news?" Josephine surprised Claire with the question.

"Fern, Laurel, and I are going into business together. The paperwork is drawn up, and we're signing this afternoon."

"I don't like change, but I appreciate you saving the shop." Josephine tucked the baby's breath into the bouquet.

"I didn't save anything. It's a partnership. Would you like a cupcake?"

"No, I only eat sweets at the Grace Writers." The woman's eyes scanned Claire. "Otherwise—."

Claire interrupted. "No worries, more for us." *Does she think I'm fat?*

Fern appeared through the workroom door, followed by Laurel. "It's happening! I'm so happy, so relieved."

"I'm off to church—prayer meeting. I put you on the list, Fern." The older woman placed the bouquet in the cooler.

"Oh … um … thanks." Fern's face flushed red.

"You need it." Josephine grabbed her coat from the hook, pushed through the door, and disappeared.

"Ouch." Fern sighed.

"A woman without a filter." Claire handed cupcakes to the sisters and picked one for herself. She lifted it in the air. "A toast to partnerships."

"Here, here!" Laurel took a big bite.

"What about a name?" Fern licked frosting from her finger.

"We all must agree, but I did come up with something … it's a metaphor of sorts." Claire pulled an old, beat-up vase from a tote bag. "I was going through my stash and …."

"It's beautiful!" Fern reached for it. "Can you see it filled with floribunda roses in peaches and pinks?"

"Oh yes," Laurel agreed. "It's so perfectly weathered."

"It's a … weathered vessel." Claire looked from sister to sister, waiting for the idea to sink in.

"The Weathered Vessel. Flowers and Antiques." Fern waved her arm as she said the words.

"Yes. And it speaks to the human condition … to all of us, right? That was the metaphor I was going for. We're all weathered vessels … going through life, cracked, worn …." Claire's eyes welled.

"Trying not to crumble completely." Fern spoke softly.

"And still beautiful." Laurel pulled her sister to her side.

"That's it, isn't it?" Fern sighed. "That has to be it."

"I think so, but do you like it, Laurel?" Claire's left eyebrow lifted.

"The Weathered Vessel." Laurel smiled. "It sings, doesn't it?"

༝

Claire waved from the corner of the diner.

Guy held Bertie's hand as they wove through tables to where Claire, Will, and Harley waited.

Harley stood. "Well, look who's here. If it isn't my favorite number cruncher."

Guy pulled him in for a quick hug. "God bless you, Harley. I've missed seeing you." Guy turned to Will and Claire. "I used to do the books for the bar—saw my buddy every week."

Harley turned to Bertie. "You look as beautiful as ever."

"Oh, stop it, you're letting your soft side show." The older woman laughed, hugging him tightly.

"I see your husband is sparing no expense in taking you out for dinner," Harley teased.

"We couldn't resist the invitation to join you. I don't think we've seen you in weeks." Bertie smiled.

"Glad you could come."

Claire listened to stories about their long friendship. She watched the soft rapport between Harley and Guy. She breathed a prayer of thanksgiving, grateful for the people sitting at the table and all the new friends she'd made. They'd lived in Walters Bluff only a few months, but it was home.

"What have you been writing about, Claire?

Guy's question startled her from her thoughts. "Writing?"

"Will said you joined the Grace Writers."

"Oh, I've written a few stories, mostly fiction. I'm just having fun."

"That's wonderful," said Bertie. "Ramona told me what a good writer you are."

"She did?" Claire tried to hide her surprise.

"Well, yes, she said you write beautifully."

"Oh, gosh, that's sweet of her."

"That's my girl," Will boasted.

"And what about the shop? I hear the paperwork is all signed, and it's a done deal." Guy took a sip of water.

"We're working with an architect, and construction begins after Valentine's Day when Greenwald's Floral officially closes." Claire's voice filled with excitement. "We'll have a grand opening of The Weathered Vessel in June. There's so much to do between now and then."

"I love the name," said Bertie. "You'll be selling your mother's antiques?"

"Yes and no. My mom had a booth at a local antique mall, and we spent many weekends filling a storage unit with our finds, with a plan to open a shop together. She was a collector of all things old and … well, weathered. I am, too."

"Will it be hard to let go of those treasures?" Bertie's voice held concern.

"I've saved a few special pieces. The memories of those times together are my most precious possessions." Claire smiled. "I'm ready to part with the rest."

⁓

Claire's mood was light as she entered the fellowship room for the Grace Writers meeting.

Ella Mae hadn't yet arrived, and the ladies were discussing where she might be.

"I'm sorry I'm late, and I've come empty-handed." Ella Mae stopped in the doorway and blew her nose into a wad of tissues. "Yesterday, when I brought in the groceries, the neighbor's dog blew right past me and chased our cat through the house." She sniffled and mopped the beads of sweat on her dark forehead. "It took George forever to shoo the mutt out the door. The thing shed fur all over the place. I've been cleaning and sneezing ever since."

"No worries, I brought a surprise." Claire placed a box on the table. "I baked a treat for us. I'll share it after I read my story."

Ella Mae's head jerked to look at her.

Is that a scowl? Claire couldn't help but grin.

"Well, I guess we won't go hungry." Ella Mae folded her arms.

"Let's get started," Rita said.

"Claire should go first since we're half-famished," Millie said.

Ramona agreed. "Great idea."

"I brought a story about Aunt Evelyn." She adjusted her reading glasses.

"You have a lot of aunts," declared Josephine.

"I don't have any, actually. They're all fiction." Claire paused. "I've always wanted an aunt or two ... so I'm adopting them." She smiled at Josephine and began.

Aunt Evelyn loved making gifts for the family. She was not, however, an artist. She admired the talents of her peers and tried desperately to duplicate their work with a creative spin.

She tried—and she failed.

Unfortunately, Evelyn did not recognize the failures. She knitted love into her sweaters. She didn't see the uneven arms and yarn sticking out like strands of spaghetti. Her pattern and color combinations turned heads—away. She crocheted, decoupaged, and strung beads with abandon, always keeping the recipient in mind while working. Her heart overflowed with talent—her hands, not so much.

Aunt Evelyn oozed joy, warmth, and love, but the dread began when a birthday or Christmas arrived. The worry was that a reaction to a gift would not match the enthusiasm with which it was given.

"I stayed up all night finishing this for you," Evelyn would say.

Her declaration only added to the foreboding
that hung over the recipient's head like a guillotine.
After a gift exchange, Evelyn flitted around, asking
how much we loved what she'd given.

"I can tell you made it with love."

"This yarn is so soft."

"I love kittens. How did you know I love
kittens?" (Her decoupage always included
magazine cuttings of kittens.)

When Uncle Red passed away, her creative spark
waned. She informed the family of her lack of
enthusiasm. "Don't expect my usual level of gifts
this Christmas," she sighed. I'm spent after Red's
passing."

We assured her she should grieve and let the
family spoil *her* this Christmas. We were sad for her
sorrow but relieved for her lack of creative zeal.

As Christmas drew near, she began to show signs
of life again. Perhaps the holiday lights or Christmas
carols sparked her muse.

She arrived at Grandma's house on Christmas
Day with a stack of uniform-sized wrapped boxes.
A palpable dread cloaked the room. She handed a
small, heavy gift to each person.

Her hands folded in her lap, she chirped,
"Unwrap your gifts."

We gingerly worked off the paper. Inside was a
shiny box tied with red and white baker's twine.
Each recipient removed the string and opened the
box to reveal a block of fruitcake suitable for use as
a doorstop. Evelyn clapped her hands with delight.
"I've added baking to my repertoire. Doesn't it
smell divine? Go ahead, dive in."

In an instant of pure genius, Grandma jumped out of her chair.

"I'll slice mine so we can all taste it."

She scurried to the kitchen, checked on the turkey, and turned the oven temperature down. Grandma sliced the cake into thin slices and arranged them on a plate. She glanced at the clock and recalculated the roasting time before setting the plate on the coffee table with a flourish.

"You go first, Grandma." Uncle Leonard smirked.

"Oh, no, I had a slice in the kitchen," she said, winking at him.

No one could outfox Grandma.

Each person in the circle took a slice and then a bite.

"Mmmm."

"Oh, my."

"Hmmm."

Aunt Evelyn perched on the sofa, beaming.

The fruitcake crossed my tongue—a shock of cloves numbing it instantly. It settled hard into the bottom of my stomach.

Grandma had a plan. "I'm so sorry, I just realized that the oven was too low—dinner will be a bit late. Perhaps we could all walk around the neighborhood and admire the Christmas lights."

The family embarked on a Christmas stroll in the snowy landscape, hoping to digest Aunt Evelyn's gift in time to enjoy dinner.

Even though I was young, I realized how much Aunt Evelyn loved us. I understood we loved her back by appreciating her gifts, even if our delight was only for her benefit.

When Aunt Evelyn passed away, we were surprised to learn that everyone had saved her gifts. No one could part with them. For some, it was the outlandish humor of the item, and for others, the tacky element that couldn't be duplicated or described. For all of us, though, it was love. Who could throw away love? We began an Aunt Evelyn gift exchange every Christmas—sharing her creations over and over brought us joy, even in her absence.

Claire looked up to see Ella Mae and Joan dabbing at their eyes.

"Oh, Claire, that was so sweet," Joan said. "I wish it were true."

"Sorry. But we can all relate to receiving a homemade gift of questionable beauty." Claire giggled. "And I brought a fruitcake to share." Claire opened the box to reveal a loaf of dark cake. Dismay shone on every face around the table. "Don't be afraid. I have a delicious recipe."

No one dove in. Claire noted the smug look on Ella Mae's face.

"Oh, you chickens, I'll try it," Millie said. She brushed a salt and pepper curl from her face and reached for a slice.

Joan pressed her coral-painted lips together, then took half of a slice.

Ramona hesitated, then quickly grabbed a piece.

Millie nibbled at the end of the slice. "This isn't fruitcake. I thought you said it was a fruitcake. My mother's was plumb awful, but this is delicious." She took a full bite. "What is this?"

"Fruitcake." Claire chuckled.

Rita and Josephine joined the others.

"Watch out." Ella Mae reached for a slice and broke off a small piece, scrutinizing it. She lifted it to her nose and sniffed. "It smells fruitcakey." She popped it into her mouth.

Everyone watched as she closed her eyes and appraised the morsel.

"Well, I'll be freckles on a fig newton. This isn't half bad."

The loaf disappeared within a few minutes, and only a wad of foil remained.

"That was delicious." Millie licked her fingers as she finished the last crumbs.

"I'm glad you like it," Claire said.

"Oh, we do." Rita dabbed her mouth with a napkin. "The day was saved. We should move along so everyone gets the chance to read. Who wants to go next?"

Claire watched Ella Mae jot something on a page in her notebook. She lifted a crumb from her napkin, placed it on her tongue, snapped her fingers, and added something to her note.

After everyone had shared, Rita said, "Our next prompt is to write about a pet peeve."

Chapter 12

A BELL JINGLED AS CLAIRE PUSHED through the door of Stuff and Things. The Christmas tree stand had gone missing in the move. Surely, Millie had one.

Millie and Harley were playing a lively game of Go Fish at the counter.

"Give me your twos," Harley said, his chuckle rumbling.

"No! I was going to ask *you* for twos. Doggone. Claire's here, and I'm being rude." She put her cards face down and strolled around the counter.

"Looks like a hardcore game you've got going there." Claire smiled.

"You should see us play Scrabble." Harley chuckled. "It's dangerous."

"We're evenly matched, so it does get a little rowdy. Most people think Scrabble is a calm, thoughtful game, but ...."

"She cheats."

"Harley Bushkin, you take that back!"

Claire watched the banter between them. They'd known each other since they were young. Millie claimed there wasn't anything else there, but … Claire wasn't so sure.

"Do you have a Christmas tree stand, Millie? We seem to have misplaced ours in the move." Claire glanced at the shelves of ornaments by the counter.

"I do. I'll go get it."

She disappeared around the corner and returned with a stand that looked just like their old one. Perfect.

"Voila." Millie had a silly grin on her face.

"I'll take it." Claire opened her wallet. "What do I owe you?"

"It's yours."

"No, really, I want to buy it. How much?" She looked at the tag. Three dollars.

"You brought it into my shop a few months ago. It's *your* stand, Claire. It's the one you misplaced, apparently." She giggled.

"You kiddin' me right now?" Harley threw back his head and laughed.

Claire chuckled. "Well, that explains it then." She dropped a few bills on the counter and hurried out.

Millie was giggling too hard to refuse.

Claire hurried home with her tree stand and set about decorating the house for Christmas.

She opened a box of ornaments. Each held a precious story. A snow-covered house for the year they bought the Cape Cod across the street from her parents, and a golden retriever for the year they'd surprised the kids with a puppy. She unwrapped another. A crystal heart, for the year her dad had a heart attack—and a stent saved his life.

Tears filled her eyes. *Why did God save him then, but take him a few years later?* Claire couldn't help but question God's plan.

He didn't make sense. In one breath, she praised the Lord for moving them next to Guy and Bertie and, in the next, doubted He knew what He was doing.

Last year, she put on a brave face, cloaking her grief in holiday cheer. With an empty nest and longtime friends so far away, Claire hoped she could muster up the merry.

Anger welled anew in her heart. Why couldn't she think of her parents without recalling the man who killed them? The deacon, the pastor who supported him, and the church tainted nearly every thought of them. Did mulling over the hurt help her process her grief, or was it an infection rotting her from the inside out?

She blinked away her unshed tears and unwrapped the nativity set. The doorbell rang as she began arranging the pieces in the bay window.

"Merry Christmas!" Fern, Sage, and Marigold stood on the porch with a plate of Christmas cookies.

"Come in." Claire stepped aside.

Fern and the kids moved into the cozy living room. "I love what you've done with this house. It's beautiful."

"Missus, is your dad home?" Sage looked up at her. His brow wrinkled.

"Her husband. Her husband is at work," Fern said.

"He'll be home soon, Sage." Claire looked into the blue eyes of the freckle-faced boy.

"Can I see his policeman car when he gets home?"

"Whenever you see his car in the driveway, you can knock on the door, and he'll be happy to show it to you."

"Cool."

Marigold took Claire's hand and played with her wedding rings. "I helped make the cookies."

"They look yummy. Should we try one now?" Claire lifted the plastic wrap from the plate.

"The kids are full of sugar and frosting. They've had enough," Fern said.

"Well, I need to try a bite, just to see if they're as good as they look." Claire winked at Marigold. She chose a snowflake smeared with a blob of blue frosting.

Marigold watched as Claire took a bite.

"Oh, my goodness, the best sugar cookies I've ever had. Wow."

A smile spanned the width of her chubby, freckled cheeks.

"Okay, let's go," Fern said, taking her daughter's hand.

"Bye, Missus." The little girl looked up and waved.

"Bye, Miss." Claire smiled.

"I'll come over when Mister comes home, right, Mom?" Sage shot a pleading look at Fern.

"Only if it's convenient for Mr. and Mrs. Baldwin."

"Come anytime." Claire ruffled Sage's hair.

She watched them leave and shut the door, eyeing the plate of sloppily frosted but oh-so-merry cookies.

Her heart filled with joy, her angst forgotten.

Claire and Will hopped into the truck and drove downtown. Oscar's tree lot looked like a scene from the North Pole. Even Bob, his basset hound, wore reindeer antlers. They parked and wandered through the forest of trees, each the perfect shape and fullness. How would they choose?

"Merry Christmas." Oscar appeared at the end of the row. His beard sparkled with hints of silver, and laugh lines accented his eyes. Claire thought he looked a bit like Santa Claus.

"Quite a scene you've created here," Will said.

Oscar scratched his beard. "Thanks for giving me the time off. Folks would have to go to Walkersville for a tree otherwise."

"I was told your lot is a Walters Bluff tradition. Far be it from me to mess with that. We're getting by down at the station—barely." Will chuckled.

Claire glanced around the snow-covered Santa's workshop, where Oscar served coffee and hot cider and collected payment for the trees. "You've outdone yourself. This is magical." Claire examined a nearby tree.

"Are you lookin' for a particular height?"

"Six feet, I think." Will stood straight, touching the top of his head.

"You'll want to look over on the second row to the right there." Oscar pointed. "Those'll be about the height you want. Let me know if you find somethin'. I'll help you load it up."

Claire and Will didn't take long to decide on a Noble fir with branches spaced neatly over six feet of height. It was a beauty and smelled divine. They returned to Santa's workshop to pay as Harley entered the lot.

"Hey, Harley," Will called.

"Hey, yourself." Harley ambled over to Will and shook his hand. He reached out to Claire for a hug.

Maybe it was the scent of the trees, or perhaps it was just Harley tugging at her heart. Claire didn't think before asking, "Do you have plans for Christmas dinner?"

He seemed flustered by her question. "What, Christmas Day?"

"Yeah, Christmas dinner." Claire smiled. "Would you like to join us?"

Will squeezed her hand.

"We'd love to have you, Harley," Will said.

"Ah … I don't think so … my sister usually has something, and well, I'm not much for celebratin' Christmas … it's just …."

"Well, if you change your mind, there's always room at our table." Claire smiled.

"I thank you kindly." He looked down at his boots.

While Harley helped Will load the tree into the truck, Oscar poured cider for Claire.

"Will's been talking about hiring someone to lighten your load down at the motor pool." Claire took a sip.

"They've been talking about hiring another mechanic for years," Oscar chuckled. "Harley'd be a fine mechanic, but he feels his ancestors tellin' him to keep the bar going. I just wish he didn't feel so tied to that dern bar."

"What does he want to do?"

"He tinkers with cars, he can fix almost anything—plumbing, electric, he used to work with wood. He's always been handy. I told him to apply, and I think he'd do it in a heartbeat if he thought he wouldn't get any guff from the family." Oscar sighed.

"That's a tough situation." Claire pondered the softhearted Harley. She could see him wanting to get out from under the bar. Since his scuffle with Buster, his heart didn't seem to be in it.

She heard Harley and Will's voices as they returned.

"Did Oscar tell ya the good news?" Harley punched his friend lightly on the shoulder.

"No, what good news?" Claire looked to Oscar for a clue. A grin spread across his whiskered face.

"I asked Laurel to marry me."

"Congratulations, man." Will shook Oscar's hand.

"When did this happen? I assume she said yes." Claire couldn't wait to see Laurel and hear all the details.

"Yes, she said yes, and I asked her last night. I was going to ask her at the Twilight parade, but I couldn't wait. We had supper at the diner, and I just up and asked her after we ate our meatloaf." Oscar chuckled. "I think she wants to plan a summer wedding."

"I'll bet she's thrilled," Claire noted Oscar's wide smile.

"I think so." Oscar's joy escaped in a giddy laugh.

"Let's get this tree home and decorated," Will said. "Thanks for the cider—and congratulations."

"Merry Christmas." Oscar smiled, his cheeks rosy, just like Santa's.

❧

Ella Mae made her famous Chocolate Almond toffee for the Grace Writers. The whoop of cheers when she lifted the cover from the container left Claire wondering what on earth could be so exciting. The silence as the ladies devoured the delicacy spoke volumes to its exquisite melt-in-your-mouth quality.

"I'm going first today since you all have your mouths full." Ella Mae announced. "I have a list of pet peeves. How can a person have only one? Here it goes…."

1. Running out of butter.
2. Copycats.
3. Underwear riding up.
4. Long lines.
5. People who don't eat carbs.
6. Hot flashes.
7. Mispelled words.

"Hold on a minute." Ella Mae giggled. "I think I spelled misspelled wrong. How do you spell that? One S or two?"

"Two," Josephine said.

"No, just one. Here, I'll look it up on my new phone." Rita fetched it from her purse and stared. Her bracelets jingled as her finger moved over the screen. "Never mind. I don't have a clue how this thing works."

"It's two," Josephine snapped, shifting in her seat. "Go on, Ella Mae. It's two. Just finish your list."

"Okay, fine, let's see, where was I? Oh yes,

8. Dogs barking in the middle of the night.

9. Snoring.

10. Ironing.

"And that last one is a pet peeve with a holy passion," Ella Mae added. "The only thing I iron is Aunt Twylla's fancy tablecloth at Christmastime. I ironed it just the other night, and I thought, this must be what hell is like."

"Oh, for pity's sake," Josephine snapped. "Why'd you have to bring up—" She leaned forward and whispered, "hell."

"It's a justifiable comparison," stated Joan.

"Agreed." Claire chuckled. She couldn't remember the last time she'd ironed anything.

"I hear that. I have all my blouses ironed at the dry cleaners." Ramona brushed an always-wayward strand of hair out of her eyes.

"Wasteful spending. There's a pet peeve for you. Why would you pay perfectly good money for something you can do yourself?" Josephine folded her arms and tilted her head as if waiting for an appropriate answer. Her lifted eyebrows added to the wrinkles on her forehead.

"Because she can. She'd rather spend money on ironing than other things." Millie mimicked Josephine's folded arms. "What's it to you?"

"Now, now," Joan said. "It's no one's business to judge where another person sees fit to spend money. There's no right or wrong."

"Hallelujah for that," Millie said.

"Humph," Josephine scowled.

Ella Mae put down her paper and grabbed the last piece of toffee. "Who's next? The toffee's gone, so we'd better start reading before the sugar slump hits."

Everyone shared their greatest pet peeves, agreeing that running out of butter was, indeed, a worthy irritation. Josephine was the last to share.

"I didn't write about it, but my greatest pet peeve is know-it-alls." Josephine folded her napkin and pushed it to the side, then placed her hands in her lap before looking up at the women seated around the table.

"She's kidding, right?" Millie's brown eyes scanned the other ladies.

Ella Mae's dark fingers swiped non-existent crumbs from the corners of her mouth. She smiled slightly and mumbled, "Takes one to know one."

"I think that's a pet peeve we all share as well, right up there with running out of butter," Rita said under her breath. She ran her fingers through her impossibly red hair.

Claire watched as Joan glanced from woman to woman— she appeared desperate to diffuse any tension.

"We're all know-it-alls, aren't we ladies ... sometimes, I mean." The pastor's wife sighed. "Lord knows I am."

Rita changed the subject. "We're taking a break for the holidays. Our next meeting will be on January fourth," she announced. "The writing prompt will be, oh, let's see ... write about an animal you've loved."

Chapter 13

"MOM, COFFEE?"

Claire looked up to see Emma's head peering around the corner. "Oh, yes."

Claire pulled the sheets off the sofa bed and pushed the mattress back into its hiding place. She replaced the cushions and moved the ottoman to the front.

Emma returned with two mugs, setting them on the side table.

They plopped on the sofa, and Claire sipped her coffee. "It's been so nice having you kids home." She studied her middle child, a woman. How did she grow so fast? She reminded Claire of her dad—same smile, same dark curly hair.

"I love that you moved here, and I love that you decided to go ahead with the antique shop."

"I can hardly believe it's happening." Claire clapped her hands together. "I'm so excited!"

"I am, too. Fern and Laurel are so fun—and talented. The bouquets they brought to dinner the other night are amazing." Emma sipped her coffee.

"They have become my friends, not just business partners," Claire said. "I'm so thankful."

"You seem happier, Mom," Emma said.

Her heart pounded. She had tried to hide her anger and grief from her kids. Emma's words both shocked and relieved her. "Good things are coming, but it's been a challenge."

Emma reached out to Claire, hugging her tightly. "I love you, Mom."

"I love you, too, sweet Em."

After a moment, her daughter pulled away. "What did you think of Michael's girlfriend?"

"Annie fits right in. I love her." She sighed—another answer to prayer.

"Me, too," Emma smiled. "She was as competitive as Kate when we played dominoes. I've never seen Michael so happy."

"He asked for Grandma's engagement ring. I think he'll pop the question soon."

"Really?" Her daughter giggled. "He didn't mention it to me. He probably knows I can't keep a secret."

"No doubt about that—oh, look at the time. Your flight isn't going to wait for you. We should go." Claire kissed her daughter on the cheek. They'd have plenty of time to chat on the two-hour drive.

As Emma lugged a suitcase to the front door, she stopped to gaze at the living and dining rooms. "Mom, you've made this house feel like our old home. It's smaller, for sure, but it's familiar. I like it." Emma pushed her hair behind her ear. "And those picture frames Dad made are amazing. The carved leaves in the corners. He did such a good job. I can't believe he's woodworking."

"I'm so thankful for Guy. Dad spends a lot of time with him."

"He reminds me of Grandpa."

"He does, doesn't he? And Bertie's a sweetheart." Claire smiled. "I wish you could have met Harley."

"Well, we didn't go to the diner. Sounds like that's where he hangs out."

"I invited him to Christmas dinner, but he couldn't come." Claire pulled on her coat. "I want to know him better."

"I like that you're giving him a chance," Emma said.

Claire looked at her daughter. "I am … trying."

Emma looked at her watch. "We should get going."

"Yeah …" Claire squeezed her daughter tight. "Would it be the worst thing in the world if you missed your flight?"

Harley opened the cupboard.

Empty.

He hadn't had a drink in a month.

Just one shot of whisky … but I can't—I won't.

When Claire asked him about the photo in the bar—the picture of him and Danielle and little Rebecca, it broke his heart … again.

The shame of letting them go—of not fighting for them, even though fighting meant slugging it out with himself, with his addiction.

What would Claire think of what I've done?

What was it about her that made him feel shame? He couldn't put his finger on it. She was nothing but kind and didn't judge him—at least, she didn't seem to. He wanted to make her proud, but why? Maybe because she reminded him of his aunt. The dear woman had tried to lead him onto the straight and narrow path, but he had better ideas—partying and reveling in his ownership of the bar were more important than anything.

Harley took a deep breath.

I'm such a foolish man.

He could descend the stairs, enter the bar, and drink away this gnawing guilt and shame. It would be so easy.

Harley lumbered down the steps, and stood behind the bar, gazing at the bottles filled with amber liquid—relief.

It had been four weeks of hell. Did he want to start all over? Did he really want to beat the booze?

I can do it this time. I'm going to change my life and find my family.

A knock on the door jarred him from his thoughts.

"Ready to go?" Buster stood on the sidewalk, shivering.

"Yeah, I'm ready. Thanks for sponsoring me—you're a good friend."

"I'm proud of you, buddy," Buster said.

My friend is proud of me.

Determination replaced the ache for booze.

The men hopped in Buster's truck and headed for Walkersville.

"I've been thinking a lot about finding Danielle and Rebecca." Harley tugged his beard.

"Your head is getting clear of the alcohol. Makes a person take stock of their choices."

"I need to make amends. I blew it. I abandoned 'em. Why didn't I quit drinkin' then? Why?" He shook his head. "I need to find 'em, make it right."

"One step at a time, buddy." Buster looked at his friend. "Ya know where they are?"

"Nah, I'll need to Boogle 'em, or Gooble 'em or whatever that dern thing is."

"Google."

"Yeah, that."

"Patsy can help you. She's good with the computer. I leave all that stuff to her."

"When I'm ready, I'll ask Claire. I think she'll know how to do it."

"Yup. When the time is right, buddy."

~

Fern swept the floor while Laurel hummed as she counted the cash and prepared the deposit.

Headlights flashed in the window. Laurel pulled back the curtain. "Ferny, it's Frank. Do you want me to tell him to leave?"

"No, I'll talk to him." Fern opened the door.

Her husband stomped his feet at the back door, ridding his boots of snow, and strode in. "Hi, Laurel. Hey Fern, can we talk outside?"

"Sure, give me a second." Fern finished sweeping a pile of leaves, petals, and stem ends into a dustpan and emptied it into a large barrel. She removed her apron, threw on her coat, and walked outside, where Frank waited.

"Deb broke up with me." Frank shifted from one foot to the other. He looked like a teenage boy in a used car salesman's body—hapless and conniving.

"So?" Fern couldn't imagine what his declaration had to do with her.

"I want to come home."

"Why?"

"I need a place to stay."

"There's a motel about a mile from here. I'm sure you're familiar with it." In the previous weeks, Fern had grown immune to his salesmanship.

"C'mon, Ferny …."

"I'm not your Ferny."

"Fern, c'mon, you can't keep me from my kids." Frank's voice grew louder.

A fire burned her chest and her cheeks. She slowly placed her hands on her hips and leaned forward. "I've never kept you from the children. You've kept *yourself* from *them*."

"You'll really make me pay for a motel?"

"Yes. Besides, we don't have room. Mother is here. She's staying until Laurel's wedding this summer, maybe longer. You've made your choices, and we haven't been one of them."

"You've changed, Fern."

Fern's anger dissolved with those three words. Her shoulders relaxed, and she smiled. "Thank you. That's the nicest thing you've said to me in a long time."

The call came as Claire and Will sat in the diner with Harley.

"Mom, I asked Annie to marry me." Michael's voice was filled with excitement.

"Well, what did she say?" Claire asked the question, but she did not doubt the answer.

"I said yes!" Annie's voice declared.

"Harley, do you mind if I put them on speaker?" Claire asked.

"Not at all."

"Welcome to the family, Annie," Will said, taking Claire's hand.

"I'm so happy for you both … and for us!" Claire's eyes brimmed with happy tears as she let the news fill her heart.

"We're planning the wedding for next December," Annie said.

"Congratulations." Harley's gruff voice broke through the excited banter.

"Thanks," Michael said. "Is that Harley? I thought you might be having dinner at the diner tonight."

"It's a Thursday night ritual." Claire giggled.

"Mom told us all about you. I wish we could have met at Christmas. Nice to meet you now, Harley," Michael said.

"Likewise." Harley sipped his coffee.

"We'll let you guys get back to dinner and talk more later," Michael said.

"Okay, we're just so happy for you." Claire touched the edge of her phone as if hugging them across the miles.

"Love you guys." Michael and Annie said the words in unison.

"We love you, too." Claire ended the call and squealed with glee.

ॐ

Harley watched the excitement as Claire and Will received the good news.

He was happy for them. He was.

But an ache grew in his heart.

Rebecca just turned twenty-four. *Twenty-four.* He'd missed twenty years of her life. How had he allowed that to happen?

Did she have a beau? Was she married? Did she have good news to tell?

He'd lost the privilege of hearing—of rejoicing in her news.

Harley smiled as he watched the happy conversation between Will, Claire, their son, and their future daughter-in-law, but his heart ached with regret.

Chapter 14

WINTER CLUNG TO Walters Bluff like icicles glued to the gutter. Claire was weary of the bone-chilling cold. On a rare afternoon when the mercury hovered just below freezing, she and Will decided to walk to the diner for a piece of pie with Harley.

Claire saw Guy pouring birdseed into the feeder as they descended the porch steps.

"Hi, Guy," Claire called.

"God bless you."

"How's Bertie?"

"She gave that cold a one-two punch with her homemade chicken noodle soup, and she's feeling much better."

"What's on the workbench?" Will asked.

"I'm working on a dollhouse for the granddaughter." Guy's face lit up when he mentioned her. "Doing the detail work now, and Bertie's sewing curtains for the windows. Little ones like that kind of thing."

"Sounds beautiful," Claire said, pulling her scarf tighter.

"If you're available, I have a project in mind," Will said.

"We can start on Saturday morning if that works for you," Guy offered.

"Great." Will reached over the low picket fence, and the men shook hands.

"Make it eight o'clock, and Bertie'll have the coffee on."

Will and Claire moseyed toward town, passing matted lawns, weary from the long winter. The setting sun cast a golden glow, their breath a glittery vapor. On Main Street, twinkle lights dripped from trees and rooftops, drawing people downtown despite the cold. The sidewalk grew crowded as they reached the heart of Walters Bluff. Like salmon swimming upstream, they wound through the crowd on Main Street. Claire and Will greeted a surprising number of people they now called friends.

They inquired about each person's goings-on, and their walk quickly became a stand as they stopped for several minutes on each block. That's what a walk downtown proved to be in Walters Bluff: slow and halted and not much of a walk at all.

They arrived at the diner a little later than planned.

"Thought you forgot," Harley grumbled.

"Never." Claire sat and patted his hand. If someone had told her a few months ago she'd choose to count Harley among her friends, she'd have scoffed. Yet here she was, happy to share his company.

"It's crowded downtown tonight. Next time, we'll leave earlier," Will said.

"Yup, if you're walking downtown, you've gotta allow time for the folks. That's Walters Bluff for ya." Harley chuckled, low and raspy. "Claire, I have a favor to ask you."

"What do you need?"

"I wondered if you might could help me find my daughter, Rebecca. I know she's out there somewhere, and I want to know if she's okay. I'm doing the twelve steps, and it's time to make things right." He looked at Claire with clear eyes.

She wanted to jump up and hug the man. Tell him they'd help him in any way they could. But knowing Harley, she needed to keep her emotions in check.

"I'm so happy for you. Of course, I'll help you with that. Come over to the house on Thursday, and we'll Google her. I think we'll find her pretty easily."

"You think?"

"Provided she didn't change her name," Will said.

"Oh, I hadn't thought of that. She could be married?" Harley looked stunned.

Claire elbowed Will. "We'll find her, don't worry."

"What a great finale for Greenwald's Floral." Claire stacked ribbons and wire into a moving box.

"We ran out of roses, and all we had left was a bucket of filler flowers and greenery." Fern sighed. "I'll tell ya, what was supposed to be a sad day turned into a celebration."

"On to the next chapter!" Laurel lifted her pointer finger toward the ceiling. "I wasn't the least bit sad yesterday. Thank you, Claire."

"Thank me? I don't know if I would have taken the plunge to open a business if you weren't in it with me."

Laurel smiled. "Well, it's going to be so good. And Walters Bluff will show up for the grand opening just like they did for our last day."

"How are the wedding plans coming along?" Claire asked the question as Laurel taped another box shut.

"Good. We'll get married at St. John's Catholic Church. The reception will be on the courthouse lawn next to the church. I reserved the tents. Of course, Fern will coordinate the flowers. What else is there?"

"Your dress. Do you have a dress?"

"That's a sore subject." Fern groaned, looking at her sister.

"I'll probably wear my mother's dress." Laurel wrinkled her nose.

"You don't want to?" Claire noticed she wasn't smiling. *A bride should be excited about her dress.*

"I broke our mother's heart when I refused to wear her dress," Fern said.

"I do. I do want to." Laurel's smile remained absent.

"Don't believe her." Fern disappeared to load a box onto the truck.

"You can believe me. My mom is so excited. It's going to be beautiful." Laurel kept her eyes glued to the box she was filling. "Did you see the headline in the paper today? A couple in Walkersville had quadruplets!"

Interesting. She changed the subject. "I did. Can you imagine that many babies at once?" Claire waited a few seconds to continue. "What about food for your reception? Have you figured that out yet?" Claire watched Laurel for a reaction.

"Church ladies. Volunteers from St. John's will make food, and Ella Mae volunteered to make cupcakes. She's just so sweet. Only four more months to go. It's so hard to wait."

"It'll go by fast. It sounds like you're right on schedule to finish it all."

"I can't wait to be Mrs. Peabody."

༂

Claire watched the Grace Writers file into the room slower than usual.

"I'm sick of winter," declared Ramona.

The others agreed wholeheartedly.

"Good morning," Ella Mae called as she waddled through the doors. She set a vintage metal cake carrier on the table and dug into her bag, pulling out a knife. "I thought it was time for a taste of the tropics." She did a little hula dance, knife in hand.

"Put down that knife." Josephine leaned away from Ella Mae.

"I brought pineapple upside-down coconut cake." Ella Mae carved it into generous slices.

The mood in the room brightened as they sampled the cake.

"Our prompt was to write about an animal you've loved," Rita announced.

"Can I go first?" Joan asked the question and put her phone in the middle of the table. She smiled as a photo of a newborn baby filled the screen. "I have a grandson. The first one after seven granddaughters! I'm flying to California today, so I must leave early."

After passing the phone around and receiving a flurry of congratulations, Joan read a story about her cat and flew out the door.

"Claire, your turn," Rita said.

"This is a story my grandmother used to tell."

I loved spending summers with my grandpa. His mansion stood three stories tall and had more rooms than I could count. I remember losing my way in the maze of hallways and hidden passages. Grandpa loved playing checkers and hide-and-seek and told tall tales of growing up in the mansion on the shore—the place he still called home.

I spent summers collecting swirling pink, yellow, and orange seashells and riding the standard poodles, Brick and Bella, like ponies.

One sunny afternoon, I sat on the bottom step of the wide stone porch, scuffing my saltwater sandals in a mound of long pine needles. The spicy scent of a peony growing beside the porch reminded me of my mother. I missed her. Breathing deep, I reached out and plucked a bloom, pressing the silky petals to my cheek. I'd been with Grandpa only a week, but an ache for home started to overwhelm my young heart.

The grand door creaked open, and a puff of pipe smoke wafted to my nose.

"Well, hello there, little one." Grandpa's voice rolled from his belly, embracing me with comfort.

"Papa!" I nearly shouted his name as I dropped the bloom and raced into his arms. "Can we play?"

He chuckled, "Of course."

Something cooed behind the peonies.

"Did you hear that?" Grandpa cupped his hand to his ear.

"Yes." I leaned toward the sound. "What is it?"

"A dove—be very quiet." Grandpa reached into his pocket and pulled out a dinner roll. He plucked tiny bits and dropped them on the ground. The bird emerged from her hiding place.

I held my breath and tried not to move.

Grandpa held more crumbs in his hand and reached out to the dove. It was cautious, hopping to and fro a few feet away. It eyed the crumbs until, with one swift flap of its wings, it hopped onto Grandpa's hand.

"Ooh," I squeaked. The bird hopped down and backed away.

Grandpa chuckled. "Here, you try." He gave me a handful of crumbs. Grandpa showed me how to move slowly and talk softly as the bird nibbled bread and seeds.

When my cousins arrived a few days later, Grandpa showed them how to feed the doves, too. A curious dove hopped over to me, tilting its head back and forth as it drew cautiously closer. I reached out my hand, and it jumped right in. With one swift motion, I lifted it to my chest. It cooed softly as I stroked its white feathers. My cousins marveled at the dove in my arms. They attempted to pick up the others to no avail.

For the rest of the summer, I was known as the dove catcher, and my cousins loved to pet the birds as they cooed contentedly in my arms. I don't know why they liked me best, but their affection proved good practice for the new baby brother born late that summer. When my mother put him in my arms, I snuggled my little brother to my chest. I whispered that I loved him and gently stroked his feather-soft cheek.

My new brother cooed, just like a dove.

"Oh, that's lovely," Rita said.

"Thank you."

"I like that you wrote the story in first person," Ramona said.

"I wanted to remember it just as my grandmother told me." Claire tucked the pages back into her notebook. She was amassing quite a collection of stories. What a blessing to have this group, inspiring her to write and share them.

"Ramona, would you like to share your news?" Rita asked, brushing back her impossibly red hair.

"Well, a small press in Seattle is publishing my book. They specialize in historical works about the Northwest. So, I should have books to sell at the Founder's Day Festival in August. All that editing and years of work will finally be complete."

The ladies burst into applause.

"We'll look forward to it," Rita said.

"I can't wait to learn more about this community." Claire wondered what it must feel like to have a book published. It was the first time she'd ever known a real author.

"You'll probably learn more than you've ever wanted to know." Ella Mae chuckled.

"It's a lot of history, fun stories, and a few secrets mixed in," Ramona said. "I can hardly wait."

The rest of the ladies shared what they'd written about their pets, and Josephine surprised everyone when she wrote about a stray cat she'd been feeding on her back porch. She admitted to inviting it into her house on occasion.

"It might have fleas, you know," Ella Mae said, her brown eyes squinting.

"I took it to the vet. She's had her shots, and she was given a flea bath. She's fine." Josephine looked different. Was that excitement? Love?

"Do you have a name for her?" Claire couldn't imagine what the woman would name a pet—especially since she claimed not to like animals.

"Precious." Josephine's voice was but a whisper.

"Precious?" Ella Mae's face hid nothing. She was shocked.

"That's a lovely name," Claire said. *The old bitty has a soft side.*

Rita announced, "Our next prompt is to write about your favorite possession."

Chapter 15

CLAIRE'S MIND WANDERED to her children as she sorted a box of antique trinkets. She thought of Michael. He had Annie now. Emma loved her career, and Kate—unsure and seeking, but smart and driven. What would become of Kate?

Claire looked out the window and saw Harley walking up the porch steps. She set aside the box.

He's searching for his daughter. What must that feel like?

She welcomed him and led him to the kitchen table, where her laptop sat.

He shifted in his seat and wiped a bead of sweat from his brow. "Could I get a glass of water?"

"Certainly." Claire retrieved the water for him. "You okay, Harley? Are you ready for this?"

"Yes, let's do it. I'm ready. I need to know where they are." He drew in a breath. "I want to know if Danielle and Rebecca had a good life."

"Did you bring a picture of them?" Claire asked.

"Here." He handed her the photo from the bar—a young Harley with a pretty wife and adorable little girl.

Claire examined the photo. His daughter's hair curled in ringlets at her shoulders, her eyes as blue as her father's, with long eyelashes. Her mouth smiled, but her eyes looked sad. "Your daughter is beautiful. Let's see if we can find her."

"I hope so."

"Okay, here we go." Claire glanced at the printed name on a sheet of lined paper. She typed *Rebecca Danielle Bushkin* into the search bar. She glanced at Harley. His eyes were glued to the screen. A page of results popped up. The first one read: Rebecca Danielle Hardy-Bushkin—curator, Wilson County Museum.

"Is Hardy Danielle's maiden name?"

"Yes." Harley's eyes widened. "She works at a museum?"

"Maybe. Let's look at the images. We'll find a photo of her."

Claire typed. Little squares, each a photo of a woman, popped onto the screen.

"I'll bet that's her." Harley pointed to the first photo—a dark-haired young woman with fair skin and shocking blue eyes. She had a natural look with just a hint of lip gloss and nothing else. She wore a gray T-shirt and waved at the camera. On her wrist, a tattoo—a heart with the initials D.L.H. Claire noted contentment in her eyes.

"Look, here's another photo of her." Claire scrolled down and clicked. "She does work at a museum. Rebecca is a curator for the Wilson County Museum. Harley, she didn't go far. She's just across the state line in Glenwood." Claire looked at Harley. "What's Danielle's middle name?"

"Her name's Danielle Louise Bushkin."

Claire typed her name into the search. The first link to appear was an obituary. *Danielle Louise Hardy died on November 5, 2022.*

"Oh, no," Harley choked.

"I'm so sorry, Harley." Claire put her hand on his arm. She stood and invited him to sit—to read the obituary for himself.

He gazed intently at the screen for several minutes, then looked away. She watched as he stood and walked to the window. He laced his fingers on top of his head, his body expanding and contracting with every deep breath he took.

Tears filled Claire's eyes.

A few minutes passed before he turned to face her. "She died of cancer." He wiped his left eye with his fist. "What do I do with this information? Should I contact Rebecca? I've gotta think this through."

"Of course, take your time and do what you think is best. It's a big step."

Claire wrote Rebecca's full name, her place of employment, and the address to the museum on a piece of paper and handed the page to Harley.

"I don't know what I thought we'd find today, but I never expected to find out that Danielle was …." Harley wiped another tear with his fist and added. "You're good with this computer stuff."

"If you ever need help with anything, I'm here for you." Claire squeezed his arm. "Really, Harley, anything at all."

She watched him meander down the path to the street—slowly, thoughtfully. Her heart broke for him, and in that moment, she realized she cared deeply for the man. He didn't smell like stale alcohol anymore, and he was taking back his life. Claire found herself praying for him as he disappeared down the street—that he would become the man he wanted to be, the man she now believed he could be.

༄

Harley headed home, each step reminding him of another detail about his short married life with Danielle. The words of the obituary swirled in his mind. She'd had to work so hard for his daughter. She did everything by herself.

Guilt hit him like a punch to the gut. His mind wandered to the night she left. They didn't live over the bar then. They had a little house on Peach Street. He worked late, drinking away his profits with Buster. That night, Buster passed out on the hardwood floor. Harley left his friend lying there to sober up and drove home. His next memory was waking up inside the car parked on the front lawn. His head rested on the steering wheel.

Pounding on the window startled him awake.

"So you're *not* dead." Danielle's fury was palpable.

An angry voice filled his ears, but he couldn't decipher the meaning. A wave of nausea punched him, and a wretch jerked him forward. The voice grew louder. *Was she cursing?* He turned his head to the voice, but his vision was blurred. As his eyes scanned the scene, the only thing in focus was the face of his daughter peering through the curtains.

Danielle packed and left with Rebecca before he could rouse himself. She left a note on the windshield.

When you decide we're more important than whisky, let me know. We'll be at my mother's. I do love you. Danielle.

Buster was scared sober. He'd just met Patsy, a sweet, church-going girl. He wouldn't risk losing her.

Both men joined AA, and Buster meant every step he took. Harley quit after the second meeting.

Alcohol was Harley's lifeblood—his livelihood. The bar was chained to his family's legacy, the shackles more comfortable and familiar than the responsibility of marriage and fatherhood.

Now, twenty years later, Harley's heart ached at the thought of his downright selfishness and stupidity.

What-ifs filled his mind. What if he had stayed sober? What if he had pursued them? What if Danielle hadn't needed to raise Rebecca alone?

What if she hadn't died?

Life could have been so much different—so much better. But here he was, playing the age-old what-if game.

He *hadn't* sobered up, and he *didn't* try to make things right.

He let them down.

What could he do now?

As much as he wanted a drink, staying sober was a good start.

Dear Wanda,

My mother insists that I wear her wedding dress when I get married this summer. It's hideous. First of all, it's high-necked and long-sleeved. Second of all, it's got a train the length of a football field. My sister refused to wear it, and I'm the last girl in the family to get married. She swears her heart will break if it sits in a box forever. What can I do?

Sincerely,
A strapless tea-length kind of gal

Dear Strapless,

My daughter didn't want to wear my dress either. If I'm honest, it did break my heart. Why do mothers always want their daughters to wear their tired old wedding dresses? The good news is that we came to a compromise both of us could live with. I handed my dress over to a gifted seamstress who altered it into a beautiful design my daughter loved. She wore the same fabric, the same lace, some of the same beading, with new touches thrown in for good measure. She was the most beautiful bride I've ever seen. The dismay of someone cutting up my dress left me the moment I saw her walking down the aisle like an angel on a cloud of tulle. Tell your momma that Georgine Tillamook (555-3258) can turn her wedding dress into precisely the dress you want at a price that can't be beat. She's not paying me to say that, either.

Laurel picked up the phone, called Georgine, and set up a meeting. She wasn't going to look like her mother on her wedding day.

～

Claire stepped into the gutted shop. The wall of the adjacent space was gone, creating one cavernous room. It was bigger than she'd expected. *Did I bite off more than I could chew?* Her heart pounded. *I can't let the girls down.* She strolled through the space, imagining the walls of the workroom, the office, and the storeroom. The short walls creating rooms within the large space would surely make it cozier. She took a deep breath. *Yes, it will be perfect. No sense worrying.*

The sisters pushed through the door.

Fern gasped. "I have so many feelings running through me right now."

"Me, too." Laurel turned in a circle, eyes scanning the bigger shop.

"They saved the workroom counter." Fern pointed to a large wooden slab leaning against the wall. "I forgot that was in the storeroom."

"I remember sitting on that counter, helping Dad peel spent rose petals, and I distinctly remember when Mrs. Witherspoon came in with her son to pick up a corsage for his prom date." Laurel chuckled.

"I had such a crush on him," Fern said. "He was so handsome."

"You were only, what? Nine?" Laurel huffed. "Mrs. Witherspoon gave you a five-dollar tip for your time. I was so jealous."

"Are you talking about Bertie?" Claire looked from sister to sister.

"Mrs. Witherspoon when we were girls, but yes, Bertie." Fern turned her head left, then right. "The place is demolished."

"It's a little daunting to see, if I'm honest," Laurel added. "I trust the process, though."

"Look at that." Claire pointed up. "The old tin ceiling goes through to the other space. Can you believe it? An ugly dropped ceiling covered it."

Laurel looked up. "Wow."

"It's going to be gorgeous when it's freshly painted, and they'll put up wood beams to cover the gaps." Claire clapped her hands. "I can see it now."

"I have a hard time imagining it." Fern clutched her chest. "Right now, it feels like a tornado swept through here. I'm both shocked and excited."

"I can see it." Laurel squeezed her sister's arm. "It'll be beautiful."

"Is everything still on schedule?" Fern asked.

"So far so good." Claire smiled. "I don't foresee any delays, but those are always famous last words."

১

At the weekly Grace Writers meeting, Clare settled into a chair next to Joan.

"I saw a daffodil." Millie sang as she hurried into the room. "It isn't open, but I saw the bright yellow petals peeking from the green. Spring is here."

"Hallelujah!" Ella Mae filled a bowl with homemade caramel corn.

"You didn't," Rita snapped.

"Oh, yes, I did," she replied.

"Goodness. You are something else." Joan pushed her blonde hair behind her ear and reached for a napkin.

"Is that?" Ramona pointed to the bowl.

"So, what if it is?" Ella Mae pushed the bowl toward Ramona.

"Well, it doesn't matter, but you should give her credit." Rita's eyebrow lifted.

"We just did." Ella Mae filled a napkin with caramel corn and waddled to the end of the table.

"What am I missing?" Claire had never been so confused.

"This isn't Ella Mae's recipe. It's Beulah Fletcher's. She goes to St. John's," Millie said. "Ella Mae had the gumption to ask for the recipe, and Beulah refused. A week later, Beulah accidentally emailed it to Ella Mae instead of her daughter." Millie popped a piece into her mouth.

"She emailed it to you?" Claire was still struggling to navigate the conversation.

"One night, I'm just checking my email like nothing special, and there it is in my inbox. The subject line said, *Here you go, honey.* I clicked on it, and honey, there it was! Her top-secret recipe for caramel corn."

Josephine rolled her eyes.

"I might have emailed her back saying, *Thanks, sweetie.*" Ella Mae threw her head back and laughed.

"You didn't!" Millie clapped her hands.

"Claire, we have an ongoing competition with St. John's. There's a dessert auction every July before Founders Day," Joan said. "Two years ago, Ella Mae lost to Beulah Fletcher."

"Really, Joan, you're telling *that* story?" The plump woman folded her arms.

"It's part of the bigger story," Joan explained. "It was extraordinary because you always win."

"I do, don't I?"

"The next year, after the email brouhaha, Ella Mae topped her Salted Caramel Chocolate Dream Cake with caramel corn from Beulah's recipe and won the whole she-bang. It was funnier than a crutch!" Millie hit the table with pure glee. "Beulah never saw it coming."

Josephine frowned.

Claire popped a piece of caramel corn into her mouth. "Let's see if Beulah's recipe is as good as mine." She savored the sweet and salty treat. "It could do with a little more salt to give it that extra *je ne sais quoi*."

"I did add a bit more salt than her recipe called for; you think it needs more?" Ella Mae's eyes squinted as she looked to Claire for a response.

"Just my opinion." Claire winked.

Ella Mae looked around the circle of ladies. She jotted something in her notebook and sighed.

"Okay, ladies, who'd like to start?" Everyone munched on caramel corn, so Claire volunteered. "The prompt was about a possession," she said. "The story I brought sort of works with that. This is about my mother, Rose, and her best friend, Nora."

Thrifty. That's the word that best described Nora Whitaker.

Her children called her cheap.

Nora could make a pound of hamburger stretch through several meals. She washed and reused plastic bags. She rarely bought anything new, finding whatever she needed at thrift stores and garage sales. The only splurge she allowed herself was bingo every Friday night. Her rationale was that she almost always won a game, sometimes two. If she compared the expense of playing with all her winnings, she didn't spend a dime.

One Friday evening before her sixty-seventh birthday, Nora won the blackout game and a mysterious gold envelope. The excitement was palpable as she broke the seal. It could be a month's worth of groceries, a piece of jewelry, or a gift certificate to her favorite restaurant. Her mind spun as she read the coupon. "Good for one free tattoo, maximum value $300." She gasped and clutched the envelope to her bosom.

"What is it? You look like you've seen a ghost." Rose grasped her friend's arm.

"Tell me what this says. I think I read it right, but I'm not sure."

Rose took the envelope and examined the coupon. "Good for...."

"Shhhhh. I don't want anyone to hear."

Rose's eyes scanned the card. "Oh, my, well, that's quite a prize."

A smile crept onto Nora's face.

"You're not going to *get* one, are you?"

"Well, I'm not going to let this go to waste. It's the biggest prize I've ever won." Nora plucked the coupon from Rose's hand.

"Tattoos last forever. For-ever. And they hurt." Rose huffed. "Surely, you're not—for heaven's sake, not at your age. What will your kids say?"

Rose was speaking, but Nora wasn't listening. She fixated on the value of the prize and the fact that she'd be able to point to her tattoo and say, "I won it at bingo." She couldn't do that with a case of microwave popcorn, a free breakfast at the Pancake House, or a tire rotation from Tire Town.

The following Friday, Nora pranced into bingo and plopped next to Rose. She leaned over and said, "I redeemed my coupon."

Rose groaned. "Do I dare ask where? Do I dare ask what?" She covered her eyes and peeked through her fingers.

Nora removed her coat and lifted the sleeve of her decades-old blouse. A bouquet of roses bloomed in a teapot—lovely, if painted on a canvas and hung on the dining room wall, but on Nora's sixty-seven-year-old arm, it was a little wilted.

"What do you think?" she asked. "I love roses and tea. It was a perfect choice."

"Whatever floats your boat," Rose said, rolling her eyes.

"My boat is afloat." Nora grinned and pointed to her tattoo. "I won it at bingo."

Claire smiled and closed her notebook.

"I love it," Millie said, smiling.

"A woman our age getting a tattoo." Josephine scowled. "I can't even imagine."

"I'd get a tattoo," Millie volunteered. "I'd put Fussy right here on my shoulder if needles weren't involved."

"A stick of butter." Ella Mae chuckled. "Right on my caboose." She nudged Josephine playfully.

Josephine nudged her back. "I believe you would." Her mouth remained a straight line.

When all the stories were read, Rita announced the next prompt, "Write about a lie."

Josephine frowned, "Why would we write about that? The good Lord knows I won't."

Chapter 16

WILL SETTLED AT A TABLE in the corner of the Daily
Brew. Guy joined him and began updating Will on all
the goings-on of his grandkids.

"God bless you," Guy called as Harley ambled through the
door.

"Hey, Guy, Will."

"Harley, are we walking to church together tomorrow, or do
you want to meet us there?" Will stood to shake his hand.

"You can stop by."

"Fine, we'll be there at six forty-five."

"What on earth—that early? I told Claire I'd go, but she
didn't tell me the service was at the crack of dawn.

"It's a sunrise service. It starts at seven. Breakfast afterward."

Guy pulled another chair to the table. "Take a load off. Have
a seat."

"Let me get some water. I'm thirsty." Harley purchased a
bottle of water and sat.

"How's business?" Guy took a sip of coffee.

"Well, I'm mullin' things over. I'm tired of running the bar." Harley guzzled half the bottle.

"Maybe you should talk to your sister—see what she thinks. She may agree with letting it go." Guy's expression showed concern.

Harley shifted in his seat. His forehead sparkled with tiny beads of sweat. "I don't know—just thinking out loud. Maybe I *will* talk to her about it." He excused himself and bought another bottle of water.

"You're awful thirsty today." Will watched him chug half the bottle.

"Yeah, I think I'm dehydrated. I spent the afternoon working on the Caddy in the sun. She's runnin' like a top, though."

"She's a beaut," said Guy. "My son's got a '67 convertible. The boys love the classics."

"You raised 'em right." Harley stood. "I've gotta run. See you tomorrow."

"Tomorrow, Resurrection Sunday." Will stood and shook his hand.

"God bless you." Guy turned to Will. "Let's go home and get busy, shall we?"

They walked to Guy's house and entered the garage through the side door. Guy helped Will cut the pieces that would be a jewelry box for Claire. She'd be fifty this year, and Will wanted to make her something special to soften the blow.

~

Claire waited next to Pastor Karl on the courthouse lawn. Over a hundred children stood behind a green ribbon held by two uniformed police officers.

Mayor Bickerstaff removed a microphone from a stand. "Ladies and gentlemen, or should I say, boys and girls?" The mayor waved his arm toward the antsy kids. "Welcome to the thirty-fifth annual Easter Egg Hunt. The First Community Church graciously gave up hosting the hunt this year, allowing me to extend the privilege to our local businesses. As your children enjoy the eggs, consider patronizing the establishments that so generously filled them." Mayor Bickerstaff stood next to a campaign table stacked with *Bickerstaff for Mayor* bumper stickers and lawn signs.

"Nothing like starting the campaign early." Pastor Karl sighed.

"Is that why First Community isn't hosting the hunt? He wanted the business owners to back him for mayor?" Claire watched the mayor drone on.

"Small-town politics. He's using the kids to gain the votes." Claire shook her head and sighed.

Sage and Marigold, all dressed up, danced behind the ribbon, waiting to bolt. Their eyes looked from one egg to another, no doubt planning their strategy.

Fern pulled Sage back as he ducked to crawl under the ribbon.

"So, without further ado." A siren sounded, and the ribbon dropped. Children ran onto the lawn like ants at a picnic. Within a few minutes, it was over. Every basket overflowed, and children huddled in groups.

The mood on the lawn quickly changed from wild excitement to something else entirely. What was an excellent idea to Mayor Bickerstaff seemed a disappointment to the offspring of Walters Bluff voters.

Instead of candy, coins, and toys, something else filled the eggs.

Claire watched Sage and Marigold open their eggs and throw colorful slips of paper to the side. She picked one up. "Twenty-five percent off a set of tires?" She grabbed a few more. Shuffling through them, she read, "The Washboard Cleaners. Thirty percent off one dry-cleaning order. The Daily Brew has a coupon for one free hot chocolate with the purchase of a latte. Goodies Bakery, one free cookie. Wait, don't they always give kids a free cookie?"

Pastor Karl scratched his head. "This doesn't make any sense."

Each child sat amidst a kaleidoscope of plastic egg halves and heartbreaking offers.

Claire watched Marigold open her eggs slowly and carefully. Her green chiffon dress highlighted her strawberry blonde curls. Her prizes included coupons, a single packet of jellybeans, and a blue bouncy ball stamped *Bluff Chiropractic*. One lightweight egg remained. She squeezed the pink shell, and a piece of yellow paper tumbled out.

Fern picked it up. "One free children's haircut from The Chop Shop on Main."

"No!" Marigold burst into tears. "I hate this Easter egg hunt!"

Her cries mixed with the groans and wails of all the other children on the lawn holding coupons for half-off eye exams from Eagle Eye Optical and a free keychain with a tune-up from Gordon's Automotive.

Fern hugged her daughter. "This is the dumbest Easter egg hunt I've ever seen."

"Where's the candy?" Sage stomped on an egg, shattering it on the lawn.

"I don't know, but that's no way to behave. Clean that up." Fern sighed. "Give Mommy your coupons, kids." Fern leaned toward Claire and dropped her voice. "No sense wasting these discounts."

"What in heaven's name is going on here? This isn't a proper Easter egg hunt." Pastor Karl pulled out his cell phone and made a call. "Joan, I need you to come to the church pronto. Get the word out to the Ladies Auxiliary and everyone in town. We're putting on another Easter egg hunt right after sunrise service tomorrow morning." He paused. "I know, I know, but you ladies work miracles. Make some calls, and let's pull this thing together."

He hung up and dialed another number. "Ella Mae? I know you're busy baking for tomorrow's breakfast, but I need you to rally the ladies to stuff eggs with candy, toys, and coins. There will be an Easter egg hunt, after all."

Claire watched as he nodded and grunted. She could only imagine what Ella Mae was saying on the other end.

"Ella Mae Walker. Are you telling me you cannot do this?" A slight smile formed on his lips.

Claire stifled a giggle.

"All right then … yes … that's what I thought. Thank you, dear."

***

Ella Mae drew in a breath.

Why did I doubt myself? She pulled the last batch of scones from the oven, setting them on wire racks to cool.

She made a few phone calls, enlisting the help of her friends. It wasn't long before she and most of the ladies in the auxiliary were stuffing plastic eggs. When they finished, eight hundred eggs filled boxes to be scattered on the church lawn after the sunrise service on a glorious Easter morning.

She hustled back home to finish the baking. As she entered her kitchen, she stopped to admire the platters of cream, orange, and ginger scones. *They're beautiful.*

Ella Mae smiled—her chest puffed with pride.

She began mixing the muffins—blueberry, lemon poppy seed, and cinnamon coffeecake—her favorites and the most requested by all her fans, or rather, her friends. As she filled muffin tins with batter, the phone rang again. "Holy poppy seed muffin-top, I'll never get the baking done." She waddled around the flour-dusted peninsula to pick up the phone. "Hello?"

"It's Rita. Genevieve's hens are sleeping on the job. I'm afraid I must go to the market and buy a few dozen eggs for the breakfast casseroles for tomorrow."

"No, we can't have sub-par eggs in the casseroles."

"What choice do we have? It's store-bought eggs, or we'll have only enough for six casseroles instead of the ten we need."

"Oh, fine. Don't tell a soul. I swear those hens are the laziest birds this side of Adelaide Creek. She spoils 'em, you know. Too much scratch. They think they don't have to work for treats and, before you know it, lazy hens."

"No one will know the difference. I probably shouldn't have called, but I know you, and you'd have noticed the color of the casserole wasn't as yellow as it usually is. You're good, Ella Mae."

"Tell me something I don't know."

"I'll send Hank to the market and get crackin'." Rita chuckled. "Pun intended."

"Good one. See you tomorrow. Oh, and keep the potholders away from the stove." Ella Mae waddled back around the peninsula and hung up the phone. She smiled.

Tomorrow's going to be perfect.

Chapter 17

AN EXQUISITE PINK AND ORANGE SKY greeted the
faithful arriving for the sunrise service at the First
Community Church. Yawning children and pillow-creased faces
crowded into the sanctuary to sing praises to the risen Savior.
Despite the hour, voices were strong and loud, filling nearby
streets with celebration. Ella Mae sat in the back row, running
through a checklist. The Resurrection breakfast was her baby—
a long-standing tradition—a potluck *and* baking exhibition.
Ella Mae directed a team of Ladies Auxiliary members each
Easter Sunday to put on a feast, always bringing a flood of
admiration.

She lived for days like this.

❧

Josephine glanced down the aisle as the congregation sang a
verse of her favorite Easter hymn.

Christ the Lord is risen today, Alleluia!
Sons of men and angels say, Alleluia!

Raise your joys and triumphs high, Alleluia!
Sing ye heav'ns and earth reply, Alleluia!

Two children lay on the pew, sound asleep despite the joyful song. Josephine shook her head. *Why do parents let their kids sleep in church on Easter morning? Why do they squander this golden opportunity to teach them the joy of celebrating the risen Savior?* Her irritation deepened the wrinkles around her mouth and between her brows. *The gall.* She turned away and closed her eyes in worship as she sang the next verse:

Lives again, our glorious King, Alleluia!
Where, O death, is now thy sting? Alleluia!
Once He died our souls to save, Alleluia!
Where thy victory, O grave? Alleluia!

Josephine thanked the Lord for the saving grace of the resurrected Savior. Having lost her parents at a young age, she knew one could be plucked from this life without warning. Aunt Olivetta taught her to live by the minutia of legalism, and she gladly embraced it as a safety net from all harm. Though she dared not stray from her aunt's strict rules, she did fall into trouble in her youth. Every Easter, she renewed her resolve to follow the precepts of God's Word.

Josephine felt called to help others do the same.

One of the children stretched and fell off the pew, landing hard on the waxed wood floor. His mother quickly picked up the sobbing child, distracting others around them.

She rolled her eyes. *I could have told her that would happen.*

Harley sat like a wayward child in the pew beside Will. He didn't sing. He stared straight ahead, his hair plastered to his head with oil. His suit jacket wasn't buttoned—because it wouldn't. The much-too-small sleeves were visibly strained around his arms, but Harley wouldn't darken the door of a church without the proper attire. His aunt had taught him that much. Today, he thought a nice suit might camouflage his hesitant heart.

Harley ran out of excuses as to why he couldn't attend church. He thought Claire would get the message—he wasn't interested. But doggone if she wasn't persistent. His hands began to shake. He excused himself to find a drink of water. Church made his mouth so dry.

❧

Josephine looked over her shoulder at Will, Claire, and Harley. *Why are they bringing a drunk to church?*

She immediately repented. *Forgive me, Lord, but you know how difficult it is to get through to a drunk. Remember his daddy? Poor Will and Claire think they know him, but they don't. They'll figure it out eventually, I suppose.*

She repented again for good measure.

❧

Harley returned to his seat. Pastor Karl began saying things like, "died for our sins," "redemption," and "eternal life." He talked about "resurrection morning," "forgiveness," and "the empty tomb."

Something seemed familiar. Déjà vu.

The words drifted over his head. He broke into a sweat. His hands shook again. He wasn't sure what to do. The room started to spin. He steadied himself by clinging to the pew. Then he left to get another drink.

He gulped down water and splashed a little on his face. By the time Harley returned to his seat beside Will, he felt better. The moment had passed. Relief flooded over him, making him a little dizzy.

The pianist rose and strode to the front. It was almost over.

As the last chords of the hymn hung in the air, Harley brushed perspiration from his brow and turned to Will and Claire. "Thanks for the invite. That was real nice."

"Won't you stay for breakfast?" Claire put her hand on his arm.

"No, I got things to do." He squeezed Claire's hand. "See you later."

He steadied himself by touching the wall on his way to the door.

⁊

Claire watched Harley leave. "Do you think he's okay?"

"He's uncomfortable. I'm just glad he joined us," Will said. "Let's stop by his place after breakfast and ensure he's still coming for supper later. Maybe something didn't sit well with him."

Will's eyes followed Harley to the door.

Claire noted concern in them.

"Yeah, I'm just glad he came." Claire chuckled. "I think he wanted me to quit hassling him more than anything."

⁊

Ella Mae hustled to the fellowship hall to finish the final preparations for breakfast. Ramona, Bertie, and Rita scurried after her to help. Everything was nearly ready. The breakfast casseroles warmed in the oven, and plastic wrap covered the platters of muffins and scones. Ten long tables were decorated with tulips, daffodils, and fragrant hyacinths. Ella Mae heard the throng heading out the front doors for the do-over Easter egg hunt.

She checked the coffee pots and searched the cupboards. "Tea, tea, tea." Her heart pounded. "Where's the tea?"

"We have plenty of coffee and …." Rita opened another cupboard. "I think we're out of tea."

"Someone needs to run to the market. We must have tea. How will it look if we don't offer tea?" Ella Mae reached for her purse, grabbed a ten-dollar bill, and shuffled out of the kitchen.

"Oh, Guy, wonderful. Would you be my savior and run to the market as fast as possible? We've run out of tea." She waved the money in front of him.

"No one will care." Bertie didn't have a showy bone in her body. "Just go with what you have. No big deal."

"Oh, Bert, it's fine. I can go to the market. It's a lovely morning for a walk."

"Walk? Oh, for heaven's sake. Hurry, the egg hunt won't take long. I'll start the kettles."

As Ella Mae pushed him toward the door, Guy turned to Bertie, giving her a peck on the cheek. "Love you, Bert." He passed Claire on the way. "God bless you, Claire."

"Happy Easter, Guy."

꙰

Josephine watched Harley stagger across the parking lot, turn on Main, and head for the bar—his home. He tripped as he crossed the street. She folded her arms. *Figures.*

The children waited impatiently as adults scattered eggs across the lawn. A whistle blew, and the giggling children scrambled to pick up as many eggs as possible.

This time, the eggs held candy. That's all the kids wanted, and their joy echoed through the streets of Walters Bluff.

Josephine observed the selfishness of the children grabbing eggs on the lawn. She'd never participated in an Easter egg hunt. She didn't know the thrill or the fun of candy-filled eggs.

Little Wyatt Bingham approached her with an egg in his outstretched hand. "Mith Pritchett, do you want one?" His blue eyes were wide with excitement.

"Oh, heavens, thank you, Wyatt." She took the egg as Wyatt bolted back to the lawn, cracking it open to find a miniature chocolate bar and five jellybeans. She popped a pink bean in her mouth. *Delicious.* Josephine closed her eyes as she savored the sweetness. She picked a green one next. It reminded her of the lime Jell-O Aunt Olivetta served with dinner every Sunday. She couldn't help smiling as the jellybean's sweetness flooded her mouth and her memory.

A crash jerked Josephine's head toward the courthouse.

Chapter 18

"*Help! Somebody help!*"

The cry sent a chill down Claire's spine.

"Where's Will?" Hank ran by—his eyes darting all around.

Before she could answer, he ran past her, up the steps to the church, searching for the police chief.

Will ran like a shot out the doors, through the parking lot, and down Main Street.

A siren blared in the distance.

"What happened?" Claire watched her husband disappear down the street.

"I couldn't see exactly, but it looks like a car hit the statue of Walter Wickham." Millie was breathless. "I hope nobody's hurt."

"I'm going to check." Claire took off running toward the scene. She could see a police car skidding to a stop. An officer joined Will, kneeling on the ground.

"Oh, Claire … Claire …" Jeannie ran toward her, still holding a coffee pot from the diner. "Claire, it's bad, real bad."

"What? What happened?"

"It's Guy. Guy Witherspoon."

"What?" Claire's heart pounded. She was sick—dizzy. "What happened? Jeannie, tell me!

"Guy's been hit. He's been hit real bad."

"Someone hit him? What?" Nothing made sense. Claire couldn't process what she was hearing. *He was just here.*

"Harley's Cadillac came outta nowhere and just …." She was breathless and pale. Tears filled her eyes. "Just ran him right over."

Claire looked over at the scene. A Cadillac rested against the toppled statue, its front grill crumpled—the windshield shattered. Harley was behind the wheel, unmoving.

Claire's legs wouldn't move. She watched another police officer arrive on the scene. He took over for Will on the ground, tending to Guy?

Claire rushed down the block, afraid of what she might see.

Will stood and pointed to her. "Don't come any closer! Go find Bertie!"

Without another thought, she turned and ran back to the church. She saw Joan standing among a crowd of people. They were watching the kids but glancing toward the commotion.

"Oh, Joan, pray. There's been an accident." Claire raced past and ran into the church.

She found Bertie adding extra chairs to the tables in the fellowship hall. Claire ran to her and put her shaking arm around her shoulders.

"Happy Easter, dear."

"You need to come with me. There's been an accident."

Bertie's eyes searched Claire's. Her happy demeanor drained

with the color in her cheeks. "What accident? What's going on?"

Ella Mae stopped what she was doing and looked at them. "What's wrong?" Her face was etched with concern.

"Gather the ladies and pray." Claire drew Bertie close. "Let's go. Guy needs you."

"Oh, my dear Lord."

Claire felt Bertie's knees buckle. She gripped her tighter as they walked.

Neither of them spoke as they hurried down Main Street.

Will saw them coming and ran to them. "Bertie."

Claire's heart pounded afresh as she looked at her husband. The usually calm, composed man was clearly distressed.

"Bertie, it's Guy … he's … he's been … it's bad. Bertie … he's gone. I'm so sorry."

The words punched Claire in the chest.

She couldn't breathe.

❧

Bertie pushed past Will and saw Guy lying on the ground. She knew it was him by his navy-blue slacks, worn loafers, and black socks dotted with colorful Easter eggs—a gift from the grandkids who loved giving their Pop-pop crazy socks. A box of tea lay smashed nearby, and a blood-stained sheet was drawn over his head. The shock of seeing that sheet stole what little breath she had right out of her.

Her hands shot to her mouth. She dropped to her knees. She couldn't blink—she couldn't look away.

The knowledge that this was the last time she'd see her Guy washed over her like a tsunami.

Bertie took his uncovered hand in hers and held it to her cheek. She kissed it, examining his fingers, knuckles, and scars from years of carving wood. This hand had held her when they'd lost their baby girl, when she'd had a cancer scare, and when each of her parents died. His hand was calloused from working and helping others. She closed her eyes, feeling his fingers, cool and rough against her cheek.

How can I live without him?

She folded her body over her knees, held his hand to her lips, and wailed, "No, no, no!"

Despite sirens and shouting, her mind swirled in disbelief. Their life together flashed through her memory as she clutched Guy's precious hand.

Pastor Karl's voice broke through her stunned silence. "Oh, my Lord, we thank you for Guy's life. We thank you for this husband, this father, this friend, this man of God. Pour your comfort and peace on Bertie, Lord. Oh, Lord … Oh, my dear Lord." His breath caught in a sob as he and Joan kneeled and placed their hands on Bertie, offering whispered prayers.

Bertie kissed Guy's lifeless hand. "I love you. I love you, I love you."

~

After Pastor Karl arrived, Will slipped away to Harley's Cadillac.

Three volunteer firefighters had extricated him from the car, and a volunteer paramedic held gauze to his head.

A siren in the distance blared assurance that an ambulance was on its way.

Blood streamed down Harley's face, drenching his beard.

"How bad is he?" Will's stomach churned.

"He's got a wicked gash on his forehead. It looks like he hit the windshield." The paramedic added, "I smell something sweet on his breath. He could be drunk, or it could be diabetic ketoacidosis."

"A witness said he looked drunk," one of the firefighters added. "He was seen walking toward the bar about five minutes before the accident. Said he didn't look right, sort of staggering. He could be on something. He has a history."

"Okay, I'll follow you to the hospital." Will looked at Harley. His eyes were closed, but he moved his head back and forth.

Lord, please—he cannot be drunk.

He checked with the officers working the scene to ensure all the *i*'s were dotted, the *t*'s crossed, their measurements precise. He couldn't risk the slightest mistake. Then he hurried back to where Guy lay. Claire stood and turned to him. He took her in his arms and squeezed her in a desperate effort to turn back time. His stomach filled with bricks. *How could this happen? What must Claire feel at this moment?* So many questions swirled in his mind as he held his wife.

Her sobs soaked his shoulder. She didn't utter a word.

Will hesitated outside the emergency department. His mind swirled with a mixture of grief and vivid memories.

He didn't know what he'd find when he arrived at the scene of the accident that night a year and a half ago.

Just like today, when he first saw Guy, Will didn't need to assess the condition of his in-laws. There was no question. They were gone.

He turned his head to speak into his shoulder mic, "Two confirmed. Roll the medical examiner and chaplain." His breath exhaled in shallow puffs as he ran to the truck resting on the wrong side of the highway.

His eyes scanned the scene, taking in bits of information while trying to convince himself it was *just another wreck*.

The road is clear and dry. No fog, clear skies. No skid marks.

The stench of alcohol stung his nose as Will approached the truck.

"Get me outta here!" Deacon Simpson struggled to find the latch to open his door. His nose was bloodied—a deflated airbag the likely culprit.

Will's stomach turned as he recognized the man.

The deacon vomited on the steering wheel and wiped his mouth with his sleeve. Anger sprang from him. "I just bought this truck!"

Will lifted the latch and yanked on the dented door. It creaked open.

The man staggered out of the truck.

"Mr. Simpson, how much have you had to drink tonight?"

The man's head jerked to attention. "Ask the other driver. They hit *me*!"

Will's fist clenched, ready to swing.

An officer grabbed his arm. "I'll take it from here."

Will stepped back. Ambulances, fire trucks, and law enforcement vehicles swarmed the scene, shutting down the highway. Claire filled his mind. She must be sleeping soundly—comfortably unaware of the devastation dancing in the red and blue lights. He didn't want to tell her—to bring this horror to his home.

The sheriff led Will to his cruiser. "I'm so sorry, man."

Will couldn't speak.

The days following the accident blurred—the case was turned over to the sheriff's office. Will couldn't work an accident where his family members were killed.

The deacon refused the breathalyzer, but the sheriff's department obtained a warrant to draw blood. Unfortunately, the crime lab mixed up the blood of three DUI cases on the same night. Due to carelessness, the charges against the deacon were dropped. He never spent more than a night in jail.

Will ran his fingers through his hair. *This* case must be handled carefully. He wouldn't give the reins to anyone else.

So much is at stake.

Will breathed a desperate prayer for help and pulled the curtain aside to the ER room, where Harley lay with gauze wrapped around his head, his arm tethered to an IV. He swallowed hard. "Hey."

"Are you gonna tell me what happened this morning? One minute I'm at church, and the next, I'm here."

"I was hoping you could tell *me* what happened." Will folded his hands to steady them. How would he tell Harley what he'd done? "Where were you going this morning?"

"Going? They told me I was in a car wreck. I didn't even know I was drivin'"

"You lost control of your car."

"That's what they tell me. I had some kind of …." He grabbed papers from a table by his bed. "Ketoacidosis. Diabetes. Man, I don't remember any of it."

"You ran into the statue of Walter Wickham … and …." Will drew in a breath. "You hit a person, too."

"No," Harley choked.

Will stepped toward him, putting his hand on his friend's shaking shoulder. "Guy Witherspoon was walking on the sidewalk and …."

"No, no, no … he's okay, though?" Two tears escaped, following the path of creases on his weathered cheeks. "Will, you gotta tell me he's okay. Please, Will." His eyes squeezed shut.

"I can't. I wish I could."

The color drained from his face. "He's not …." Harley's voice stuck on the word. The rough, tough man caught his breath in a loud squeak. A wail escaped as his eyes implored desperately.

"He's gone, Harley—he died instantly." Will clutched Harley's shoulder tighter. It shuddered with each sob.

"What have I done?" Harley's voice sounded like someone else entirely. He put his face in his hands and sobbed.

Will hated the sound of fresh grief. He'd heard it so often in his career—strangers in the throes of pain and loss. Now, hearing Harley's voice morph into dark despair—it was surreal and jarring.

"Bertie." Harley gulped as he said her name. "She ... she must be ...."

"Devastated." Will caught his breath in a stifled sob.

"No, no, no ...."

He held Harley's shoulder as raw emotion coursed through him. Will contemplated the enormity of the situation. He squeezed his eyes shut as his friend groaned in grief. The ache of tears seared the back of his throat. It was too much to fathom.

He couldn't imagine Harley hearing the news from anyone else, regardless of how painful it was to tell him. It was a long while before Will could do what he had come to do.

"Harley, I have to ask you some questions. I'm law enforcement first and foremost today. I know you understand—I must set our friendship aside for a moment."

"Yes."

"Did you drink at all this morning?"

"No, nothing. Just water. I haven't had a drink since before Christmas." Harley hesitated, rubbing his eyes. "But, I don't remember anything about this morning. I can't ... I don't remember drivin' and I don't remember drinking. The doc said I tested negative for alcohol and drugs."

"He did? That's good to know. What about other substances? Drugs, marijuana, are you on any medications that could have affected your judgment?"

"No, never, and I haven't been to a doctor for twenty-odd years."

Will felt a bit of hope. "Will you consent to a Portable Breath Test?" He reached into his pocket, retrieving the instrument.

"Yes, of course."

Will administered the test and took in a deep breath, as if he had been underwater all morning. "Zero point zero, zero," Will announced. "One more thing. Follow my pen with your eyes."

Will moved the pen slowly, Harley's eyes tracking without the tell-tale movements of intoxication.

Will remembered the comments of the volunteer firefighter. *'He has a history.'* People were already assuming Harley was drunk—already talking. "Harley, with your consent, I'd like to take a blood sample so we can send it to the state toxicology lab." Will jotted notes on a pad and sighed. "I believe without a doubt you're sober. I have the proof I need, but it may be wise to obtain undeniable proof." His eyebrow rose as he looked into his friend's sorrow-filled eyes. "For those who doubt."

"Yes, that's fine. I understand."

Chapter 19

JOSEPHINE DIDN'T BELIEVE the news at first. Guy wasn't gone. He couldn't be.

But it wasn't long before everyone spoke of the tragedy, and the reality hit.

The congregation assembled in the sanctuary to pray. One by one, First Community cried out to God for comfort and answers. How could this have happened? Why did He allow Guy to die?

After hours of prayer, sorrow, comfort, and questioning, breakfast was forgotten. Some nibbled on a scone to tide them over, but most had lost their appetites. Eventually, everyone left, shuffling to the parking lot as if in a daze.

Josephine was the first to say what she was sure everyone was thinking. "Harley didn't look well this morning. I'll bet he was drinking." She picked up a basket of muffins and started for the kitchen.

"You don't know that," Rita said.

"Would it surprise you if he were drunk?" Josephine waited for an answer. *When I'm right, I'm right.*

"No, I suppose not," Rita whispered.

Josephine grunted. "It was a matter of time. I can't believe he …." She wiped a tear. "I hope he rots in jail. I'm just sick for Bertie."

"No one knows for sure what happened," Rita muttered.

Josephine rolled her eyes. "I'm willing to bet I do."

☙

Ella Mae sat in the sanctuary, staring at the empty cross. Tears streaked her upturned face.

"It's hard to believe, isn't it?" Joan sat next to her.

"It's my fault," she whispered. Another tear rolled down her cheek.

"That's silly." Joan put her arm around her quaking shoulders. "Why would you say such a thing?"

Pastor Karl joined the two women. "Ella Mae, why on earth would you blame yourself?"

"I sent Guy to the store. I thought it would look bad if we didn't have tea. I didn't want to look like I didn't have my ducks in a row. You know how I am."

Joan reached for a box of tissues.

"If I hadn't sent him to the store, he would be safe at church with Bertie and all of us. He wouldn't have been hit. Bertie wouldn't be a wi—" She put her face in her hands and sobbed. "A widow."

Pastor Karl moved to the other side of Ella Mae. "Did you know before you sent him that he'd be killed?" He pulled a few tissues from the box.

Her face shot up from her hands, "No, of course not! How could I have known?"

"Exactly," Pastor Karl said, handing the tissues to Ella Mae. "Don't do this to yourself. Only God knows what's coming next. We can make up stories and blame ourselves—but ultimately, God has a plan to prosper us, not to harm us, to give us hope and a future. It's times like these ... I wish I could understand how it all comes together because this pain—it's so hard to bear."

❧

Claire stayed with Bertie until her oldest son, John, arrived.

He, his wife, and two little girls arrived in town just hours after the accident, undoubtedly speeding the entire way. Claire brought sandwiches and movies over for the girls to watch—anything to distract them from the grown-up business of losing their Pop-pop.

Claire trudged up her porch steps. She crossed the threshold, shut the door, and leaned against it to keep the pain from following her inside, but it seeped in through the cracks and enveloped her.

She fell to her knees.

You took Guy? God, how could you do this to Bertie? To their boys? To Will? How could you do this to me? And Harley? Lord, why? Why? He came to church this morning! She pounded the wood planks. Hadn't God brought Guy and Bertie into her life to help her through the loss of *her* parents? Why would a loving God allow Guy to be killed, too?

Here we go again. Is this a game? Do You like poking Your children where it hurts?

Claire's stomach turned. She ran to the bathroom, slammed the door, and fell to the floor in front of the toilet. She wretched until the wave of nausea passed. She pulled herself up and caught her angry reflection in the mirror. Puffy eyes raged red. Her mouth, painted and smiling when she'd left this morning,

was dry and stiff with fury. She stared at herself for a moment—
Who is that woman?

Claire didn't want anything to do with the woman in the mirror. Bitterness etched her face. She leaned against the door—her back slid down the wood panels, and she sat on the cold tile.

Claire looked up at the ceiling. "God, what plan could you possibly have? Right now, I cannot even fathom that good is possible." She didn't know what else to say to Him. She sobbed for Bertie, for their sons, for Harley, for Will, and for herself. She couldn't pray—she could scarcely put thoughts together at all.

After what seemed like a long time, Claire stood and splashed cold water on her face. She looked into the mirror again. The anger she'd seen before had changed to sorrow. She looked broken and lost, and she was. The day had utterly shattered her heart.

But she had to prepare for guests. The family was coming into town to support Bertie for the funeral. She offered their home as a place to stay. She had to do *something* to help—anything to ease Bertie's sorrow and stress.

Claire listened to Joan rally the ladies for the coming days. In an emergency meeting of the Ladies Auxiliary on Easter evening, the gathered women discussed meals and housing for those coming to town and food for Guy's service.

"Bertie told Karl, and I quote, 'Guy wasn't one to be sad and mopey, and he certainly wouldn't want anyone to be weepy and dismal at a sad-sack funeral. It will be a celebration of his life,'" Joan announced. "So, we will provide all the food and drinks for the memorial. Let's start with drinks, shall we? We'll need punch and coffee and tea…."

With the mere mention of the word, Ella Mae lost her composure. She jumped up and ran from the room.

"What did I say?" Joan looked around the room for an answer.

"Tea," Rita said. "You said tea. She sent Guy for tea at the Wickham Market, and Ella Mae feels responsible for his death."

"Oh, for heaven's sake." Millie's eyes welled with tears. "That's just silly."

"Silly to you, but to Ella Mae, it's not silly at all." Rita dabbed her cheeks.

"I'll go after her," Claire said.

She found Ella Mae in the bathroom, splashing water on her face. "Ella Mae, are you all right?"

"No, I'm not. I'll never forgive myself." Ella Mae dabbed her face with a paper towel.

"There's nothing to forgive, and if I'm honest, I feel responsible too. Will and I invited Harley to church, and he didn't look well when he left. I should have been more insistent that he stay for breakfast, but I didn't want to nag." Claire's vision blurred with tears. "I chalked up his sweating and shaking to being in church. I should have asked more questions. I might have been able to help him—and prevent the accident."

"Josephine said he was drunk."

"He stopped drinking months ago.." Claire's stomach churned. "At least he said he did." Did the morning at church make him fall off the wagon? Did he need liquid courage to come to church?

"Josephine said he was a drunk, and Harley owns the bar, so I just assumed."

"Will said he was diagnosed with ketoacidosis. He had diabetes and didn't know it." Claire drew in a breath.

Doubt niggled at her. Did she believe him when he said he was sober?

"It will be good to uncover the truth, but the fact remains that I sent Guy to his death. I was so set on the Easter breakfast being perfect. It was silly. Who cares? Bertie even told me then that no one would care if we had no tea."

"That sounds like something Bertie would say." Claire smiled.

"But oh no, it was all about me. Me, me, me." A sob hitched Ella Mae's voice. "What would people think of *me* if we ran out of tea? Silly. Selfish. If I hadn't sent him to the market …."

"If I had paid closer attention to Harley, our *guest* at church, maybe I could have stopped him from getting in his car."

"Oh, well, it *is* your fault then." Ella Mae chuckled half-heartedly and hugged Claire. "You know I'm kidding."

Claire held her tight. "We'll share the blame. How's that? I'll take half of the burden. Now, isn't that better?"

"Not really. I can't believe we're doing this, Claire, planning for Guy's memorial service."

"I know. I keep praying it's not real—that I'll wake up and realize it was all a horrific nightmare." Claire looked at her friend. "Let's cut ourselves some slack so we can be there for Bertie."

"Yes. For Bertie."

Chapter 20

CLAIRE OVERHEARD Josephine talking to someone on the next aisle in the Wickham Market.

"You know he was drunk. He came to church yesterday drunk as a skunk. Just like his daddy, that Harley is." She sniffled. "I just can't believe it."

She'd know that voice anywhere. Her face flushed hot as she pushed her cart down the aisle. She wanted to defend Harley. Will said without a doubt he was sober. "Don't say that. You don't know that."

Josephine swung around, eyes red with emotion, and squared her shoulders, "I *do*."

Claire gripped her cart, brow furrowed. "How do you know?" Looking at the older woman face to face caused her courage to wane. *Why did I butt in?* "He was sick."

"Hmmmph." Josephine dabbed her nose with a tissue and glared at Claire. "Why are you defending Harley? He's always been a drunk. His wife left him because of it. He didn't even go after her or his daughter."

Claire felt her stomach churn. She wasn't wrong.

The woman Josephine was talking to turned her cart and left.

Josephine sighed. "You don't know him as I do. I've lived here much longer than you."

"No, I don't think *you* know him at all. He wasn't drunk. He stopped drinking months ago. When was the last time you talked to him? When was the last time you shared a meal with him?" *I'm wasting my time.*

"Well, I …."

"That's what I thought. You know someone by spending time with them, not by supposing what they're thinking or doing." Claire clung to the handle of the cart, fighting back tears.

"But …."

"You can't just assume people did something unless you have proof." She stopped herself before she said something she'd regret. She gave Josephine a stiff smile and pushed her cart to the register.

It was too familiar—stories swirling about. Just like last time, she knew what was true. The irony of the situation hit her as she placed the groceries on the conveyor belt. Now she defended the one who killed another. Claire wanted to yell at the top of her lungs. *"Harley wasn't drunk, but the deacon was!"*

Oscar scratched his beard and assessed the damage. Walter's nose was buried six inches beneath the sod.

Hank arrived on a backhoe with the tools needed to remove the statue's remains from the courthouse lawn.

They'd have to replace the damaged marble before setting Walter back on his perch. Luckily, Walter didn't seem to have suffered more than a dent or two.

"Poor Walter," Hank said as they began to clean up the mess.

"Poor Walter? He's not feelin' a thing." Oscar sighed. "Bertie and Harley are the ones in a world of hurt." He began filling a wheelbarrow with small pieces of marble.

"I've known Harley a long time, but I don't know if I can forgive this." Hank shook his head and leaned on his shovel.

"I heard he was sick. Keto something or other. Diabetes. It can make you look drunk."

"Nah, he was drunk. Rita heard it on good authority."

"Will says he wasn't. Wouldn't Will know for sure?" Oscar's face warmed.

"The truth will come out ... either way." Hank motioned to a hunk of marble, and the two men moved it aside.

"He's my friend. We've been friends for decades. I support him." Oscar adjusted his gloves. "He needs his friends now more than ever."

"You'd still be his friend if he killed Guy when he was drunk?" Hank wiped his forehead. "I believe in forgiveness, Lord knows I need it, but ...." The older man didn't finish. He lifted his fist to his eyes, swiping at a tear. "Guy was my dear friend. I know he was yours, too."

"I'm praying that's not true." Oscar wanted out of this conversation. The idea that Harley was drunk hadn't entered his mind until this moment. Was that what *everyone* thought?

The men worked in silence. Oscar contemplated the horror of what had happened as he examined the pieces of marble and figured measurements and angles in his mind. He could fix this statue, but this tragedy, the loss of Guy, this mess Harley found himself in ... Oscar didn't have a clue how to begin to set it right.

෨

Buster stopped his truck in front of the bar. He let himself in and hung a sign in the window: *Closed Indefinitely.*

The buzz in Walters Bluff was that Harley was drunk, and although a few knew the truth and tried to spread it, people were angry and happy to believe the worst. People who thought they knew Harley were just plain disappointed.

Buster hopped back into his truck and sighed. He recalled the conversation with his wife, Patsy, the day before. "I put fresh sheets on the guest room bed. I'll help Harley monitor his blood sugar and make sure he eats right. He's welcome to stay as long as it takes him to settle into his new normal," she had said and held his hand. "It'll do him good to be away from the bar."

A wave of relief washed over him. He didn't know how to help his friend, but just like that, his sweet Patsy had the answer. "I'll ask him if he'll stay with us. As a nurse, I can help him get used to monitoring his blood sugar. He's in a bad way. I don't think he should be alone right now anyway."

And that was that.

Buster drove to the hospital and presented his offer.

"Stay with us for a while," Buster said. "Just 'til things settle down."

"I wasn't drinking." Harley's eyes held a look of defeat.

"You know that, and I know that, but some will take a bit more convincing. We'd love to have you stay with us, buddy."

Harley remained silent.

Buster breathed a prayer.

There was another reason he wanted Harley with them—he worried for his friend. He knew Harley's heart was broken—shattered, more like it. His conscience convicted him of crimes he hadn't committed. Harley was, at one moment, filled with self-loathing and, in the next, full of anger for the hand fate dealt him.

"I can take care of myself, but I see what you're doing. I suppose it's a good idea." His mouth turned up in a slight smile, but Buster saw nothing but sorrow in his friend's eyes.

☙

Claire picked up *The Durham County Herald*. The headline read: "God Bless You, Guy Witherspoon. Tragic Accident Takes Much-Loved Walters Bluff Resident."

She sat, somewhat shaky, and read the article. It was a fact-filled account indicating Harley had a medical emergency, but it left the question on everyone's mind unanswered: *Had he been drinking?*

Claire turned the page. A photo with the caption read: "Cherry Trees on the Courthouse Lawn Festooned with Blossoms."

Festooned—such a happy word. Her heart felt so heavy she could scarcely breathe. She laid her head on the desk and looked at the photo of her parents across the room. This weight was too familiar. Her mind drifted to the night her parents were killed. The shock, the bargaining with God—*please God, I'll do anything if You'll just turn back time and give them life again.*

The days following her parents' accident were a cacophony of what-ifs, incoherent prayers, and recollections of words spoken and unspoken. Memories were dissected, and regrets, though few, churned in Claire's mind.

Now, she wondered if she'd told Guy how grateful she was for all he'd done for them—for loving them, for spending time with her and Will. Did he know how much he meant to them—what a gift he was? A tear crossed the bridge of her nose, and she lifted her head. She took a deep breath and willed herself to dress. Claire was well aware that life continued after a loss. Perhaps that was the most brutal realization. Her grief didn't matter to everyone. Her agony didn't close the bank or stop the mail. Bills still had to be paid, and dinner cooked. Life moved on. There was never time for grief.

This morning, she had to shower, cook breakfast for her house guests, gather her things, and attend the Grace Writers meeting.

❧

Claire trudged through town, her feet slogging as if through mud. Harley's blood test wouldn't be processed in the state toxicology lab for a few weeks.

"Rumors are swirling already," Will had told Claire on Easter afternoon. "I asked him to submit to the toxicology screen—I figured we'd need it to stop the gossip."

The test would typically take months with the backlog at the toxicology lab, but Will had pulled a few strings and called in favors to shorten that time. Claire recalled what Josephine had said in the market, and her blood boiled anew. Was she still telling those lies?

This scenario was just what she feared. *Will Josephine turn the church against Harley? I can't let that happen.* This was all too familiar. She entered the fellowship room filled with angst.

Claire chose a seat next to Ella Mae. Across the table, Josephine stared down at her papers.

Rita suggested they share stories about Guy—about his legacy. One by one, the ladies shared anecdotes, tears, and even laughter. They agreed to polish their essays and print them for Bertie.

Mostly, though, they comforted one another. Claire's heart relaxed a bit, mostly because Josephine said nothing about Harley—a small win for now.

Claire strolled home and breathed the fresh spring air, sweetened with lilac. While it should have brought a smile to her face, a tear fell. She looked up and saw Bertie walking Daffy on Butternut Street. Usually full of energy, the dog walked close to her with slow, measured steps, glancing up at Bertie with seeming concern.

Claire turned and approached her.

"Bertie!"

"Hello, dear." Bertie stopped. "Thank you for taking in my brother's family. I love having everyone here, but I had to sneak out to walk Daffy." She patted the dog's head. "No one wanted to let me walk the dog alone. *No, Mom, someone must go with you,* as if I'm an invalid." She chuckled half-heartedly. "As afraid as I am of being alone without Guy, I really need time to myself."

"Oh, I'll leave you alone then." Claire took a step back.

"No, no, honey, walk with me. If you promise not to treat me like a lost puppy, I'd love the company. Can you tell I don't know what I want? My mind is so befuddled."

"That's understandable. I've loved having your brother and his family. They're sweet people."

"It's been so long since we've all been together—I just wish Guy could be here with us. He would have loved this … well, this reunion. Why does it take something like a—we should have gotten together more often." Bertie sighed. "The house is so loud and busy, and oh my, I'm exhausted." She stopped walking and looked down.

A moment of silence hung between them.

"I had him cremated. It's what we discussed years ago." Bertie brushed a tear. "Mayor Bickerstaff called and wants to put a plaque in the rose garden by the statue of Walter Wickham. I'll sprinkle his ashes among the roses. The plaque will say: *In memory of 'God-Bless-You Guy.'* They'll add his name and the dates of his life. It'll be real nice … real, real nice."

"That's wonderful." Claire looked at her friend, a mountain of strength wrapped in a short, soft package.

"Of course, they'll have to get the statue put back up before that can happen." Bertie wiped a tear.

They meandered home, and somewhere along the way, Bertie reached for Claire's hand and held it. Claire felt like she was holding her mother's hand. She didn't want to let it go. The women hugged in front of Bertie's house. "I love you," Claire said. "And I loved Guy too."

"I love you, too, and so did Guy."

She watched as Bertie walked away, with Daffy lumbering slowly beside her.

Chapter 21

ELLA MAE HAD TO GO all the way to Walkersville to get the semi-exotic, semi-sweet chocolate for the cookies she'd bring to the memorial. Chocolate-dipped almond shortbread— Guy's favorite. She'd spent two days making four double-batches, and while the last cookies cooled, she drove to Walkersville. She didn't even clean the kitchen in her haste. With a storm brewing, she didn't want to get caught in the wind and rain. It was hard enough for her to keep a vehicle between the lines without the wind adding to the challenge.

She arrived at Betsy's Candy Cupboard just as Betsy unlocked the doors. "What brings you to Walkersville?" she asked.

"I need the absolute best chocolate for dipping shortbread."

"Just got a shipment straight from Belgium. I had a little taste—quality control, don't you know? And it's divine."

"Load me up, sister. I've got hundreds of cookies to dip, only the best for Guy." Ella Mae heaved her purse onto the counter.

"I heard. Such a tragedy. I'm so sorry, dear."

"The shortbread must be perfect, which is why I'm here. I could have dipped the cookies in chocolate from the Wickham Market, but no sirree. It must be special." Ella Mae rummaged for her checkbook.

Betsy filled a large bag with the semi-sweet and gave her a sample of leftover white chocolate Easter eggs while she rang up the sale.

"Thank you." Ella Mae handed her a check.

"Come back soon and bring some shortbread for me next time."

"Will do." Ella Mae turned on her heels and waddled to the door.

She drove home slowly. Rain began falling in sheets as the wind blew. Cars whizzed by as if it were another sunny day.

She finally arrived in her driveway to see the mudroom door wide open.

Her heart raced.

A thief? Did I forget to shut the door? Did George come home from work early? No, his car isn't in the driveway. Did the wind blow it open?

Ella Mae tiptoed around the car, slightly hunched over, holding her purse by the strap—ready to swing if the need arose. She peeked around the open door. There, on the kitchen counter, three raccoons ravaged the shortbread.

"Holy shishkabob!"

The raccoons glanced her way, unconcerned, and returned to their feast.

She couldn't believe her eyes. George had warned her against feeding the raccoons, but she didn't listen. Ella Mae dropped her purse, waddled across the garage, and picked up a broom. Entering through the front door, she approached the critters from behind and shooed them out the back door, yelling unholy things as she did. She kicked the door shut with a thud, hoping the neighbors didn't hear her tirade.

She squeezed her eyes shut. "Dear Lord, if ever I needed a lightning bolt, now is the time. Strike the beasts dead!"

She opened her eyes and examined the destruction. The cookies were annihilated. Not only that, the critters helped themselves to the eggs she left on the counter as well. Egg whites slithered down the lower cupboard into a puddle of goo on the checkered linoleum.

Ella Mae did the only thing she could think to do.

She sat on a chair and cried.

Dark storm clouds spat rain against the window as big, wrenching sobs poured from her.

Lord, why would You allow this to happen? The memorial service is tomorrow morning! What will I do now?

Half an hour passed before she composed herself.

I'm doing it again, aren't I, Lord? I'm worried about how things look. I want to shine when it isn't about me. It's about Guy... it's about You. Guilt rose in her heart as the phone rang.

"Hello?"

"Hi, it's Claire. I wondered if you'd mind if I brought cookies to the memorial. I want to honor Guy in some small way. I have Bertie's recipe—the shortbread he loved so much. Is that all right? I know you said it was all covered, but ...." Claire's voice trailed off.

Ella Mae sighed.

"If you don't want me to, it's fine," Claire added.

"I *do* want you to. You're a lifesaver. This is a gift straight from the Almighty. Thank you, dear."

"Oh, good. Okay, I'll get busy then."

"See you tomorrow."

"Yes, tomorrow."

Ella Mae hung up the phone. She trudged around the peninsula to put the phone on the hook and stepped on smashed cookies mixed with spilled milk and egg slime.

Is that raccoon poop on the floor?

She began to laugh despite herself.

"It had to come to this, Lord? I must be one stubborn old woman." She opened the bag of chocolate and ate a square. It didn't stop there, unfortunately. Several squares disappeared before she was ready to clean up the mess.

Josephine snipped the stems of a bunch of daffodils.

With Greenwald's Floral closed, Fern and Laurel volunteered to make the flower arrangements for Guy's memorial at cost. The construction of The Weathered Vessel was at full speed, so the fellowship hall at St. John's turned into an explosion of blooms as Josephine, Fern, and Laurel worked feverishly, sorting, trimming, and arranging flowers.

"I hear Harley has diabetes," Fern said.

"Psssht! Brought on by too much drinking, I'm sure," Josephine said.

"You don't know that." Laurel's eyes flashed in her direction.

The look startled Josephine. "Don't I? You know as well as I do he's a drunk, just like his daddy." She stood straighter—her face hot with indignation.

"Will said he has diabetes. Keto … dosis—something or other. He could have died. He passed out at the wheel." Fern put down her clippers. "And Will said he was sober. No alcohol in his system at all."

"Hmmmph." *No way, he's a drunk.*

"We shouldn't jump to conclusions. I've always liked Harley. He must be devastated by what happened." Laurel pulled another bucket of roses to the table. "I don't think we've ever had so many orders for a funeral."

Josephine had to prove her point. "Harley was at the early service on Easter, and he was acting funny—like he'd had a few too many before breakfast. Shameful. He kept walking out of the sanctuary. He was probably taking nips from a flask in the foyer." She couldn't help herself.

"Josephine Pritchert, stop that!" Fern put her hands on her hips.

"I saw what I saw."

"I hope you're wrong," Laurel said.

"I do, too," Josephine said. But in her heart, she relished the thought of being right.

～

Bertie led her family through the sanctuary's side door. The hum of conversation hushed instantly. Somber silence enveloped the room. She glanced at the crowd as she led the long line of relatives to sit in the first two rows.

The First Community Church bulged at the seams.

The congregation sang a couple of Guy's favorite hymns. As the last chords of the piano faded, Pastor Karl lumbered to the pulpit. He shared a short message of comfort, then added, "I'd like to share with you something that Guy shared with me."

Bertie caught Pastor Karl's gaze. She smiled softly at her friend, seeing the emotion welling in his eyes.

"I asked Guy once why he always said, 'God bless you,' and you know what he told me?" Pastor Karl paused, swiping a tear. "He said when he was young, he didn't have anyone in his family who knew the Lord. But a neighbor said, 'God bless you' each time he saw him. He thought it was silly at first, but then he began to appreciate the blessings because the man meant it.

He prayed for the people he blessed and took the time to talk to them. Eventually, that man led our Guy Witherspoon to faith in Christ. He sounds a lot like our Guy, doesn't he? The pastor sighed. "Our friend planted many seeds of faith throughout his life. I know many have come into the fold because of his bold faith. If anyone would like to share a memory of Guy, now is the time to bless the Witherspoon family with your story." He looked over the congregation. People began to rise and form a line at the microphone.

Bertie's cheeks were wet with tears, but her heart filled to overflowing as, one by one, people shared a time that Guy had spoken a blessing at precisely the moment their hearts needed to hear it. Many gave their testimony of faith, of which Guy was a part.

After quite a while, Pastor Karl said, "I know others have stories to share, and I'd encourage you to write them down and give them to Bertie. Send them to her in the mail. She'll appreciate the blessings in the days ahead."

Pastor Karl asked everyone to open the hymnals.

"As we all know, and as the testimonies of many in this room demonstrate, Guy loved to bless each person he encountered. This song epitomizes how he lived his life. May we strive to fill the gaping hole of blessing left by Guy's passing. Join me in singing, *Make Me a Blessing*."

Bertie opened her hymnal and sang,

> *Out in the highways and byways of life,*
> *Many are weary and sad*
> *Carry the sunshine where darkness is rife,*
> *Making the sorrowing glad …*
> *Make me a blessing, Make me a blessing,*
> *Out of my life, may Jesus shine*

Make me a blessing, Oh savior, I pray …
Make me a blessing to someone today.

As Bertie received hug after hug, she was comforted—yet, as much as she mourned the loss of Guy, she felt an unbearable ache for Harley.

Chapter 22

AFTER A FEW WEEKS at Buster's house, Harley ached to go home. His heavy heart longed for solitude.

He could scarcely hold it all in, but at Buster and Patsy's house, he had to. He couldn't let them know the weight of his sorrow.

He had wanted to attend Guy's memorial service, but fear kept him away. How could he face Bertie? How could he face *anyone*?

Buster drove around the back of the bar. "You sure about this?" he asked.

"Yeah, I need time to myself." Harley turned to face his friend. "Thank you for everything."

"If you're sure you're okay, I'll be by tomorrow."

"You're a good friend." Harley meant it more than ever.

He watched Buster's truck round the corner and stuck the key in the lock.

As he crossed the threshold, something caught his eye—a folded piece of paper shoved under the door. He picked it up and unfolded it.

Leave town.

Harley's heart sank. His stomach turned. He couldn't catch his breath.

In the weeks since Guy's death, he'd been quarantined from suspicion and accusation. Here, the reality of what people thought of him hit Harley like a sucker punch.

He slogged up the stairs, and stopped short. Shattered glass caught the mid-morning light like hundreds of sparkling daggers across the floor.

His eyes scanned the apartment—a broken window.

A rock lay in the middle of the floor—a note rubber-banded to its surface.

Harley picked up the rock and removed the note.

You should have died, not Guy.

Pain seared Harley's heart. He threw the rock across his living room, hitting the lamp.

It crashed to the floor.

He recalled the moment he learned of Guy's death—Will's face as he broke the news. The powerful punch in his chest. The realization that he'd killed someone. Guy Witherspoon died because of *him*.

Tears filled his eyes. He felt an awful slug to the gut. This time, though, it twisted and clenched. He struggled for breath and heard a wail.

Is that my voice?

Great heaving sobs poured from his body as his head pounded with anguish.

Do it. Kill yourself. No one cares. No one will miss you. You deserve to die.

Harley fell to his knees. Glass pierced his flesh—the pain a welcome punishment. He deserved misery, guilt, and grief. He deserved to ... die. *Why Guy? Why not me?*

It would be so much easier if he did himself in. *I can't live with this guilt.* His heart had never pounded so hard.

Yes. I should end it.

After all, if the reward for *finally* being clean and sober was killing Guy, his life wasn't worth another breath.

He staggered to his bedroom and opened the drawer of his bedside table.

The Smith and Wesson met his gaze.

Harley checked the cylinder.

Empty.

He rummaged through the drawer in search of ammunition and thought of Danielle—about the vows he'd promised to keep. He'd failed as a husband—chose alcohol over his beautiful wife.

His mind reeled as he remembered Rebecca's dimpled cheeks and heard her sweet voice saying, "Daddy." He'd abandoned his precious daughter. *What kind of father abandons his only child?*

Darkness closed in as elephant-sized grief crushed his chest. He choked back a sob.

I've ruined everything I've touched, and now I've killed a man. Not just any man, either.

My friend.

He lifted a box of rounds from the back of the drawer, flipped open the cylinder, and loaded the bullets.

He snapped it shut and whispered, "For once, I'm doing the right thing."

He lifted the gun to his temple.

The only sound in the room was a clock ticking the final moments of his life.

Harley took a breath.

His last.

He straightened his finger, feeling every pull of muscle, tendon, and flesh. He began to curl it toward the trigger …

"Harley, are you in there?" A woman's voice broke through the heavy stillness.

As if ripped from his hand, the gun dropped to the floor with a clunk.

"Harley, are you here? I need to speak to you."

Did I leave the door open?

"I'm here," he called, his voice hoarse with despair. *Why did I answer?*

Harley's legs shook as he staggered to the bathroom to splash cold water on his face before descending the stairs.

The door *was* open.

Why did I leave the door open?

Bertie and her oldest son stood just outside.

His first thought was, *they're here to kill me.*

It'd save him the trouble if *they* did the job.

No—Bertie is nothing but kind.

"Harley, I'm glad you're here. Do you remember John?"

John looked at him and dropped his eyes to the ground, his mouth a straight line across his somber face.

Harley nodded—saying nothing. He wanted to run up the stairs and finish the job he'd started.

Why are they here? Why didn't I pull the trigger when I had the chance?

Bertie reached out and touched his arm.

The warmth of her hand was an electric shock, causing words to explode from the depths of his soul. "I'm sorry, I'm so very sorry." He choked back a sob. "I didn't mean to kill Guy. I didn't mean to, I ... I'm just so sorry."

"Harley, oh, Harley." Bertie squeezed his arm with both hands as a tear slipped down her cheek.

"I wouldn't've drove if I'd known I was sick. I should have taken better care of myself. I'm so sorry." Harley's voice was strained with emotion. Tears flowed down his weathered cheeks.

"God allows things to happen for a reason, and I don't understand why this happened, but I trust He has a plan." Bertie took in a breath. "It's real hard right now, but I know it's hard for *you* too."

Harley looked at Bertie.

What is she saying?

John gazed at the floor, his hands in fists at his side.

Bertie's eyes met his. "Harley, I forgive you. You didn't mean for this to happen. If we spread the grief between us, it might be a little easier to bear."

Harley leaned against the doorframe, dropped his face into his hands, and sobbed. "You...? What?"

"I forgive you, and I believe Guy wants to give you this message ...." Bertie stood up a little straighter. "God bless you, Harley."

Harley lifted his head from his hands and examined the woman's soft face. "Guy said that to me every time he saw me." He swallowed hard. "I saw him at the coffee shop the day before I ... before he ... he said he'd been praying for me."

"Well, that's also why we're here. I have something to give you. I found the notebook where Guy wrote some of his prayers. I removed a page for you. I thought it might bring you comfort to have it." She held a folded piece of paper. Bertie unfolded it and handed it to her son.

John's brow furrowed.

"Read it out loud." Bertie nodded to him as if to impart confidence.

John took it and read: *"Dear Lord, I saw Harley today. He didn't look well. More than that, he looked lost. Lord, I ask you, once again, to shake him up so he will see his need for You."* He paused and cleared his throat. *"So many years I've prayed for Harley, and still he's stuck. He clings to his life without You."* John's voice broke. He brushed away tears, took a breath, and continued. *"You, Lord, are not slow in keeping your promise, as some understand slowness. Instead, You are patient with us, not wanting anyone to perish but everyone to come to repentance. Thank you, Lord."* Tears streamed down his face. He lifted his eyes to meet Harley's.

Silence hung between them for a moment. Harley held his gaze as if transfixed.

"Dad cared about you very much." John turned to his mother as if seeking a morsel of her courage.

Bertie took the page from him and squeezed his hand.

John sighed. "Maybe all of this—maybe it's all part of a bigger plan."

Harley looked from Bertie to her son—words nowhere to be found.

Weight floated from Harley's shoulders. Forgiveness? For killing Guy? It's been only a few weeks since the accident.

"Well, that's why we came by." Bertie handed the paper to him.

Harley held Guy's prayer as if it were a precious jewel.

She smiled tenderly. Her eyes held less sorrow than they had a moment ago. "If you ever want to talk, I'll listen. I'd love to tell you more about Jesus."

Harley wiped his tears and tried to speak, to no avail.

John stretched a protective arm around his mother. His eyes met Harley's. They were softer. His mouth turned up on one side.

"How is your health?" Bertie's eyes searched his. "I hope you're feeling much better."

"I am. I … thank you for giving me Guy's prayer. It means a lot to me. I … I'm just … thank you."

Bertie stepped toward Harley. She reached her arms around him and squeezed.

Her embrace was illuminating, causing the darkness in his mind to skitter away like so many cockroaches.

"God bless you, Harley." John's voice, so much like his father's, caused a joy-filled sigh to escape from the depths of Harley's soul.

How can this be?

Harley watched them disappear around the corner. He shut the door and locked it. His knees buckled, and he nearly tumbled as he sat hard on the stairs. He read Guy's prayer for himself.

I am lost—but am I a lost cause?

He took a deep breath.

Bertie forgave me.

John might.

Would Guy? Yes, of course, he would.

He rubbed his knees, cutting his finger on glass still stuck to them. He looked down to see spots of blood soaking through his jeans.

What if she had come a moment later? He imagined the scene she would have discovered, only adding to her grief.

He took Guy's prayer, climbed the stairs, and entered his bedroom.

The gun lay on the floor. Harley picked it up, feeling its weight in his hand.

What was I thinking?

Guy would never want me to ....

He hoped for better things for me, and I nearly ....

His heart pounded—this time filled with relief.

With hope.

Maybe he *could* make something of this life. Maybe it wasn't too late because Bertie—forgiveness—knocked at his door.

Harley flipped open the cylinder, removed the rounds, and carried both to the top shelf of his closet—out of sight.

Chapter 23

HARLEY, BUOYED BY THE VISIT from Bertie, decided to return to Buster's house. His apartment over the bar didn't feel like home anymore.

He made repairs around the house for Patsy and tilled the garden to prepare it for planting. Patsy portioned his meals and snacks, forbidding him to eat anything not on her strict menu. Harley felt better than he had in years, despite the turmoil inside his mind and outside the haven of Buster and Patsy's farm.

It wasn't just his physical body that felt better and lighter. Deep down, his heart did, too. When he woke with a start—several times a night—he'd remember the events of the past few weeks and feel a punch in his chest.

But then he'd remember Bertie's visit, Will and Claire's kindness, Buster and Patsy's generosity, and Guy's prayer, and the pain of the punch faded—just enough to keep him from diving back into the depths of despair.

In a small town, rumors grow like a smear in a petri dish, vile and ugly. It didn't matter that Will, Claire, Bertie, and others knew he wasn't drunk. It didn't matter that they spoke out in his defense. Many people wouldn't believe the truth.

The toxicology lab's results would be proof positive that he wasn't drunk, but when would they know the results?

Claire turned the key in the lock. The door swung open.

The shop was nearly finished. Just painting and fine-tuning, and it would be done. It was time for the real work to begin.

Fern pushed through the door. "It's so roomy!" She walked to the workroom and hollered, "Have you seen this?"

Claire followed her. "Wow. I love the repurposed tabletop. Is the cooler big enough?

"It's perfect. The same size we used to have. When do your antiques arrive?"

"The first shipment will be here next week." Claire smiled. "It will be a nice distraction from all the … grief."

"I agree. Many people are looking forward to the grand opening of The Weathered Vessel simply because it's a happy event."

"The shop has been a lifeline these past weeks." Claire sighed. "Let's have fun. That will honor Guy, and Bertie looks forward to the grand opening. She told me so last night."

"I still can't believe he's gone," Fern said. "I saw Bertie at the market, and she looked good. A little thinner, but good."

"She's doing okay. John left last week, so she's alone for the first time." Claire sighed. "Will and I check on her."

"Oh, good to know. I will too. I'll have the kids draw her pictures, and we'll bring them over." Fern smiled.

"Hey, her birthday's coming up. Let's plan a little shindig."

"Let's do it. Something small. She won't want to be alone on her birthday." Fern sounded excited.

"Oh, how fun!" Claire smiled. Planning something for Bertie would be another welcome distraction. She began a mental list of guests to invite. She looked up and noticed Fern's pensive gaze.

"How are things going with Frank?" Claire asked rather cautiously.

"It's rough. He came to the house and moved out the rest of his things. It upset the kids, but he didn't seem to care."

"I'm sorry," Claire said.

"Yeah. My mom's been wonderful, though. She's a sweet grandma, and the kids are happy she's here. I am, too. I think it does her good to be needed. She's been lonely since Dad died a few years ago."

"I like your mom. You're fortunate to have her." As Claire said the words, she thought of how much she missed *her* mom. "She's a blessing, Fern."

"And now we're about to open The Weathered Vessel. I couldn't be more grateful," Fern declared.

A knock on the door startled the women. "The painters must have arrived," Claire said. She propped open the door. "So close," she chirped.

~

Will's heart pounded as he opened the envelope. His eyes scanned down the page to the results. *Alcohol Concentration: 0.000 gram of ethyl alcohol per 100 milliliters whole blood (99.73% confidence interval).*

The report concluded that Harley wasn't affected by any substance whatsoever.

Thank You. Thank You. Thank You, God. Finally, there is irrefutable proof.

Will ran his fingers through his hair. He took a long, deep breath and exhaled.

The air seemed sweeter. Had he even been breathing for the last few weeks while rumors swirled?

"Knock knock." Bertie stood at the door of his office, holding a paper cup.

"Bertie?"

"Hi, Will. I was walking downtown, and I just … I wanted to pop in and thank you."

"Thank me?"

"You work so hard for our community, and you've done so much for me. I'm just grateful for you. Here." She gave the cup to him. "Black coffee with a splash of hazelnut. Claire said it was your favorite."

He took the cup and sipped from it. "Perfection."

"Wonderful. I wanted to talk to you about something else."

"What's on your mind?"

"A lot of people have asked me if I'm going to sue Harley for killing Guy." Bertie's eyes welled. "They say that he was drunk."

"I've heard those rumors as well."

"I believe you when you say he wasn't. I believe the breath test, and I trust that it was accurate. Most of all, I believe Harley. He's not a liar."

"Agreed." Will's mouth turned up in a smile.

Bertie's head tilted as if confused. "Will, I hardly think this is something to smile about. I'm sick and tired of it, and I don't know what to do. I can defend Harley 'til the cows come home, but most of those folks won't believe it. And I would never sue him."

"I'm smiling for a reason." Will grabbed the report from the desk. "Here's the proof. I'm going to ask Harley to sign a release so the paper can write a follow-up to the story."

"I'm thrilled!" Tears filled Bertie's eyes. "That will quiet the gossips. What did Harley say when you told him?"

"I haven't told him yet. I just received the report."

"For heaven's sake, Will, tell him!"

"That's what I was just going to do, but you showed up with coffee and …." Will winked at the older woman.

"I'll leave you to it." Bertie hugged him. "Love you, Will."

"Love you too, Bertie. Thanks for the coffee."

She headed out the door and turned to wave before disappearing around the corner.

Will picked up the phone and dialed Harley's number. No answer. He'd likely be at Buster's, or maybe he wasn't answering his phone. He drove his cruiser to the bar. Pulling in, he saw a window open upstairs.

He rang the doorbell and waited.

Harley appeared at the door. "Will, you here on official business?" Concern filled Harley's eyes.

"I have news for you," Will said.

"You get the blood test back?"

"I did," Will said, his mouth bending into a smile.

"And? What'd it say?"

"Said you were clean as a whistle." Will laughed and pulled his friend in for a hug. "Time to shut down the rumor mill."

"Did you doubt?"

"No, I always believed you. And I had the proof of the breathalyzer. I'm just happy we have the undeniable proof to convince the naysayers."

Harley leaned against the doorframe as if the wind was knocked out of him.

"You okay?"

The gruff guy with the tender heart looked his friend in the eye. "I am. It's been rough."

"I didn't know how to convince everyone," Will said. "That's why I felt we'd need this definitive report."

"But now what?"

"I requested a consent form from *The Durham County Herald*. If you sign it, they will print a follow-up story reporting the undeniable proof that you were not drunk." Will produced the document and a pen. "It's up to you. I think it will go a long way to shut down the gossip.

∂

Harley signed the paper and watched Will's patrol car as he drove away. The events of the past several weeks swirled through Harley's mind. The pain of conviction welled in him—an urgency—requiring action.

Harley rushed to his bedside table and examined the page Bertie had given him—Guy's prayer. He reread it. The words pierced his heart.

Lost, stuck, clinging to his life without You. Shake him up so he will see his need for You.

"Shake him up?" He took in a breath. "Shake him up so he will see his need for You?" *God answered Guy's prayer.* Harley pondered that for a moment.

The words of Guy's letter, Bertie's forgiveness, and his friends' unwavering confidence all pointed to one thing. *God must really love me.*

Harley didn't know what to do, so he knelt by his bed, folded his hands, and decided to give prayer a shot.

"God, are you there? Do you love me?" He reread the prayer. "God, forgive me for all the years I was drinking and trying to do life without you. I'm sorry. I need you. Come into my life and change me. And thank you for sending Bertie and John that day."

Harley opened his eyes. Did he feel any different? Yes. It was the same lightness he felt when Bertie forgave him, except today, the weight of a thousand wrongs lifted from his heart.

And something else.

Bertie returned home and left him by himself, but right now, in his apartment over the bar, Harley was no longer alone.

Chapter 24

CLAIRE UNWRAPPED a silver teapot and set it on the matching tray. An antique walnut dining table held the treasures as she unpacked them. Heavy glass paperweights, bone china teacups, leather-bound books, sterling thimbles, a collection of miniature pottery vases, and so many knickknacks. With every paper-wrapped treasure she lifted from a box, another memory sprang to mind. A flea market day with her mother, the conversation they shared, something they laughed about, or a colorful person they met while shopping.

Miraculously, she smiled more than she wept as the scenes played out in her mind.

"Claire, you in here?" Bertie appeared around the propped-open back door to the shop.

"Yes, I'm here."

"Do you mind if I take a peek? I saw your car our front and couldn't resist."

"Not at all. Let me show you around." They strolled through the empty shop, stepping around boxes. "The painting was finished last night, and I'm so happy with how everything turned out."

"I'm thrilled for you. I'm thrilled for all three of you!" Bertie clapped her hands with joy. "There is another reason for my visit." Her demeanor softened a bit. "Will left a message asking if he could come over and finish a project he and Guy were working on. Would you let him know he's welcome to come over any time?"

"I'll tell him. How are you doing, Bertie?"

"Oh, well … I haven't even been in the garage since … I avoid it. I keep the trash bags and the extra paper towels out there." She hesitated. "But I've just bought new rather than go into Guy's shop. I'm not ready for that."

"Maybe when Will is there, he could bring some things inside for you. Would that help?"

"It seems so silly. Do you think he'd mind? Maybe that *would* be nice."

"He'd be happy to." Claire smiled.

Bertie meandered to the back door. "Are you going to the diner to meet Harley tonight?"

Her question surprised Claire. Was Bertie comfortable having dinner with Harley? They were close before, but was it too soon? "Yes, he said he had something to tell us. I hope he's doing okay."

"The article about his test results sure took a load off his mind. Took a load off mine as well. I'm anxious to hear what he has to share." Bertie's face showed no sign of angst. No sign of anything but peace.

Claire saw Harley waiting for them at their usual table. She, Will, and Bertie wove through the tables to the back of the diner.

"You're lookin' trim." Will shook his hand.

"I feel good." Harley hugged Claire and Bertie.

Jeannie arrived at the table, pen and pad in hand. "Harley, I read the article in the paper, and I want you to know, I never believed the gossip."

"Thanks, I appreciate that." Harley smiled. "I've had a few folks apologize for doubting. I can't say I blame 'em."

Jeannie squeezed his shoulder, then took their orders.

"I have good news," Harley announced.

"Spill it." Bertie reached over and patted his hand. "I love good news!"

"You know that prayer you gave me when you came over and forgave me?"

"Guy's prayer." Bertie's voice was but a whisper.

"I've read it a bunch of times. The other day, I read it again. Guy said I was clinging to my old life, and he was right. I asked God to forgive me, and He did. I gave it all to Him—my old life, my sins, my guilt."

Claire looked from Bertie to Harley. The older woman sobbed into a napkin with her left hand, holding Harley's hand with her right.

"Bertie?" Harley lifted his eyes to Claire and Will, his brow furrowed.

"That is the *best* news." Will's eyes appeared misty.

"Guy is rejoicing with all the angels in heaven." Bertie struggled to dry her tears.

"He is?" Harley's eyes welled. "You think so?"

"I know so!" Bertie squeezed his hand. "God has always loved you—and so did Guy."

Tears streamed down Claire's face. Her relief and joy at the news left her speechless. She couldn't have imagined she'd be in the diner with Will, Harley, and Bertie, crying tears of *joy* when, not long ago, grief consumed them.

"Do you have a Bible?" Bertie asked the question with determination in her voice.

"I did when I was younger, but I don't have it anymore."

"Guy had several. I'm giving you one of his. I read one of his old Bibles, and seeing his handwriting in the margins brings me comfort. Maybe you'll like that too."

"Are you sure?" Harley brushed a tear from his cheek.

"Yes, sir, I am. I'll bring it to you tomorrow."

"Thanks."

"Harley, this is just the best news." Claire's heart overflowed—yet something he mentioned stung her conscience.

Bertie forgave Harley.

≈

Will scanned the list of items Bertie needed from the garage and set to work bringing them in before closing the door to face Guy's workshop. He understood why Bertie wouldn't want to be here. Looking around, he heard Guy's voice instructing him how to make a cut, measure an angle, or fit a dovetail.

Guy's essence still lingered in the garage. It was unnerving.

Tools hung on the pegboard like soldiers standing at attention. No one had been here since that awful day. Even Guy's jacket lay on a stool like he'd been working there this morning. Will looked around for the box he'd been making for Claire. He found it off to one side of the workbench.

In the center of the workbench lay a panel. A scene carved by Guy's hand—it looked like the backyard. Two birds splashed in the birdbath. The only part left to carve was the tree off to the right, and the lilac bush sketched in pencil on the left. It was beautiful. Will looked around to see if he could discover what Guy had planned for the panel. Behind the table, he saw a towel draped over something square—the bottom of a box, probably a jewelry box. It was finished, aside from the panel for the top. Will could attach the two, leaving the carving undone. He didn't want to touch what Guy had wrought.

He set to work putting the box together. Perhaps Guy was planning to give it to Bertie for her birthday. Yes, Guy had always been a good giver of gifts.

Claire didn't know how to act around Josephine when she arrived at the Grace Writers meeting. Josephine must know by now that Harley wasn't drunk—that it was all gossip and assumptions. Claire wanted to stand up and shout, *I told you so,* but somehow, she resisted the temptation.

Josephine didn't look at her. She appeared a little forlorn, like someone had stolen her thunder.

Keep your mouth shut, Claire. She took a deep, cleansing breath.

Ella Mae unveiled a plate of chocolate chip cookies, and the ladies started grabbing.

"Your chocolate chip cookies are just the best," Joan said.

Ella Mae plucked a cookie off the plate, her mouth bending into a smile.

"The prompt so long ago was to write about a lie, but we've been so discombobulated for the past several weeks that we sort of forgot about that one," Rita said.

"I forgot all about it." Millie licked her fingers.

"I brought a story about a lie," Claire said. "It's a story about my mother's old neighbor—and it's about spite."

"Spite is sinful." Josephine folded her arms. She glanced at Claire and looked quickly away.

"Oh, Josephine." Millie said, "Go ahead, Claire."

Ike Winthrop, a wealthy and generous bachelor, lived a quiet life in a modest home. He was a bit of a hermit, and although he enjoyed solitude, sometimes he wished he had a family.

One spring evening, Ike wandered downtown for supper. Eating alone didn't bother him. He enjoyed watching people, and the restaurant was a treasure trove of observation.

He ordered fried chicken, just like his mother used to make it. Every bite took him back to Sunday afternoons at his mother's dining room table: a starched linen tablecloth, mashed potatoes piled into a fine china bowl, green beans mixed with bits of crunchy bacon, and a Jell-o mold sitting atop a crystal pedestal, shimmering in the sun.

Those were the days.

Ike snapped to attention as the door swung open.

"I don't want dinner. I want ice cream!" A girl of about six years stomped her feet as she pitched a hissy fit of epic proportions.

"Honey, stop yelling. You're disturbing everyone." Her mother stroked her hair. "You have to eat dinner first."

"I don't want to," she screamed.

Ike cringed. His peaceful supper screeched to a halt.

The drama increased as the brat screamed, and her mother passively cajoled her.

Ike's regret over not having a family diminished with each exchange.

The waitress approached the table to take their order.

"I want ice cream!" The girl snarled at the waitress.

"She'll have a grilled cheese sandwich," her mother said.

"No!" The girl pounded the table, toppling the water the waitress had just poured.

"After you eat your sandwich, you can have ice cream. Mommy will buy you ice cream." The waitress dropped a stack of napkins with which to clean up the spill, rolled her eyes, and walked away.

The screaming continued, and several customers stormed from the restaurant.

Ike stayed put.

The waitress arrived with his check and apologized for the commotion.

Ike leaned toward her and whispered, "I would like to buy all the ice cream you have—to go."

Her eyes grew wide, and a smile crept onto her face. "*All* the ice cream? We have at least ten gallons in the freezer."

"Every last bit of ice cream you have," Ike whispered.

"As you wish." She curtsied happily and turned on her heels.

Ike paid his check, added a hefty tip, and headed to the door. A busboy waited with a non-descript box holding several large tubs of ice cream.

Ike winked at the little girl as he passed by the table and said, "It's been a pleasure."

The girl stuck out her tongue.

He hesitated by the exit as the waitress asked the mother if she wanted dessert.

"A large bowl of ice cream, please."

"I'm sorry, we're out of ice cream." The waitress glanced at Ike as he pushed his way out the door, satisfied.

Ike Winthrop had dished up his own dessert: Spite à la mode.

"Good for Ike. Please tell me that's a true story," Ella Mae begged.

"It is. Isn't it satisfying?" Claire closed her notebook.

"So satisfying." Millie giggled.

The rest of the ladies shared stories with the group, and when they were done, Rita announced, "Our prompt this week is to share a story about a trip. Hank never wants to go anywhere, so I'll have to write a fiction piece, but that's neither here nor there."

"Good one." Millie chuckled.

Chapter 25

"THIS IS MY COMMANDMENT, *That you love one another as I have loved you.*" John 15:12 (ESV)

Claire listened to Pastor Karl read the passage from the pulpit. Thoughts of dinner with Harley and Bertie swirled in her mind. Bertie loved people well—and Guy. He loved and blessed people wherever he went when he was alive.

And Bertie forgave Harley. Of course, she did—but when? Days after? How?

Claire looked to her left. Bertie sat with her hands in her lap. Was she thinking of Guy? Probably. She looked to her right. Harley sat at the end of the pew.

Bertie forgave Harley. But how could *she* forgive the drunk deacon who remained unpunished for what he did? He was guilty. Harley wasn't.

Claire thought of the Grace Writers. She hadn't written a thing for the meeting. Honestly, she wasn't inspired. She was bothered more than anything. More accurately, Josephine bothered her. How could she live with what she'd done? Her gossip had hurt people, specifically Harley. He wasn't a drunk anymore—he hadn't been for months, and now he was saved and forgiven.

There was that word again.

Forgiven.

❧

Josephine looked at the clock. Three in the morning. She tried to go back to sleep.

Something nudged her wide awake. What was it? Oh yes, it was May twenty-ninth. She closed her eyes and tried to think of other things—her to-do list. It was Tuesday. She'd go to the Grace Writers.

Claire would be there.

Didn't she give her the cold shoulder at church on Sunday? Josephine couldn't blame her. But if she was honest with herself, she was nothing but kind.

My conscience is bothering me. That's what it is.

I should make things right with Claire—apologize for gossiping about Harley.

Ultimately, she knew she should apologize to Harley as well.

She rolled over. How did she get herself into this mess? Maybe if she waited it out, gave it time, everyone would forget what she'd done. Yes, that was her plan. Who could blame her for thinking what she did?

Relief washed over her.

Josephine tossed and turned until six o'clock, when she shuffled to the kitchen and put a kettle of water on the stove. She dressed and tied her walking shoes. Today would go smoother if she took a brisk morning walk. She poured the hot water into her favorite cup and dipped a tea bag beneath the steam. As tea stained the water, she read the Dear Wanda column:

Dear Wanda,
 I'm at my wit's end. I was told my neighbor is having an affair. Now his mistress is pregnant, and his wife has no idea. What am I supposed to do with this information? I don't want to know all of this. It's keeping me up at night, and when I see my neighbor's wife, I just want to cry! Should I tell her? Help!
 Sincerely,
 Knows too much

Dear Knows too much,
 You don't KNOW anything. You've heard gossip. It may be lies and speculation. Keep your mouth shut! Only your neighbor and God know what is going on, and nothing may be happening. If you stick your nose in their business, it will be lopped right off your face.

Josephine sipped her tea and folded the paper. *Hmmph. It seems like someone should do something. That wife deserves to know.*
Guilt washed over her.
Well, it could be false. She read it again.
Okay, maybe Wanda's right.
She finished her tea, put on a sweater, and ambled out the door. It was a beautiful day. Beams of sunshine cut through the trees, and the fragrant air brightened her mood.
"Hi, Josephine." Ramona waved as she stepped out of her car.
"Hello, it's a lovely morn-*oh!*" Josephine stumbled and dropped to the sidewalk like a rag doll. She heard a crack and felt an electric jolt in her arm and ribcage. "Oh, my lands!"
"Are you all right?" Ramona ran across the street to her side.
"My arm—oh my—my ribs, I think something broke." Josephine attempted to stand, and gave up. "Oh, my heavens."

"Stay put. I'll grab my phone and call for help." Ramona ran to her car.

Josephine sat on the sidewalk, trying to find a position that didn't make her want to cry out in pain.

Oscar Peabody's truck screeched to a stop on the other side of the street. He jumped out and ran to her, kneeling beside her. "Are you all right? What happened?"

"Oh, gracious. I think I broke my arm, and my ribs hurt. Ramona's calling for help. I just tripped, and here I am … oh, my goodness." A tear slipped down her cheek.

Oscar grabbed his phone from his coat pocket and made a call. "Hey, we need an ambulance down here on Barley Street. Oh, it is? Can an officer run Josephine Pritchert to the hospital? It appears she's got a broken arm, possibly a rib or two as well."

"Who are you calling?" Josephine asked.

"Will."

"Oh, heavens."

"Okay, great, yes, we're on Barley Street behind the library." Oscar pushed a button on his phone and took off his jacket. He draped it around her. "That arm is definitely broken."

"Yes, I felt a snap. I can't believe this is happening." Josephine steadied herself with her good arm and tried not to move unnecessarily. It looked like a plum had taken root under her skin just below her elbow. It throbbed with each beat of her racing heart.

It wasn't long before Ramona reappeared, running down the sidewalk. A police cruiser arrived just as she reached them.

"Josephine, what's happened to you?" Will knelt beside her.

She noticed how official Will looked in his uniform. She'd never been the subject of police attention, and she was quite uncomfortable, even in this circumstance. "I think I broke my arm, and my ribs hurt too." She tried to keep her voice strong.

"From the look of things, I'd say you're right. Listen, I'm going to apply a splint so it doesn't move, and then I'll give you a lift to the hospital in Walkersville. Our ambulance is transporting someone from Shady Pines, so I'll be your driver today." Will pulled a first aid box from his trunk and applied a splint to her arm.

"Ooooh, that's too tight," she moaned. Will loosened it a bit before he and Oscar gently helped her to her feet.

Will opened the back door to his patrol car.

"Can't I sit in the front?" asked Josephine. "I'll look like a common criminal sitting back there."

"If you sit in the front, you could bump your arm on the door when I turn. That would be painful," Will explained. "You're welcome to, but I don't think it's wise."

"Okay, fine." The last thing she wanted was to bump her arm or move her torso. She could scarcely talk with the pain she was in, and now her hip throbbed as well.

"Is there someone who can meet us at the hospital?"

"I'll follow you," offered Ramona.

"Perfect." Will helped Josephine pull the seat belt around and buckle it. Josephine turned her head from side to side as Will stretched his arm around her body.

"Excuse me," he said.

Will jumped in the front seat and turned the car around.

"Do you have to drive right through the center of town?" she asked.

"It's the only way to Walkersville." Will smiled at her in the rear-view mirror.

Josephine put her head down. Even moving her head seemed to hurt her arm. She thanked God she wasn't taller, confident no one would be able to see her now.

As they approached the First Community Church in the middle of town, the car slowed, and Will rolled down his window. "Hey, Pastor Karl, I'm on my way to Walkersville. What do you need?"

Josephine's eyes popped wide open. *Pastor Karl? Land sakes! What will he think when he sees me in the back of a police car? He'll think I've been picked up for shoplifting or drunkenness, or Lord knows what he'll think …*

"I just got a call from Ramona, and she said Josephine fell, and I'm wondering if I can help?" Josephine slowly lifted her head and looked out the window.

"I'm taking her to Walkersville right now. It appears she may have a broken arm." Will rolled down the back window. Now, Pastor Karl could see her with his own eyes.

"Oh, my dear, I'll alert the prayer chain. You're in good hands with Will. I won't keep you."

Josephine didn't detect a speck of judgment. She felt foolish for assuming he'd think the worst. Why would Pastor Karl think she was a criminal? He always thinks the *best* of everyone. It was *she* who imagined the worst. Conviction washed over her heart.

"Thank you, Pastor." She reached her good arm out the window and squeezed his hand.

☙

"You need to fill out these forms here and also these, and this one here as well." A woman with a blue streak in her hair and tattoos on her forearms pushed a stack of paper across her desk to Josephine.

"I can't write," Josephine announced.

"I'll write for you." Ramona took the pen and clipboard and began to ask questions. "Do you have any allergies?"

"Yes, sulfa."

"Do you smoke cigarettes?"

"No."

"Do you drink alcohol?"

"If you count communion. I dip my bread in the wine. Does that count?" She looked at the tattooed woman, waiting for an answer.

"Doesn't count," she sighed, scratching her neck.

"Oh, here's one." Ramona grinned. "Could you be pregnant?"

"My lands, really? No, I'm not pregnant. For heaven's sake."

Ramona giggled, then moved to the next question. "Have you ever had surgery?"

Josephine inhaled a deep breath. "Well, I …" She looked down.

"Either you have, or you haven't, which is it?"

"Yes. Yes, I have."

"If yes, what and when?"

"That's not on there. What do they need to know that for?"

"Josephine, they need to know. It's important. The next question is about anesthesia. There's no tellin' if you'll need surgery to fix this arm up. What difference does it make?"

"It's just that … it's too personal."

"Female surgery? Did you have a hysterectomy or something?" Ramona whispered. "You can tell me. We're friends. I'm not going to blab it anywhere."

"It's not female surgery. Well, it wasn't a hysterectomy."

"What then? Did you have plastic surgery, a facelift?" Ramona tapped the end of the pen on the clipboard.

Josephine looked at her friend, tears filling her eyes. "I don't want you to think of me in any kind of way."

"Josephine, I'm sitting here, trying to help you, and you are acting like your past surgery will change our thirty-eight years of friendship. Did you hit your head when you fell?"

"I had a cesarean section." There, she said it. Why did she feel so exposed yet so much lighter?

Ramona began to write. "Wait, what? You had a baby?"

"Shhhhhhh!" Josephine was crying now. "See, I told you, it's too personal. It's nobody's business."

"Why haven't you ever told me this?"

"I don't want anyone to know about the indiscretions of my youth."

Ramona handed her a tissue, and Josephine wiped her eyes with her left hand.

"Honey, you've been sorely misled if you think you have the corner on indiscretions."

Josephine's sorrow flowed in the tears she tried so discreetly to mop.

"Let's finish this questionnaire and get you patched up. We can talk about this later. I don't think any less of you, that's for darn sure."

"Yes, let's finish." Josephine looked at her friend. "Thank you."

❧

Claire was about to head out the door for the Grace Writers when she heard a knock. She peered through the peephole and saw the top of Amos Kicklighter's fuzzy head.

She opened the door. "What brings you by this afternoon?" Claire couldn't believe her eyes. Amos had never darkened her doorstep, not once.

"I need a favor."

"How can I help?"

"I didn't go to Guy's fun'ral, and I have something to give the Widder Witherspoon."

"You mean, Bertie?"

"Isn't that what I said?"

"Well, no, you called … never mind."

Amos held a tattered cardboard box in his hand. "Can you give this to 'er?"

"You can give it to her yourself. She's home."

"Nah. Don't want to go that far." Amos sniffed loudly.

"But she's right next door."

"Don't want ta disturb."

"Oh, you won't disturb her."

Amos thrust the box at Claire. "You give it to 'er, and if she wants to know who gave it, tell 'er I did."

"Okay, may I ask what's in the box?"

"Nosy ain'tcha?"

"Well, is it time-sensitive? Cookies or something perishable?"

"I don't bake. Men don't bake." Amos's caterpillar eyebrows kissed in the middle of his forehead.

Claire sighed. "I just wanted to be sure because I can't run it over to her until later."

"Since you mentioned baking, that there apple cake you made a long time ago—Wickham Market's isn't as good, even though yours needed more cinnamon, and I was wonderin' if you fixed your recipe."

"Do you want me to make you an apple cake, Amos?" Claire was both annoyed and strangely flattered by his veiled request.

"Suit yourself." He turned and trudged down the brick pathway to the gate.

Chapter 26

CLAIRE RANG THE DOORBELL and soaked in the warm sunshine while waiting for Bertie to answer.

"Oh, come in, dear."

Claire took her by the hand and pulled her onto the porch. "The sun feels wonderful."

"Oh, my, it does. What is that in your hands?" Bertie's eyes landed on the tattered box. "My birthday isn't until tomorrow, and I have a strict no-gift policy."

"It's not a birthday gift. I don't know what it is. Amos brought it over and asked me to give it to you. I'm dying to find out what's in it."

Bertie eyed the box. "Good heavens, what on earth would Amos want to give to me? I haven't so much as said hello to the man for months."

"Well, open it, and we'll both know." Claire set it on a little table flanked by two rocking chairs.

She tugged on the top flap of the box. It popped open. "Oh, my." She lifted a hand-carved dog from the box. It was the spitting image of Daffy. "You don't think …."

"Did Amos carve that?" Claire admired the detail of the bright, eager eyes. The nose appeared to be twitching, and her fur was rendered in exquisite detail—curls hugged her collar and twisted down her back.

"It's probably been fifteen years ago. Guy showed Amos some carving techniques but didn't think he paid attention. He was impatient and cut the lesson short. My goodness, this is beautiful."

"I'm in shock. Who'd have thought that man could produce something so incredible? He's so … odd."

"There's more to that odd man than meets the eye. Guy loved him. He always stopped to talk to Amos when he walked Daffy." Bertie gazed at the carving and smiled. "I'm going over there to thank him. Come with me."

Claire followed her to Amos Kicklighter's weathered gate. He was sitting on his porch smoking a cigarette.

"Amos, can we visit for a moment?" Bertie called from the gate.

"Suit yourself."

Bertie and Claire carefully picked a path along the broken walkway. "Thank you for the carving of Daffy. It's absolutely beautiful."

"I was makin' it fer Guy, and then he upped and died."

"He would have loved it."

"I know. He taught me how to carve. He was a good man. Busts me up he's not here no more." Amos took one last drag from the stub of a cigarette.

"Well, if he *were* here, he would be very grateful for the carving, and he would say, 'God bless you, Amos.'"

"I know that."

"He liked you very much. Your carving is displayed on the mantle, next to his chair." Bertie smiled. "That's where he would have wanted it."

"Well, if he were here, I'd of given it to him, but since he's not, you get it."

Claire looked at Bertie. What would she say to that?

"Amos, I'm having a birthday party tomorrow night. Would you like to come?"

"Nah, I'm s'busy, I can't. It's not going to be loud, is it?"

"You mean with music and shouting?" Bertie smiled at Claire.

"We'll try to keep it down, Amos." Claire giggled.

"We done here?" Amos stood.

"No. Just one more thing." Bertie walked over to Amos and hugged him. The astonished look on Amos' face was priceless. He stood as stiff as the porch post, and when Bertie let go, he made a quick exit into his house. The door shut with a slap.

Claire heard the deadbolt latch.

The two ladies strolled silently down the path, exited the gate, and turned to the right to return to their homes. When they were clear of Amos' sight, they looked at each other and giggled.

"I'm so happy you moved next door," Bertie said. "No one understands when I try to describe Amos, but you do. You understand perfectly."

"I do. He's starting to grow on me—he's so awkward and … I can't believe I'm going to say this. He's rather sweet."

Claire stepped back from the group, beside Will, grateful that two of Bertie's sons and their families made the trip to Walters Bluff. Guy and Bertie's closest friends were also in attendance, hoping to make her first birthday without Guy a happy one. Gathered in Will and Claire's living room, everyone sang to her and watched her blow out the candles on a huge German chocolate cake, baked by Ella Mae.

When the smoke cleared, Will presented her with a gift bag. "What's this?"

"It's a gift. What does it look like?"

"Well, I can see that, Mr. Smarty pants. I thought the invitation said no gifts, please." She wagged her finger at him.

"It's not from me." Will stepped back and took Claire's hand.

Bertie looked at Claire.

"Not from me either."

"Well, who is it from?" She looked around the room.

"Just open it," Will said.

Bertie removed the tissue from the bag and peered inside. "What in heaven's name?" She covered her mouth. "Where did you get this?"

"I found it on Guy's workbench. It was almost finished, so I put it together as it was." Will squeezed Claire's hand.

She held the box with a delicate touch as if it were a delicate bloom. "It's beautiful. Guy made this for me?"

"Yes … and I found something else in his workshop. It's inside."

Bertie tipped the lid open. Inside was a little velvet box. "Oh, my heavens," she whispered. She opened the box to find a gold band, beaded at the edge. She gasped, dropped her head into her hands, and began to cry. "Oh, Guy … you are such a dear." She sniffled and blinked to focus on the ring.

Bertie slid it on her ring finger and held her hand out for a look. "I lost my wedding band many years ago, but still had my engagement ring. Guy wanted to replace it, but I told him not to spend the money. You all know me. Frugal. He brought it up occasionally, and I'd shush him—tell him not to bother." Bertie's voice cracked with emotion. "But it looks like he just went ahead and bought it for me. That sweet man—oh, my goodness, he really did it this time." She wiped her tears, but then she began laughing simultaneously. "Sure beats the frying pan he got me for our first Christmas."

With that, everyone laughed through their tears as they passed the box around the room to be admired.

Claire watched as Bertie rebounded from the sweep of emotion, and in that moment, she knew her sense of humor would carry her through. Guy and God were looking out for her from above.

☙

Claire, Fern, and Laurel worked tirelessly to prepare The Weathered Vessel for a very grand opening. "I think we're ready, ladies," Claire announced as she placed one last bouquet in an old vase—one last weathered vessel on the antique buffet in the picture window by the door.

"Beautiful. Just beautiful." Laurel placed her hands on her hips, scanning the inviting, homey space. The floral area was near the counter, where folks could grab bouquets from the cooler and pay for their treasures. It was perfect.

"What are we going to put here?" Fern asked. She waved her hands around as she stood in the center of an open space.

"I have an idea." Claire excused herself to the workroom.

She returned with a vintage oak bistro table and placed it in the space. She left again and returned with a couple of stools. "A place to chat."

"I like that!" Fern clapped her hands. "We can have coffee brewing to inspire people to stay."

"We'll have cookies and coffee tomorrow, so let's see what happens, but I love the idea of having a space for folks to visit." Claire placed an arm around Laurel's shoulders.

Fern joined them. "I'm so excited I can hardly stand it."

"Me too. I'm so grateful." Laurel sighed. "I didn't imagine a shop like this. I just hoped we wouldn't have to close forever."

"God always has better plans." The words tumbled from Claire's mouth, catching her by surprise. *Does He? He must.* She breathed a prayer: *Lord, I'm trying to believe that with all my heart.*

꙰

Claire baked cookies until the wee hours of the morning—sugar cookies in the shape of daisies, violets, and forget-me-nots—every cookie piped and frosted in detail until each ironstone platter became a blooming bouquet.

Will ambled into the kitchen as she finished the last one. "I'll clean up," he announced and immediately set to work loading the dishwasher.

"You're my hero." Claire moved the platters to the table and sat, pondering. *I hope the day goes off without a hitch.* But she assumed it wouldn't. Wasn't there always something?

Will finished the work and stretched with a loud, wide yawn.

Bone-tired, Claire wrapped her arms around him.

He squeezed her tight, and they fell into bed to chase a bit of sleep before the grand opening of The Weathered Vessel.

The alarm sounded, it seemed, just as Claire's head hit the pillow.

Excitement filled her as she stood before her closet, scanning the choices. Her fingers ran over the fabric of a dress she'd never worn. She bought it for her parents' fiftieth anniversary party, but days before, they were gone. It was colorful and happy with a full, swinging skirt. No occasion had warranted removing it from the closet, but perhaps today was the day. She pulled it on and twirled, much like she did as a girl on Easter morning. Claire paused in front of the mirror. Her face glowed with excitement. Gone was the fresh pain of loss. Instead, hope filled her eyes.

She and Will loaded the car with platters of cookies, fancy napkins, and a few extra trinkets to add to the shop.

"I'm proud of you." Will kissed her and held her tight. "This is a big deal."

"It is." Tears threatened as she thought of her mom. Their dream of opening a shop together, and the fact that she would have loved what she, Fern, and Laurel had created. Both of her parents would have been so proud.

"I'll drop in later today. Have … fun." He said the last two words like an admonition.

He knows me so well. But how could she *not* have fun with Fern and Laurel?

She arrived at The Weathered Vessel before the others. Breathing in the fragrance of flowers, fresh paint, and antiques, Claire silently thanked God for this most important of days. She placed the platters of cookies on a table near the counter and started two large pots of coffee.

Fern and Laurel pushed through the back door.

"Good morning!" Laurel sang the words, her face radiant with excitement.

"The cookies look amazing," Fern announced. "Is there anything you can't do?"

Claire rolled her eyes. "Pssht, most everything else."

A knock sent Claire to the storefront. She opened the door. Ella Mae stood outside holding a box.

"Thank you for coming, but I'm sorry, we're not open for another hour."

"I know. I brought cookies as a little grand opening whoop-de-do."

Claire didn't move from the doorway.

"I've baked my award-winning bars. You know how lemon bars and brownies just draw people in? Well …" She stopped mid-sentence and scowled. "Are you going to let me in so I can put down this box, or do I have to stand here with a growing hitch in my back?"

"Oh, I'm sorry, come in."

"So—wait, what's all this?" Ella Mae stopped halfway through the door, her eyes scanning the antique platters of beautifully decorated sugar cookies. She set down the box and pointed a limp finger. "Who? Where did you get those? Goodies' Bakery doesn't make those. Did you buy them in Walkersville?"

"No. I made them," Claire said.

Fern appeared through the workroom door, her mouth bent in a smile. She didn't say a word as Ella Mae's eyes grew bigger— her ebony skin glistening with little beads of sweat at her hairline.

"You? Oh, how nice. Do you mind?" She reached for a cookie.

"Not at all. Enjoy." Claire watched her choose a miniature daisy. She lifted it to her lips and took the tiniest bite, letting it rest on her tongue before tasting it with an almost imperceptible smacking of her lips. "Tahitian vanilla or Madagascar?"

Claire smiled. "I use only Madagascar vanilla. You?"

"Of course." She took another bite. "European butter?"

"I prefer regular salted butter for cookies and European for cakes."

"Mmm-hmmm."

Claire stifled a chuckle. She fiercely loved the competitive woman.

Ella Mae popped the rest of the cookie in her mouth and rummaged through her box. She produced two large plastic containers.

"I don't think I have any extra platters, but as my cookies disappear, I'll fill the empty spaces with yours." She took the bars from Ella Mae and placed them on the counter. "What a treat."

The plump woman drew in a long breath. "Well, I told everyone to come here for treats, so they might be disappointed if my lemon bars aren't out."

Laurel scooted past Fern and opened one of the containers. "Mmmm, brownies. My favorite."

"Such a shame they won't be displayed." Ella Mae sighed.

"I'll set them out as soon as there's room. If you'll excuse me, I need to put cash in the register before we open." Claire grabbed the boxes of bars, winked, and scooted past Fern into the workroom. Safely behind the swinging door, she giggled and dug through a couple of boxes in the back where there might be a platter she could wash and use.

"Look what I found." Claire presented another platter filled with lemon bars and brownies.

Ella Mae scooted the other platters around on the table to make room for her bars in the center front. "There." Her shoulders relaxed. "Perfect."

"You're so thoughtful."

"It's what I do. I love to help."

Claire put her arm around the woman and squeezed. "It's so nice to know our little venture has such wonderful support," she said.

Ella Mae returned her squeeze. "You should try one of my brownies."

꙼

At ten o'clock sharp, Claire turned on the "Open" sign and unlocked the door to a line of people eager to see The Weathered Vessel. A steady stream of customers from Durham

County and beyond filed through, purchasing flowers and treasures and gobbling cookies.

Folks enjoyed the grand opening, and many lingered much longer than expected after completing their purchases—eating cookies, sipping coffee, and chatting with neighbors and friends.

By five that afternoon, the ladies plopped onto stools. Claire sighed a long, satisfied breath and smiled. "I don't think the cash register has stopped all day."

"Thank you for saving the shop." Fern's eyes held a misty sincerity.

"I really didn't want our family's legacy to end," Laurel added.

Claire looked from one sister to the other. Who saved whom? What would she be doing if not opening this shop? Mucking around in the mire of grief, self-pity, and bitterness? Perhaps, but Claire hoped she'd have been stronger than that. "I'm grateful the opportunity presented itself at precisely the right time."

"Divine intervention." Fern chirped.

"Yes." Claire agreed. And it was.

"Here comes Ella Mae again." Laurel giggled as she opened the door for her.

"How-do!" Ella Mae made a beeline for the cookie table. Two platters held a scant number of cookies. "I see they were a hit."

"Yes, they sure were." Claire declared.

"I'm here to pick up my containers and ..." She looked around the shop. "I'll just take another look around."

Ella Mae wandered about as Laurel retrieved the plastic boxes.

"Tell me, Claire, are any of these platters for sale? I do need to pretty-up my presentation. Your cookies were lovely on the white ironstone." Ella Mae ran her finger around the edge of one of the platters.

"I'd be happy to give you that one. The others are my mother's. I couldn't part with them." Claire moved toward her. "You're welcome to it. It's yours."

"Free?" Ella Mae's hand grasped her generous bosom. "I couldn't take it without paying you."

"I insist. You so kindly baked cookies …."

"Bars, actually," she mumbled.

"Yes, and you know how bakers need to support each other." Claire's sincere smile defied the underlying manipulation. She'd disarm this competitive woman if it were the last thing she did.

Ella Mae's smile appeared nervous—a little unsure. "Well, that's awfully sweet of you."

"And I'll leave some sugar cookies on it in the bargain." Claire held the platter toward her.

She looked at the cookies with a raised eyebrow but grasped the platter with both hands. "How nice."

༚

A few days later, Claire prepared a pot of coffee and drummed her fingers on the counter as it brewed.

I want to keep that friendly grand opening vibe going every day.

Last week's paper caught her gaze. She picked up *The Durham County Herald.* The headline read: "Grand Opening of The Weathered Vessel This Weekend."

> *Eight months ago, Fern and Laurel Greenwald thought their flower shop's 30-year legacy would end.*
>
> *"We didn't know what to do. The shop's revenue had fallen, and we couldn't pay the bills," Fern Greenwald said.*
>
> *The sisters decided to sell the shop. They posted a sign in the window, and within hours, Claire Baldwin (wife of Walters Bluff Police Chief Will Baldwin) saw the sign and hatched a plan. The Weathered Vessel.*

Baldwin is an antique collector. After recently losing her parents, Baldwin stated, "I needed a new start. Fern and Laurel have the passion and drive, and I have a dream, motivation, and the capital to make this collaboration work."

"This is a timely union," said Mayor Donald Bickerstaff. "The Chamber and I were in the process of inviting and encouraging antiques dealers and artisans to open shop in our fair metropolis."

As a refueling point near the interstate, Walters Bluff has struggled in recent years to be more than a convenient stop for snacks and gas. "The idea of nurturing an art culture in Walters Bluff melds well with our founding," Bickerstaff said. "Our city was founded on fine craftsmanship and creative ingenuity."

Walter Wickham, the man for whom our town is named, sold his finely carved furniture, fruit, vegetables, jams, and baked goods in his store, where the cider mill stands today.

The Weathered Vessel is a welcome addition to the Walters Bluff Chamber and a wonderful reimagining of the Greenwald sisters' flower shop. The grand opening is on Friday and Saturday. Like all Walters Bluff downtown businesses, the shop will be closed on Sunday and honor Family Day on Wednesdays by closing at 3 p.m.

The Weathered Vessel offers antiques, flowers, and will soon offer a curated collection of local art. It will host an art fair on the lawn at City Hall this summer. "We look forward to celebrating creativity and inviting artists and creators from Durham County and beyond to share their talents and support our community," Baldwin said. Applications to sell at the fair and in the shop are available at The Weathered Vessel.

The Durham County Herald *extends a hearty Walters Bluff welcome to The Weathered Vessel.*

Claire hadn't had a chance to read the article until now. What a lovely story. And Walters Bluff had come through for them.

❧

Harley took a seat in the oak chair by the cluttered counter. It had been so long since he'd sat in Stuff and Things and spent time with Millie.

"I heard the news, Harley … all the news. I want you to know something about the test results—I didn't doubt, in case you wondered." Her face showed concern.

Did she worry about me? "Thanks—it's been a dern awful time, but it made me see my need for God. He saved me. He really saved me." Would he ever tell Millie about the day Bertie forgave him?

He wanted to.

Millie smiled. "I'm so glad you're feelin' better. You're lookin' better too."

"Say, I've been thinkin', and I have an idea that may or may not work. I wonder if we could talk over dinner sometime."

Her face flushed. "You askin' me out on a date, Harley?"

"No, I'm not asking you out. I'm asking you to have dinner with me so we can have a discussion. Don't go gettin' any ideas." Harley chuckled. He liked Millie, but he'd never considered dating her. *She's out of my league.*

"Well, the answer's yes, I'll have dinner with you. The diner tomorrow night?" She smiled.

"Six o'clock?"

"It's a date." Millie winked at him.

His face warmed, and a chuckle rumbled from his pounding heart.

❧

Josephine watched Ramona stride into her house and close her front door. Would they talk about … *no, I'm not ready.*

"How's the patient?"

"Sore. My arm feels better than my ribs and hip today, and it hurts to walk and sit." Josephine adjusted herself on the couch.

"Can I put a kettle on for tea?"

"Help yourself." *Oh no, she's staying.*

Ramona disappeared into the kitchen and returned a moment later. "Hey, Jo, I wondered if we could talk about the other day."

"About what?" Josephine drew a calming breath. *Here we go.*

"You know what I'm talking about. Don't play games with me."

"Oh, yes, that."

"About the baby. You never told me you had a baby. What happened to him?" Ramona leaned forward.

"Her."

"Oh, a daughter." Ramona's eyes softened. "Tell me the story, Jo."

"It's a long one." Josephine's mind whirled. *I've never told a soul.*

"I have all day."

"Oh." There was no escape. "Well, my Aunt Olivetta kept me under her thumb—and most of the time, I didn't mind it. The rules felt safe—secure. I craved that. But then I met Jack."

"Who's Jack?"

"A boy from another school. I met him at a baseball game. I wasn't allowed to go to the games, but Aunt Olivetta was away for the afternoon, so I went with my friend. I wish I hadn't. Well, that's not exactly true either." Josephine adjusted her arm on a pillow. "Jack and his friends sat next to my friend and me, and we talked. He was sweet—well, he was a sweet talker. He asked me to go to a show with him. I didn't know what to say, so I just said yes. I lied to my aunt and said I would be at my friend's house. I tell you, it was a slippery slope once I started down the path of deceit."

"I hear that." Ramona excused herself to take the kettle off the stove and returned with two cups of tea.

Josephine took a long sip. "Well, that summer, I was a lying, cheating sinner. I hate to admit that. I think back to that time in my life, and I'm so ashamed. Then, one September night, I gave in to temptation."

Josephine looked at Ramona for a reaction. She didn't see a hint of judgment.

"We snuck away from a football game to his house. His parents weren't home, and that was that. He broke up with me the next day. It devastated me. My aunt didn't understand why I was so heartbroken, and I certainly couldn't tell her. Then, I started feeling different. I didn't have my cycle on time, and by the time my skirt was getting tight, it occurred to me that I might be pregnant."

"What did you do?"

"Well, I had to tell my aunt. She took me to a doctor in another town, and the test confirmed my fear. Aunt Olivetta was profoundly disappointed in me. She sent me away to a home for unwed mothers the next week. My aunt told everyone I went to live with another relative for a while."

"Oh, my."

"So, I lived with a nice old couple in a big house with several extra bedrooms. There were three pregnant girls there. When I went into labor, there were complications, so they rushed me to the hospital for a cesarean section. I was so scared."

"I can't imagine."

"They put me to sleep for the operation. When I woke up, they asked if I'd like to see her, and I said I would." Josephine's eyes welled with tears. "I remember her soft cheeks—like velvet. Her little fingers clung to mine, and for a moment, she opened her eyes and looked right at me. She stared and stared, and then she yawned. Every time I see a baby yawn, it takes me right back to that moment." Josephine dabbed her eyes with a tissue. Her voice was barely audible. "I told her I was sorry, that I loved her. Then a woman came into the room and said it was time."

A long, sorrowful breath left Josephine.

"She just took her from my arms." All the emotions of the day returned to her pounding heart.

"I signed the papers even though I didn't want to. I had no other options. I don't know where my daughter went or if she had a good life, but I've thought about her every day for so many years, and now I think about her often and … The day I broke my arm was my daughter's fifty-second birthday."

"Oh, Jo …."

She looked at the floor, pondering. "I pray she's been safe and loved."

"Why haven't you shared this before?" Ramona blinked away tears as she asked the question.

"Because I'm ashamed."

"You think you're the only person who had a baby as a teenager?"

"No, but I'm not like the other girls who sleep around and have babies. I had a single indiscretion and paid a hefty price for it. I'm not one of them, and I've spent my entire life proving it to God—and myself."

Ramona chuckled. "You think you have to prove that? Do you think God's making little hash marks for all the bad things you do and keeping score?"

"No, of course not." Josephine winced. "Well, yes, kind of."

"Listen, Jo, none of us is better than another."

Josephine stared straight ahead. *Is that true? Do I think I'm better?*

"You may have accepted God's forgiveness, but you still need to forgive yourself."

A tear slid down Josephine's cheek. She brushed it with her left hand. "I suppose you're right." She readjusted her arm. "Why don't you think badly of me? I kept this secret from you. I had a child out of wedlock. I'm not who you thought I was."

"I thought you were an insecure, judgmental, fragile, sweet, godly woman. How does that change with this new information?"

"I am judgmental, aren't I?"

~

Millie couldn't help but laugh. "You're what?" Surely, he was kidding. She wanted to be charming on her first date with Harley, so she giggled even though the joke wasn't all that funny.

"No, really, I'm not joking. I'm selling the bar."

Millie looked at the man across the table. He'd lost more than some weight and the scruff of an unkempt beard. He'd lost his marbles as well. "Are you sure, Harley?"

"I talked it over with my sister. Even though the bar is mine, free and clear, I wanted to consult with her to make sure I wasn't disrespecting our family legacy."

"What'd she say?"

"My sister's happy to see it go. It's time for our legacy to change. I got a job with the city—a mechanic. I'll be working with Oscar on all kinds of maintenance. I like that kind of work. I start on Monday."

"Harley, that's wonderful."

"I'm settling down. At forty-five years old. It's about time, huh?"

"If that's what you want, I'm thrilled for ya."

"It is ... it is what I want to do, Millie."

"Well, what did you drag me out on a date for?"

"It's not a date."

"Whatever you say, Harley, what are we doing at the diner, just you and me, having dinner together?" Millie chuckled as she locked eyes with her old friend.

Harley's drumbeat chuckle made a smile bloom on Millie's face. She liked to make him laugh.

"I have an idea," he said.

"Spill it. I'm listening. What's your idea?"

"Well, I'm sellin' the bar, but I don't want to lose the stories of this place. So, I want to set up a sort of museum." He scratched his beard. "The camera shop next door is closin' down, so I thought I'd buy that smaller space with the money from the bar."

"Great idea. I'll help you," Millie said.

"You will?"

"I've got lots of ... stuff and things to contribute." Millie laughed at her joke. Her hazel eyes sparkled. "It's like you've been reading my mind or something. Golly, I've had a corner of my shop behind a rope for months. The walls of the bar are covered with all kinds of history. Why wouldn't we join forces and create a museum of some kind?"

Harley's smile spanned the width of his face. "I thought I'd have to convince you."

"Heck no, let's do it." Millie took a bite of her macaroni and cheese. "This is so dry. Next time you take me out, you'll have to spring for someplace with better grub."

"Millie, this isn't ... oh fine, next time we'll go to Walkersville."

"That's what I'm talkin' about."

ॐ

Claire watched Josephine and Ramona enter the fellowship room.

"She's back," Ramona exclaimed.

"You look wonderful. How's your arm, dear?" Joan jumped up to pull out a chair for her.

Josephine drew in a breath. "You know when someone gets in an accident, and they find cancer in a blood test, and instead of being upset about the accident, they are grateful that it happened because they found the cancer?"

Claire gasped.

"I don't know how much more I can take. It's too much. Honest to gumdrops, I can't take another sad thing. I just can't." Ella Mae grabbed a napkin and dabbed her eyes.

"No, Ella Mae, I'm just asking, do you know how that happens?" Josephine's blue eyes sparkled.

"How does what happen? How people have cancer?" Rita asked.

"No, how one thing exposes another thing. That was a bad example. I don't have cancer." Josephine adjusted her arm.

"Well, yes, but why would you say the C-word? I'm as fragile as an eggshell. You can't just go tossing that word around." Ella Mae dabbed at her eyes. She looked around the table. "Is everyone else as confused as I am?"

"My point is, breaking my arm helped me heal in other ways, that's all. That was a bad analogy. I just broke my arm and bruised a couple of ribs and my hip. I'm in perfect health otherwise."

"What a relief. I can't take any more upset, I swear to sugar." Ella Mae shook her head. "Here, have a ginger snap." She passed a plate of cookies to Josephine.

"I'm so happy for you, Josephine. Maybe someday you can write about it. But for now, I'm thankful that you've been blessed, even if it took a broken arm to do it." Joan smiled.

"I'm sorry it had to come to this." Josephine shifted in her seat.

"Who would like to begin? The prompt was to write about a Hallelujah moment. I think Josephine just told us all about hers," Rita said.

"I'll start," said Ella Mae. "I didn't write either. I'm just going to tell you all about what happened on Sunday." Ella Mae brushed cookie crumbs from her mouth before she began. "Have you heard the saying, *No man has ever been shot while doing the dishes?*"

"Yes," Rita spoke for all the ladies.

"Unfortunately, my George has never had the opportunity to find out if that is a true statement—until recently. Our Sunday routine is much like everyone else's. I put a hunk of meat into the oven to slow roast while we're at church. When we arrive home, I make the side dishes and usually a dessert. When we're done eating, I clean up. George, however, trudges into the den and sinks into his Barcalounger to take a long Sunday nap. If there's a game on, he lets the action lull him to sleep. I've asked him to help with the dishes a thousand times, but he always says, 'Elly-Lou, Sunday is a day of rest.'

"I've had many long conversations with God about the situation. I want to be a good wife, but Lord have mercy, I'd give just about anything to hear my George offer to help with the dishes." Ella Mae sighed.

"Last Sunday, it was my week to help with children's church. My favorite Sunday of the month—no disrespect to Pastor Karl, Joan."

"None taken." Joan chuckled.

"This week, a little girl told me all about a fight her mommy and daddy had on the way to church, and I explained to her what a proper secret was. I said, *Sometimes Mommy and Daddy say things that aren't nice, and it's important that we don't repeat them at church.*" Ella Mae chuckled. "Then a little boy decided to ask Jesus into his heart. I laughed so hard I nearly piddled myself as he named all his sins, including cutting his big sister's hair while she watched television and dropping the cat in the toilet. But he choked up as he asked for forgiveness, and I thanked the Lord for the little children and the opportunity to serve them." Ella Mae patted her bosom as she spoke.

"Well, the parents came to claim their children, and George appeared in the doorway to claim me. The day progressed like every other Sunday, except for one thing. After dinner, George took our plates to the sink." She paused and looked around the circle of ladies with astonished eyes. He said, 'Elly-Lou, why don't you go to the den and relax while I do the dishes?'

"You could have knocked me down with a feather. Instead of going to the den, I ran out on the front porch, threw my hands in the air, and hollered, *Hallelujah!* Then I was so fidgety I couldn't sit still, so I organized my recipe box."

"Later that night, I asked George why he decided to do the dishes. He said Pastor Karl preached a sermon that spoke to his heart, and I thanked the good Lord I was serving in children's church. The Holy Spirit convicted his heart far better than my elbow ever has." Ella Mae laughed. "And that's my Hallelujah moment."

"The sermon was about serving one another," Joan said. "How wonderful George had an immediate response to the Word."

"Wonderful doesn't begin to cover it, honest to oatmeal." Ella Mae reached for another gingersnap.

One by one, the ladies shared what they had written, except for Josephine, since she couldn't write. Claire noticed her smile was softer as she listened intently to each story.

"Ladies, our next prompt will be to write about a romance," Rita said.

"Romance? Oh, how fun!" Millie clapped her hands.

"You have a romance to write about?" Claire whispered the question to Millie as she jotted the prompt in her notebook.

"Nah." Millie drew in a breath. "Not yet."

Chapter 27

CLAIRE EXAMINED THE GRAIN of the wood on the pew as Pastor Karl preached.

"Ecclesiastes 3:11 says, 'He has made everything beautiful in its time.'" Pastor Karl paused as he always did when reading scripture.

The words steeped in Claire's heart. *Everything?*

Her mind wandered to Harley, Guy, Amos, and his beautiful carving of Daffy. She smiled. Then—Bertie forgave Harley. Harley accepted Jesus as his Savior. Beautiful. Yes.

After church, Claire moved clothes from the washer and shoved them into the dryer, still pondering the verse as the doorbell rang.

"Just a minute," Claire called, pushing the button to start the dryer.

She ran to the door and opened it. "Oh, hello, Josephine. Come in."

Her arm in a sling, Josephine stepped through the open door and looked around. "You have a lovely home, Claire."

"Thank you. What brings you by?" Claire didn't know what to do. Why would Josephine come to visit?

"I need to talk to you. Can we sit down?"

"Of course. I'll get us something to drink." Claire motioned to the sofa and excused herself to fetch ice water from the kitchen.

She returned with two glasses as Josephine shifted in her seat.

"Josephine, is everything all right?" Claire took a sip.

"No, it isn't. I need to tell you something."

"Oh."

"First of all, I need to apologize. I've said some terrible things in the past months, and I feel awful about it. I gossiped about Harley, and I regret that. I've apologized to him as well." Josephine's voice shook a bit.

Claire couldn't believe her ears. "I forgive you. And I'm sorry I haven't always been kind in my responses to you." A twinge of guilt stabbed Claire's heart.

"Well, I'm sure I've deserved it." Josephine looked at her hands.

"You said, first of all. Is there a second of all?"

"Yes. I feel compelled to admit that I'm not as perfect as I've tried to make everyone think I am."

"I knew that." Claire giggled. "I mean, really, Josephine. No one is perfect."

"I know. I'm working on being a little more … well, Ramona says I need to be softer."

"I'd agree with that." Claire took in a breath. *Maybe that was a little harsh.*

"You would?" Josephine wrinkled her nose.

Claire nodded, feeling her heart warm to this already softer woman.

Josephine gently unfolded the story of her daughter. Claire, though surprised, heard humility in every word.

"Well, I feel better," Josephine said, sipping her water. "I thought it would be harder to ask for forgiveness. And to forgive myself for my past. But I'll tell you, Claire. Forgiveness is a beautiful thing. It sets you free."

The two women chatted until Josephine announced she had to talk to Bertie next.

As Claire watched her walk next door, Josephine's words pierced her heart.

Forgiveness is a beautiful thing. It sets you free.

๛

Fern signed her name on the dotted line and put down the pen. Tears welled in her eyes, and she blinked them away. She'd cried enough tears for Frank—he didn't deserve even one more.

She took off her wedding ring.

Fern married Frank after knowing him for only five months. Her mother tried to talk sense into her, but she was in love, and he was persuasive. He sold himself to her like he sold lemons at the used car lot.

Now it was over. The persistent infidelity was more than she could take.

She put the ring in her jewelry box and rubbed her finger to erase the mark left by eight years of wear. *I never imagined I would be divorced.*

Fern shut the jewelry box and looked at the papers on the dresser. She stood there for a few minutes, pondering. The divorce, final.

๛

"I brought sugar cookies today—hearts—since we're sharing our romantic stories." Ella Mae lifted the foil off a milk-glass pedestal covered with red and pink frosted cookie hearts.

"Oh, Ella Mae, I love your sugar cookies." Rita reached for a pink cookie with white sprinkles.

"How do you make them so soft?" Claire asked.

"Cream chee—" Ella Mae caught herself. "It's a variety of ingredients."

"She said cream cheese." Millie giggled and jotted the information in her notebook.

"Did not," Ella Mae snapped.

"For accuracy's sake, she said cream chee." Joan chuckled.

"Someone's got loose lips. You know what they say—loose lips, big hips." Millie giggled.

"They don't say that. It's ships. Loose lips sink ships." Josephine took a bite.

"The dessert auction is coming up, Ella Mae," Millie warned. "You'd better watch yourself."

Ella Mae nibbled a cookie and looked around the table. "What happens in the Grace Writers stays in the Grace Writers. Can I count on you ladies to keep my little indiscretion quiet?"

"Mums the word. But you can't ask us not to use the information for our benefit." Claire raised one eyebrow as she gazed at Ella Mae. She tried very hard not to smile.

"Fair is fair," Ella Mae conceded. "I'm not worried at all."

"With that scandal settled, who would like to begin? Maybe I'll start today. I actually tried my hand at writing a romance." Rita looked a little excited. She shared a story about a waitress who fell in love with a prince.

"Claire, your turn. Did you write a romance or another of your stories?" Millie sipped her coffee.

"This is a story about our neighbor back home." Claire put on her reading glasses.

"Isn't Walters Bluff home now?" Ella Mae's brow furrowed.

"Yes, you're right. That means a lot." Claire's heart pounded. "This is about Cyrus. He is the one who inspired my mom and me to plan to open an antique store."

Cyrus Murphy pulled the last cartload of treasures into his assigned space. While he set up, his mind turned to Mona. She loved arranging knickknacks on bookshelves and setting an old dining table with china and teapots. Unfortunately, Mona could do nothing to help as she watched from heaven.

He didn't have a dining table today, but he did have a few trunks, dressers, side tables, and several boxes of whatnots. After arranging the furniture, he began unwrapping the smaller pieces. His calloused hands fumbled with the delicate handles of teacups and thin stems of wine goblets. As he worked, he noticed his neighbor struggling with a steamer trunk.

"You need help, young lady?" Cyrus asked, ready to assist.

"Young? Ha!" She giggled. "Yes, I could use a hand."

Together, they lifted the trunk and set it in a corner of her space.

"Thank you," she said, brushing gray hair from her face.

"You're most welcome. I'm Cyrus Murphy." He extended his hand. "And you are?"

"Dorothy Nesbit," she said, offering her small hand to his large one.

"Looks like we're neighbors, at least for today." Cyrus grinned and continued setting up his booth. As he worked, he glanced at Dorothy to ensure she didn't need more help. She moved with the beat of the music piped throughout the auditorium-turned-antiques market. Cyrus smiled.

The doors opened to the public, and streams of people wandered through the maze of booths. Cyrus sold two sets of candlesticks, books, records, a dresser, knickknacks, and a set of lamps. He glanced at his watch to discover it was already two o'clock. He pulled a little cooler and a thermos of coffee from behind a table and looked at Dorothy. She sat in a wing chair, flipping through an old photo album.

Cyrus's stomach flip-flopped. *What on earth?* He hadn't felt his stomach do that since he and Mona were dating.

Guilt flooded his heart. Then he remembered what his son had said, "Mom would want you to find someone. She wouldn't want you to be lonely."

Cyrus agreed, but no one could replace Mona.

"Cyrus?"

He looked up to find Dorothy standing in front of him. She held out a crisscrossed cookie.

"Peanut butter. You want one?"

It smelled just like the ones Mona used to bake.

"Thank you," he managed. *Is my face red? It's so hot.* "These are just like my ..." he stopped mid-sentence, took a bite, and savored the sweetness. "These are delicious, Mona."

"It's Dorothy," she giggled. "Who's Mona?"

His face flushed. "I'm sorry, Dorothy. Mona is my wife." Cyrus noticed Dorothy's hazel eyes look away. "My late wife. She passed two years ago."

"Oh, I'm so sorry to hear that." Dorothy's eyes showed compassion. "She made peanut butter cookies, too?"

"The best." He looked at the treat in his hand. "They were just like these, actually, with chunky peanut butter and milk chocolate chips. Wow."

"I add extra salt to cut the sweet and ...."

"Showcase the peanut flavor." Cyrus finished her sentence.

"Yes, that's right. It's what my teacher said at a baking class." Dorothy smiled.

"You didn't happen to take the class at the Riverside Community College, did you?" Cyrus's heart pounded.

"Why, yes, that's the one. Let's see. It's been about four years. We made peanut butter cookies and scones and ...."

"Cinnamon rolls." Cyrus finished her sentence again.

"Yes, cinnamon rolls."

"That was my wife," Cyrus said.

"The instructor?" Dorothy paused, smiling. "She was a lovely woman."

"Yes. And you're a good student. Your cookies taste exactly like hers." Cyrus took another bite and blinked back a watery feeling in his right eye.

They discussed baking and antiques between sales, and Dorothy told Cyrus about her late husband and his passion for cooking. "That's why I took the baking class," she said. "My husband was a chef. When I lost him, I realized how much I depended on him. I had to learn how to cook for myself."

"You're doing fine," Cyrus said, and then he surprised himself. "Would you like to get a bite after we're done here?"

"I'd love that. I really would." Dorothy smiled and reached into her tote bag. "Here, to hold us until dinner." She handed him another cookie.

Cyrus felt Mona's nod of approval with every bite.

"Oh, that's so sweet," Joan said. "It's a true story?"

Claire nodded. "They were eventually married."

"I love that. There's hope," Millie said, then added, "As if I would ever get married again." She rolled her eyes.

"Huh. You never know, Millie." Ella Mae pushed the platter across the table. "Have another cookie."

"Who wants to go next?" Rita looked around the circle of ladies.

They read their stories of romance one by one. Josephine didn't share but announced that her arm would be freed from the sling in a couple of weeks.

"No prompt this week. Ramona has a special treat for us at our next meeting," Rita said. "See you then."

Chapter 28

CLAIRE PUSHED through the door of The Daily Brew. Harley waved from a table across the room.

She settled into a chair as he pushed a folded paper across the table to her without a word.

She put on her glasses and read the handwritten note.

Harley was silent until she set the note back on the table.

"What do you think?"

Claire looked at him through her welling tears. "I think it's beautiful. I think your heart is on that page, Harley."

"You think she'll write back?"

"I don't know. That's something your daughter will have to decide, but for your part, you've expressed yourself well, and your apology is honest and genuine."

"It's sincere, but is it too much? I don't want to come off phony." He stroked his neatly trimmed beard.

"No, I wouldn't change a thing." Claire liked how he wrote, the same way he spoke—to the point—nothing fancy.

"Okay then. I guess this is it." Harley folded the page and inserted it into an addressed, stamped envelope.

"You're a changed man, Harley."

"God's grace."

Claire surveyed her friend. He sealed the envelope, and they gazed at it on the table for a moment. A question niggled at the corners of her mind. Should she ask? She had to know.

"Hey, can I ask you a personal question? I just need to know something."

"Sure. Ask away." Harley's eyes bore into hers.

"You mentioned that Bertie forgave you."

"Yes. She's an amazing woman. I don't know if I could have done the same."

"When did she do that? I know that seems …." Claire hesitated. "I just need to know."

"Bertie forgave me a coupla' weeks after the accident. She saved my life, Claire. No, God saved me." He took another sip of coffee. "Why do you ask?"

Claire's heart pounded. She'd suspected as much from Bertie, but confirming her assumption flooded her heart with … what was that feeling?

"Claire, are you okay?"

"Yes. I'm fine. I'm just … there's something you don't know. At least, I don't think you know."

"What?" Harley's brow furrowed. "Is something wrong?"

Claire noted his worried expression. "It has nothing to do with you, Harley, nothing at all."

"Okay. What is it?"

"My parents died almost two years ago."

"I knew your parents had passed. Will mentioned a car accident, but I don't know anything else about it."

"A drunk driver killed my parents."

"Oh." Harley's eyes dropped to the table.

"The man who killed them was a deacon at our church." Claire sighed. "The evidence that he was drunk was ruined, and he lied, telling everyone he was sober, but Will was there. He knows without a doubt he was very drunk."

"I'm sorry."

Claire clasped her hands to keep them from shaking.

"Many people at our church were sympathetic to the deacon. They said I should forgive—that he was grieving too." Claire hesitated. "The people I'd known all my life sided with him, leaving me to grieve with the bonus of piling on guilt for my anger—and I can't get past the judgment I felt. The idea that I should gloss over what happened because of the supposedly upstanding man who caused it."

Harley didn't say a word. His eyes were fixed on the envelope.

"I was devastated. And my grief seemed to annoy them." Claire paused. "I didn't think I'd ever trust church people again, but First Community has been a lifeline. The people there restored my faith."

"Why are you sharing this with me, Claire?"

"Because Bertie forgave you, Harley, but I haven't forgiven Richard." Claire's breath caught in her throat. She hadn't uttered his first name since the accident.

"I see." Harley's steel-blue eyes held Claire's.

"He didn't ask for forgiveness." As soon as she uttered the words, she remembered the letter. She knew what it was when it came in the mail, and she didn't want to read it—and she still didn't.

"Well, then?"

"How can you forgive someone if they don't ask?" She hesitated. The letter. She knew all along. Her voice dropped to a whisper. "But … God has forgiven us already. All we have to do is take it and *be* forgiven."

"I thank the good Lord for that."

"And in my heart, I know we can do no less for those who hurt us. Just like Bertie did for you."

"I see where you're going. You want to forgive."

She glanced away from Harley's gaze, then bore her eyes into his. "I *don't*." There. She said it out loud. She didn't want to forgive. Claire didn't want to read the letter. She deserved to be angry—to be hurt. Who could argue with that? "I don't want to give him another pass."

"Another?" Harley's brow furrowed.

"Since the drunk driving case against him was botched. He was charged only with first degree negligent driving, and that's it."

"Oh. I see what you're saying, but …." Harley looked at Claire. "You're not giving him a pass. I still suffer from the pain of what I did, even though it wasn't intentional. It still hurts."

"But you weren't drunk. He was. Very drunk." Claire felt her face flush with anger.

Harley touched her hand. "All I can say is that Bertie said she misses Guy every day. She grieves for him. But she has … what did she call it?" Harley scratched his beard. "I think she called it perfect peace."

And there it was—exactly what Claire longed for.

Ella Mae backed through the St. John's sanctuary door—in her hands, a masterpiece. She was the first to arrive. Perfect.

Three tables draped with white tablecloths waited expectantly on the stage. Eighteen numbers, six on each table—it would be a long, satisfying night.

Ella Mae carried her triple-chocolate mousse cake to number eighteen. She always ensured her entry would be the last to be auctioned—the pièce de résistance. But honestly, it had nothing to do with order. Her talents were well-known. People waited every year to bid big money on *her* dessert. A smile crossed her lips as she positioned her cake on the table, turning it to capture the best light. Three layers in varying shades of delicious chocolate mousse—white, milk, and bittersweet, separated by sponge cake brushed with hazelnut liqueur. Artfully placed curlicues of tempered chocolate completed the masterpiece. Excitement—mixed with pride—rose in her chest.

One by one, ladies began to fill the tables with subpar desserts. It was cute, and they looked so proud. Elle Mae tried to check her attitude. It didn't work.

The dessert auction wasn't an official contest, but every year, the dessert bringing the highest bid afforded the winner bragging rights for a year. To her, it was akin to winning the lottery. She typically won, but enjoyed seeing the efforts of her peers.

The cakes, pies, and other delicacies were beautifully decorated this year. Impressive. If ever there was a time to go hog wild with garnishes, this was it.

When eighteen desserts lined the tables, and there was standing room only, it was time to begin.

Mayor Bickerstaff climbed the three steps to the podium and strolled by each table. "My goodness, what a line-up we have this year!"

He began the auction with Joan's lemon meringue pie. "Would you look at that meringue? It's as tall as Mount Everest! Who will start the bidding?"

Someone bid ten dollars, and after a short back-and-forth, the pie sold for thirty-six. Gingersnap whoopee pies passed the lemon meringue with a bid of thirty-eight bucks.

Ella Mae watched from the back of the room, pacing like a lion in a cage. When the bidding heated up, she made little snorting sounds. Her dark skin glistened with beads of nervous perspiration. She found a tissue in her sleeve and dabbed at her forehead and chest.

Caramel corn with a fudge ripple—a large tin filled to the brim—took the lead with forty-five dollars until chocolate mint truffles whizzed past them with a bid of fifty dollars and fifty cents.

A wave of nausea slapped Ella Mae as the gavel pounded after a dozen cream-filled chocolate cupcakes decorated with buttercream wildflowers sold for fifty-one dollars. She waved Pastor Karl off his chair.

"You okay, Ella Mae?" He helped her descend into the seat.

"Fine, just worked up."

Claire's dessert, a four-layer carrot pineapple cake with cream cheese icing, stood eight inches high and was decorated with piped icing carrots all around the sides. Will began the bidding at thirty dollars. It rose in five-dollar increments but stalled at fifty-five dollars. Having what seemed like the winning bid, Buster Simpson waved a wad of bills.

"Sixty," a voice called from the back.

"Sixty-five," yelled Buster, turning to the back with a scowl.

"Seventy," the voice hollered.

Ella Mae watched as Claire turned to look for the mysterious bidder.

"I'm wiped out. It's yours." Buster put his arm down in defeat.

"Going once …"

"Seventy-five," Harley called, waving his hand. "We'll pool our resources, Buster. I want a piece of that cake."

"Eighty," the voice called.

Ella Mae noticed Claire's smile growing with each bid. *She looks a mite smug.* The room began to spin.

"Well, looky here, we've got ourselves a bidding war for a carrot cake!" Mayor Bickerstaff's hand waved back and forth as the bidding continued until Harley bid ninety-five.

"One hundred dollars," the voice called from the back.

"What in tarnation? I'm not goin' over a hundred. I'll ask Claire to bake another. That's just crazy." Harley slapped his knee. "Let him have it."

"Going once, going twice … sold to …." Mayor Bickerstaff put his hand on his forehead as if looking into the sun. "Who made that bid?"

"Amos Kicklighter here."

"Well, Amos, you've set a new dessert auction record. The night's not over, though. We have three more entries." The crowd applauded, and the bidding began on a plate of buckeyes as big as golf balls.

Ella Mae fanned herself.

They brought a whopping fifty-dollar bid.

People are being so generous—what if everyone's broke by the time my cake is up for bid? Ella Mae stepped out of the sanctuary to splash cold water on her face. *Why do I do this every year? What on earth am I thinking? My heart can't take this.* She returned to the sanctuary to see Fern's caramel apple cheesecake sell for seventy-five dollars. *What was it with folks this year? Isn't the economy in a slump?*

"Ladies and gentlemen, the last entry of the night is a triple chocolate mousse cake baked by Ella Mae Walker." The mayor strolled to the end of the table and pointed to a cake that looked more like the leaning Tower of Pisa than the cake Ella Mae had set there an hour ago.

"Cheese and crackers! It's tipping over." She hustled down the aisle to rescue her cake. As she neared the table, the top layer slid onto the floor. The entire room gasped as the second layer broke in half and slid onto the table. Ella Mae stopped short, hands on her bosom, mouth agape.

Mayor Bickerstaff broke the stunned silence. "Well, there's still a layer and a half there. Do I have a bid?"

"Fifty dollars." George waved a wad of cash in the air. "I licked the bowl, and I know it's delicious."

"Seventy-five." Will raised his hand as he bid.

"Oh no, you don't—one hundred dollars." Mayor Bickerstaff pointed to himself. "I've wanted an Ella Mae entry for five years, and I've been outbid every time. That's not happening this year."

No one challenged him.

"Going once, going twice, sold to me." Mayor Bickerstaff pounded the gavel on the pulpit.

Ella Mae stood by her toppled cake, scarcely breathing. She felt arms envelop her in a warm hug.

"We won." Claire's voice didn't sound smug at all.

"No, you won, Claire. I don't claim charity as a legitimate win. The bragging rights are yours." Ella Mae sighed. "Your cake is beautiful, and I'm sure it tastes divine." She squeezed Claire tightly but turned her head to Claire's ear. She whispered, "I'll get you next year."

❧

Claire settled Amos Kicklighter's cake into a box and brought it to him as he waited off to the side of the sanctuary. "Thank you for bidding, Amos. I hope you like it," Claire said.

"I like carrot cake. It's hard to ruin." He scratched his armpit before reaching for the box.

"I used carrots from the garden, and I have lots more. I'll bring some over if you'd like," Claire offered.

"Nah, I like my carrots in a cake, not on a plate. I'm no rabbit." He turned and disappeared out the side door into the balmy night air.

Chapter 29

HARLEY TOOK A SIP of ice water while waiting for Will
and Claire. His mood was wistful as he thought about the
letter. Maybe she didn't get it. Perhaps he'd never hear from her.

The bell on the door jingled as Claire and Will pushed through.
Harley waved. The sight of his friends elevated his mood.

They ordered dinner, and the conversation flowed easily.
He'd never been much of a talker, but there was something
about these two. They cared. He could trust them. They'd seen
him through his darkest hours.

He took a bite of his salad.

"Have you heard anything yet?" Claire's eyes bored into his.

"No." His voice sounded more sullen than he'd expected.

"When did you send the letter?" Will asked.

"It's been two weeks," Harley said. "I doubt that she'll reply.
But at least I tried, right?"

"Don't give up just yet. She may need time to think and put
her thoughts on paper. You never know," Claire said.

Her words tossed Harley a thread of hope.

"You're changing before our eyes. How much weight have you lost?" Claire's smile exuded pride.

"About thirty-five pounds. Between Patsy and Millie, and even Jeannie, here, I'm not gettin' to cheat on my diet." Harley chuckled as Jeannie took away his empty plate. "I've never been so hungry, but if I'm honest, it's gettin' easier and easier. Sweets don't tempt me much, and I haven't had a French fry in three months."

Will huffed. "That's determination right there."

He'd stopped drinking, cleaned out his apartment over the bar, and moved to a little house on Walnut Street. The bar was up for sale, and he'd tried to make amends with his daughter. Best of all, his newfound faith had afforded him inexplicable peace.

They finished dinner and began the stroll home. The clouds were dark, and a summer storm threatened, so they quickened their pace as they turned onto Walnut Street. Before they parted ways, Harley pulled on the door of his mailbox and removed a handful of papers.

A blue envelope caught his eye.

"What's this here?" He turned it over to see the postmark. "It's Rebecca," he said, feeling his knees buckle.

"Open it," Claire squealed.

"Let's give him privacy," Will said. "He may not want to share something so personal."

"I'm glad you're here. Let's go inside."

Harley led them into the gray cottage. The living room was filled with handsome new furniture Millie had chosen for him. They sat on the comfortable sofa, and he ripped open the envelope.

He read the page silently. *"Dear Harley, Thank you for your letter. I've thought about you often. Mom spoke only kindly of you, but she said you were sick. I didn't know what she meant, and she wouldn't elaborate. I could tell she missed you. It made her sad when I asked about you.*

Mom died a couple of years ago. Cancer. She left me information about you and how to make contact.

I went to the address, but I chose not to go in when I realized it was a bar. I supposed you were an alcoholic, so the bar confirmed my suspicions. I didn't want to be disappointed—to have to accept that booze kept you from us all these years.

I do forgive you. Thank you for asking. I hope you can maintain your sobriety for the rest of your life.

You said you want to see me. I would like that. I remember you. I've thought about the way you used to read books to me before tucking me in at night. I remember going to the creek to feed the ducks. I've missed you. Sincerely, Rebecca." Harley handed the letter to Will and Claire and trudged down the hall.

He dropped to his knees on the floor by his bed, tears streaming down his face—tears of sorrow for the loss of Danielle and gratitude for her kindness toward him all those years, for speaking kindly and not turning his daughter against him, tears for the privilege of apologizing to Rebecca and, most of all, her offer of forgiveness.

He'd see his daughter.

Thank you, God.

Harley returned to the living room, his eyes puffy and joy-filled. "It's a miracle. I'd resigned myself to the idea of never seeing her again. I didn't expect this."

"Harley, what a kind letter. What a loving young woman she became." Claire put her hand on his arm.

"She's just like her mama," Harley said, wiping fresh tears from his eyes.

༄

Claire sat next to Josephine, filled with excitement. She couldn't imagine all the work and effort involved in Ramona's new book, nor fathom the pride she must feel holding that work in her hands.

Ella Mae waddled in with a large metal cake carrier. "We're celebrating today, so I thought the occasion deserved a proper cake. Three layers of chocolate bliss for my favorite ladies." She lifted the lid and began slicing generous wedges.

"Ramona, we're just so proud of your great accomplishment. You wrote a *book*." Rita lifted her hands and clapped them together, bracelets jingling. The room erupted in applause. "You are center stage today. We turn our attention to you and chapter one, hot off the presses."

"Thanks to all of you for your editing help and letting me tell your stories. I hope you like it." She lifted a stack of books from her tote bag and passed them around the table. "A copy for each of you before I begin. My gift to you for all the encouragement along the way. I couldn't have done it without you."

Claire looked at the cover—a shot of Main Street back in the day.

"Okay, here we go, and for the record, I've taken liberties— no one can know every detail for certain." Ramona looked around the table. A giggle escaped.

Walters Bluff is a small town in Washington State surrounded by dairy farms and vast fields of wheat, barley, corn, and alfalfa—there's not a bluff for miles.

The story of Walters Bluff begins in Colorado with the birth of Walter Wickham. Born in 1853, Walter was the youngest of three boys. He grew up hiking in the mountains, building forts beneath the pines, sketching birds and wildlife, and fishing rivers and streams. Walter was tall and thin—a mop of auburn curls adding to his height.

His father and grandfather built fine furniture and taught the boys the craft. Walter, however, overflowed with creativity, carving tall trees in the legs of tables, birds, and animals in the striations and swirls of maple and pine. But he also had an itch for adventure. He'd heard good things about the new state of Washington and longed to see it for himself.

He left home after his twentieth birthday, traveling several weeks before passing through Walkersville, a settlement known for fertile soil. In the distance, he heard tinkling, like chimes in the wind. Walter followed the sweet sound to Adelaide Creek, a picturesque stream of clear water. Along the banks, apple trees dripped with pink blossoms and the promise of a hearty crop.

Cresting the hill just beyond the stream, a cabin was set back from the road, surrounded by newly planted fields. A tidy fence of thin logs protected a small garden off to the side. In it, rhubarb sprouted, and peas peeked just above the soil.

A weathered sign hung on a fencepost. *'Welcome.'* His stomach rumbled, and with nothing to lose, he knocked on the door.

The decision changed his life.

A young woman answered.

Flustered, Walter stuttered, "I s-saw your sign and wondered if you'd have something to eat?"

The girl smiled. Her periwinkle eyes made Walter's knees buckle.

A large man appeared behind her. "I'm Larson Miller, and this is my daughter, Rebecca." The man offered his hand. "Supper's almost ready if you'd like to join us."

Walter shook Mr. Miller's calloused hand and tried not to stare at beautiful Rebecca. "I thank you kindly."

"I'll set another place at the table." Rebecca blushed and hurried away.

After a hearty meal, Mr. Miller invited Walter to stay in the barn for the night. The next day, he asked Walter for help moving the cattle to greener pastures, and over the next few weeks, he taught Walter how to tend the livestock.

While Walter worked, Rebecca stole his heart. When it was time to harvest the corn, Walter asked Mr. Miller for her hand in marriage.

With the help of neighbors, the two men built a cabin on the rise by the creek. It was finished as the first snowflakes fell.

Walter and Rebecca exchanged vows under a frosty tangle of grapevines twisting over an arbor in the garden.

Walter whittled and carved in front of the fire that first winter, re-telling his grandpa's stories to his bride.

When spring melted the snow, Walter built a workshop, carved a sign, and hung it on a post by the road: "Wickham's Fine Furniture." The sign's beauty compelled anyone passing to knock on the door. By autumn, Walter filled orders for tables, chairs, and cupboards—enough business to keep him building and carving through the following winter.

A few years and three mop-haired boys later, Walter had a glowing reputation, and his business thrived. He built a proper shop by the road, and Rebecca lined the shelves with jars of preserves and vegetables from her large garden. They stocked cloth and sundries to sell to their neighbors and those passing through.

Folks began settling beyond the creek.

One stormy summer day, Harley Bushkin blew into the area. He was rough around the edges, and folks weren't sure what to make of him.

Walter invited Harley to dinner.

"We need a watering hole in these parts," Harley said as he licked his plate.

He built the saloon, and business boomed as travelers and neighbors wet their whistles after buying supplies at Walter's shop.

It wasn't long before another building began to take shape across the road from the saloon.

Harley didn't notice. He was too busy playing poker and winning the money of unwitting travelers after getting them drunk.

Walter built a little clapboard church.

One day, as Walter and Rebecca stocked the shop's shelves, Harley burst through the door. "Why did you build a church across from my saloon?"

"We need a place where folks can worship God together." Walter smiled.

Harley scowled and marched out of the shop.

A few days later, papers tacked to fences and doors fluttered in the breeze, announcing a meeting on the banks of Adelaide Creek.

On a warm fall evening, families arrived with pies and cobblers to share. The air hummed with voices discussing why Harley Bushkin would call such a meeting.

They didn't wonder for long. He heaved his portly physique onto a stump. Talking ceased, and the only sound was the trickling creek. All eyes were on Harley, and Walter thought he looked a little uneasy.

"I called this meetin' to declare that I'm the new mayor of a town heretothere ... er ... heretofore established on the land between the creek and the hill beyond the Smiths' place." His voice cracked slightly. He paused as if to let his announcement sink in. "I'm calling it Bushkinville."

Someone coughed or perhaps choked, and Walter heard a few folks chuckle.

"Now, wait just a minute, Harley, that's not how it works. We need to vote," a farmer said.

One of his faithful customers disagreed. "Harley's proved himself a savvy businessman. He'd be a fine mayor."

Walter said, "I think a vote is a proper way to proceed. We'll vote on Sunday after church."

"We don't need to vote!" Harley appeared flustered by the suggestion.

Walter watched the back-and-forth between supporters and dissenters. They battled with words for a few minutes before their fists clenched in preparation for a brawl.

Walter jumped onto a log and lifted his arms. "Wait, just a minute. Surely, there is a better way to work this out."

Harley swung his head to look at Walter, his bloodshot eyes wide open. "I have an idea, Walter," he said. Why don't you and I settle this? We'll play a hand of poker for it. Five-Card Draw. I win; I'm the mayor. You win; everyone votes." He put on a smug smile.

"Name the day," Walter said, surprising Harley and everyone else with his agreement.

Rebecca shot Walter a look of disappointment. There was a collective moan from the anxious crowd. It was a foregone conclusion that Harley would win.

"Saturday night, in the saloon," Harley snarled.

"Saturday night, on the church steps," Walter countered.

"Walter!" Rebecca's eyes flashed blue fury. "Poker on the church steps?"

"Have it your way." Harley turned and trudged away.

"What *are* you thinking, Walter? Have you lost your mind?"

Rebecca's angry brow set Walter back. "Trust me."

"I hope you know what you're doing." Rebecca lifted her skirt as she climbed the hill toward home.

Saturday night was chilly, but folks arrived early for the showdown despite the weather.

Harley and Walter sat on the wide wooden planks leading to the church's door. The local farrier dealt the cards—five to each man, face down. Harley and Walter scrutinized them.

Harley's eyes revealed nothing.

Walter looked at Rebecca and mouthed, "Not good."

Harley didn't blink. He laid down a card, and he was dealt another.

Walter examined his cards. After a moment, he lay one down.

Harley's face remained unreadable.

Walter grimaced. He scratched his head. Looking at Rebecca, a deep sigh left his chest.

The tiniest of smiles formed on Harley's dry lips.

"Gentleman, it's time to reveal your hands," the dealer said in a cracking voice, beads of sweat glistening on his brow.

Harley slammed his cards on the table with a whoop. "Full house; queens full of fives."

Walter's face fell.

Harley stuck out his chest and stood up. "Whatcha got there?"

"Well, it's not good, Harley." Walter slowly laid his fan of cards on the step. "For you."

Harley cursed. A royal flush. His face turned red as he asked, "You said it wasn't good."

Walter laughed, then shrugged. "I guess you're not the only one who can bluff."

Most of the crowd cheered, except a few who quietly shuffled toward the saloon to drown their sorrows.

Harley followed them, kicking dust along the way.

"The election is tomorrow after church," Walter announced. "We'll vote for our mayor and the name of our new town."

The small crowd buzzed. But no one questioned who would be mayor.

The following day, Walter led the first church service. He prayed for a blessing on the election and their new town. He asked God for wisdom in choosing a name that would honor both God and the community. He prayed that this piece of the country would be a resting place for the weary and a haven of God's grace to all who called it home.

A cowbell called the locals to the church for the vote. Folks trickled in and cast their ballots. A total of forty-two votes were counted by Mayor Bell of Walkersville.

"Your new mayor is Mr. Walter Wickham, and your new town shall be called Walter's Bluff." Most of the townspeople cheered, but a few turned and walked to Harley's place to drink away the sting of defeat.

Walter gave a humble acceptance speech, thanking his neighbors for their confidence. At home, he carved two signs to post on the road, one facing east and one facing west, to let travelers know that they were entering the fine community of Walters Bluff. The apostrophe was dropped in a humble effort to remove the focus from himself.

The story was told for miles around. Walter was a hero, defeating Harley at his own game. Those whom Harley had swindled stopped at Walter's store to shake his hand.

Though Harley was a sore loser, kindness is hard to resist. A few days later, Walter strode into the saloon with a freshly baked blackberry pie.

"Just put it on the bar—and tell Rebecca I thank her kindly," Harley called over his shoulder.

"Will you join us for supper this Sunday?" Walter asked.

"Nah," he grunted.

"The offer stands," Walter said, tipping his hat.

A few weeks passed before the offer was accepted. Harley couldn't resist Rebecca's plate-licking good grub—or Walter's friendship.

Ramona closed the book and looked up at the faces circling the table.

"I love that story," Rita said, flipping through the book. "I'm just so proud of all your hard work on this project."

"I've lived here for over twenty years and haven't heard that story," Joan added.

"Well, I did take creative liberty in places, but it's the story that's been told and retold in our family for generations, and I'm certain it's fairly accurate."

"What a wonderful account. I had no idea. I always wondered where the bluff was," Claire said. "That story explains a lot about our Harley's roots." Claire held the book to her chest as if it were a treasure. "It gives me a greater perspective of where he came from and how far he's come."

"It does," Millie agreed

Josephine took Claire's hand. "How far we've all come."

Chapter 30

A CIRCLE OF COLORFUL TENTS transformed the courthouse lawn. Artists and community organizations set up shop to celebrate Founders Day. A stage erected at one end faced a vast expanse of green grass where people would sit on blankets and enjoy music and entertainment all weekend.

Claire traipsed along the sidewalk in a row of ladies, each clutching a box of books. It was a beautiful day—the air thick with excitement. They found Ramona's table draped with a banner: *Ramona Wickham, Local Author.*

"You're a celebrity!" Claire set her box on the table.

Ramona's face flushed. "The library made that sign. It seems so boastful."

"Boastful? How?" Joan said. "You *are* an author.".

"If I ever become an author, I'm going to knit me a sweater that says *Ella Mae, Author* right smack on the front of it. Mark my words, I'll do it." Ella Mae didn't crack a smile.

"I suppose I still don't think it's real," Ramona said.

Josephine reached over and pinched her on the arm.

"Ouch—what did you do that for?"

"Oh, it's real, Ramona, it's real." Josephine pulled the lid off a box.

Walters Bluff, Stories of a Small Town by Ramona Wickham. With a background of aqua and a scene of Main Street circa 1912 in sepia, the stunning cover invited people to explore the history of a little town filled with characters.

Claire arranged the books on the table, leaving enough space for book signing.

"You don't really think anyone will want me to sign a book, do you?" Ramona clutched Claire's arm. "That's silly."

"Of course they will. That's what authors do," Claire said. "I have mine in my bag. As soon as you sit down, you're signing it."

"Oh, for heaven's sake. Who will sit with me and keep me from running away?" Ramona's eyes, filled with fear, looked around the circle of ladies.

"Me," Josephine said. "I'll do it."

"I will, too," Joan said.

"I want to," announced Rita, and the other ladies volunteered as well.

"We'll take shifts then," Ella Mae said.

And so they did until Ramona ran out of books early Saturday afternoon.

"I am so blessed," she said as she and Claire folded the tablecloth. "Everyone's been so nice, and they've said such kind things. It was worth all the hard work."

"I'm glad. It's a wonderful tribute to this special place." Claire smiled. "You have every reason to be proud."

"I am … I am a little proud."

Harley fidgeted at a table in the corner of The Daily Brew. He watched the door, his heart pounding. He'd waited a long time for this day. What would he do when she approached him? Should he hug her? Hold out his hand for a shake?

I'll let her make the first move.

The door swung open, and a petite woman with dark brown hair and shocking blue eyes glanced around the shop. Harley stood, watching. His mouth turned up in a smile as the woman spotted him. She headed toward him, but Harley, forgetting his decision, also approached her. He held his hand out, but she brushed it aside, embracing him.

He remembered a scene from twenty years before. Harley opened the front door as Danielle tucked Rebecca into bed. Rebecca heard him come in and ran to him, jumping into his arms. That was the last time he'd held her. Now, she squeezed his neck. She sniffled. He smelled her perfume and touched her hair.

His daughter was a woman now—the ache of squandered time filled his heart.

"You look so different," Rebecca said.

"You're beautiful. Just like your mama." Harley blinked away tears as they wandered to the table.

"I was so happy to receive your letter. I have vivid memories of you. I always dreamed you'd get well, and this moment would happen."

"I wasn't sick. I chose alcohol over my family, and I'm sorry I made that choice. I abandoned you and your mother, and I know I caused a lot of pain. I robbed myself of time—time with your mama, with you. What grieves me most is that I can't make it up to you, and I am so very sorry. I wish I could have told your mom how sorry I was before she died."

"I do, too. She was disappointed. She never married again. She felt rejected." Rebecca looked down, then back to Harley. "I'm not saying this to hurt you. I just think you should know."

"I need to know it, even though it's hard to hear." Harley took a breath.

"She'd be happy we're meeting today." Rebecca touched his hand. "She wanted this; she told me so before she died."

It took him a moment to digest her words. He wanted to turn back time—to fix all the wrongs he'd done. But he could offer this: "If you see fit, I'd like to be a family again."

"I'd like that. I've always wanted that." She hesitated a moment. "As long as you're sober. I don't want to be around a drunk."

She sure doesn't mince words.

Just like her mama.

"I'm sober. I haven't had a drink since before Christmas. And I want to tell you something else about me." His blue eyes found hers. "I don't need alcohol. I've accepted the grace of God—He is all I need."

Rebecca's smile grew. "I had a speech prepared to tell you all about my faith, about God's grace. I spent hours practicing in the mirror." She laughed.

"I'm learning a lot about grace, about God's plans. Golly, I have stories to tell you."

Rebecca moved her chair next to his. "I have something else to tell you." She held up her left hand. "I'm engaged."

"You don't say? Tell me about him." Harley laughed, his voice low and steady, as he relaxed in conversation with his daughter.

"His name is Lyle. He's a history teacher at our local high school. We met about a year ago. He came into the museum, and I showed him around, and the rest is history—pun intended." She giggled. "That's our schtick when people ask us how we met."

Harley chuckled. "I hope I can meet him someday."

"You can meet him now if you don't mind. He's just around the corner, waiting in the car. He wanted to be nearby in case you were a disappointment." She smiled. "You aren't."

Relief washed over his heart. "Bring him in."

It was a two-for-one kind of day. Harley was getting a son in the bargain. The three talked for hours, moving their meeting to the diner for lunch. Questions were plentiful and difficult, and the answers lengthy.

Jeannie quietly refilled drinks as they talked.

As the afternoon wore on, Dottie set slices of blackberry pie before them without a word.

Harley shared the story about Guy. He told them about the accident, the gossip, and how Bertie saved his life with her forgiveness. As he shared, he wept. "I don't like to think it took Guy's death to lead me to Christ, but it took me down to rock bottom and left me with nothing. Sometimes that's what it takes to see the need for a Savior."

When the time arrived to say goodbye, Lyle cleared his throat. "Mr. Bushkin, I'd like to ask you for your daughter's hand in marriage. I know it's a little late, and I asked her first, but I want to do this right since you're here and you'll be a part of our lives—May I marry your daughter?"

A sob hitched in Harley's voice. His mind flashed to the day months before when Claire and Will received the joyful call from their son at this very table. Harley recalled the pain of regret and his acceptance that he'd never feel that joy.

How can this be happening?

"Son, I'd be honored if you'd marry my daughter." As he said the words, his heart cried out in thanksgiving to the God who allowed him to utter them.

Chapter 31

CLAIRE STOOD amid a plethora of boxes, some empty, while a few remained unopened. It was the last of her mother's antique stash. The storeroom in the shop was nearly full, but the thought of going to flea markets to stock the shelves excited her. She stacked a set of china on a shelf. The smattering of tiny blue forget-me-nots on each piece brought a smile. She was with her mother when she purchased the dishes at an estate sale two summers ago. Surprisingly, it felt good to sell it. Claire sighed. She'd had exquisite taste—nearly every piece sold as soon as it was placed on a shelf. *Thanks, Mom.*

She brought a small, heavy box to the table and cut through the tape. The flaps opened to reveal a ball of bubble wrap. Claire looked at the side of the box. In her mother's hand, one word: Keep. She began peeling away the tape. Inside, an old blue and white Asian pitcher with jagged veins of gold running through it. A paper fluttered to the floor as she tipped it over to look for a mark. Claire picked it up and saw more of her mother's writing:

God uses kintsugi.

Claire held the pitcher in her hand, examining it. It was beautiful, the gold shimmering against the blue, making the white shine like a cloud on a summer day. She ran her fingers over the jagged gold lines—barely an interruption in the smooth porcelain. It *was* broken. Repaired with *gold*?

Claire grabbed her phone and searched *Kintsugi*. She discovered that when pottery was broken, instead of seeing it as garbage and worthless, the Japanese tradition was to repair it and make it more beautiful—more valuable.

A message from Mom ... from God.

Tears filled her eyes as she pondered the metaphor in her hands. Was forgiveness the gold with which God would redeem her pain, bitterness, and grief?

Claire placed the pitcher in the box and hurried home.

She made a beeline to her closet, pulled the carved box off the shelf, and carried it to her desk. *"Help me, Lord."* She ran her fingers over the hills and valleys of each carved flower, leaf, and letter of her name, thinking of her dad and mom. A tear dropped to the box.

But then Claire's mouth bent into a hint of a smile. This box held peace. It had the whole time—she was too stubborn to accept it. The deacon's—Richard's—apology would end this awful cycle of bitterness and anger.

It was time.

Claire moved the latch and lifted the lid. The envelope met her gaze. She picked it up and ran her finger under the flap. It popped open easily. She removed the page and unfolded it.

Claire,
Someone overheard your conversation with Gina in
the women's restroom last Sunday. They said you were

angry that I didn't admit to being drunk.

I wasn't drunk, Claire. I'd had two drinks. Two drinks are hardly a problem. Unfortunately, I dropped a french fry and looked down at the floor to find it. That's when I ran the red light and hit your parents' car. My refusal of the breath test meant nothing more than bad judgment amid utter despair.

It was an accident. I am sick that it happened. Do you think I don't mourn them, too? Do you think I wanted this to happen? Do you think I don't care? I just want the facts to be accurate.

I forgive you for telling lies about me. Your parents would want us to heal. Don't you think?

In Him,
Richard

The page fell to the floor as darkness moved in from the periphery. She blinked her eyes and gasped for breath.

A rebuke? He wrote me a rebuke, and all this time, I thought it was a letter of apology.

Heat rose from her chest to her face as anger and resentment fought for supremacy. She deserved to feel both. He deserved all her rage.

The letter dropped to the floor—her hands squeezed into fists.

But something was different. Her anger didn't satisfy, not even in this moment.

Her softened heart couldn't bear the stinging thorns of bitterness.

Her gut wrenched as she thought of the man who taught Sunday school every week and served communion. He was a fixture at her old church for all the decades she attended and probably still was—even though ....

Claire began to mull the pain she'd suffered, and somehow, her mind moved to Richard's life as well. At first, she resisted the thought. *Why should I care about him?*

"Because God does." The truth jumped out of her mouth.

No amount of anger and bitterness had changed what he did. How many tears of rage had she shed—and for what?

Forgiveness was still the answer. It was still the only way to .... Harley's words filled her mind. "Bertie said she has perfect peace." His gravelly voice echoed the words in her mind over and over.

Perfect peace.

She knew what she had to do.

❧

Claire called Will to tell him her plan, threw a change of clothes and a toothbrush into a bag, and drove all night. She arrived in the town she used to call home at nine o'clock in the morning.

She stopped next to a row of manicured boxwood—a perfectly kept yard. Tears threatened her resolve, but she blinked them away as she unbuckled her seatbelt. She'd rehearsed what to say repeatedly in the hours it took to drive here, but now she couldn't remember a word she planned to say.

Was Richard home? What if his wife answered the door? What if they were on vacation?

Claire looked at herself in the rear-view mirror. "Forgive him."

Excitement rose in her heart. No fear, no angst, nothing but peace. It was as if she were backing a dump truck to the deacon's door—unloading the bricks of the wall she'd allowed the enemy to erect against grace, peace, and all the good things God wanted to give. She nearly flew to the door and pushed the bell.

No answer.

No sounds came from the house.

No one was home.

Claire wasn't sure where to go, so she drove to her old church. She pushed open the large glass door and breathed in the familiar scent of pine cleaner and old books. Her eyes scanned the church attendance board—a relic from her childhood. Her heart ached—so many memories tainted by so much hurt.

She wandered to the sanctuary. The pews were gone, replaced with padded chairs. The carpet was blue rather than the maroon of the eighties. Life here had continued despite all that had happened.

Claire heard a booming laugh coming from a conference room.

Richard.

She froze momentarily and listened, then headed down the hall to the voices wafting from the open door.

All conversation stopped when she entered the doorway.

"Claire." The deacon said her name, nothing else. Another man sat with him—two Bibles open on the table.

"I'd like to speak with you privately, if possible." Claire's calm voice surprised her.

"There is no need for privacy." Richard's smile was large and forced. "What can I do for you?"

Is his lip shaking?

"I don't need anything, but I have something for you." Claire took a breath. "I forgive you for driving drunk and killing my parents." Claire looked into his eyes. It was the first time he'd made eye contact with her since the accident.

"I wasn't drunk."

"You and I and Will know the truth." Claire held his gaze. "God knows the truth."

The deacon looked away and turned to the other man. "What a bitter woman."

The man stood. "I should go." He grabbed his Bible and hurried from the room.

Claire watched him leave. "You're right. I have been bitter, but I won't hold onto the hurt anymore. I can't. It's too much of a burden." She stood taller. "Isn't the burden heavy for you, too?"

She focused on Richard. He averted his eyes, looking to the floor. Silence filled the room. He appeared to be overwhelmed with fear—fear of the truth? Fear of everyone knowing what he'd done? Was he afraid to face it himself? *How exhausting that must be.*

"Richard, even though you deny what you have done, I still forgive you." Claire exhaled.

The weight of nearly two years of striving fell from her shoulders.

Peace flooded her heart.

He opened his mouth as if to speak but said nothing. Richard's eyes met hers.

Claire held his gaze. A few silent moments passed. "Well, I suppose that's all I have to say." She turned and headed toward the door.

There's one more thing.

Claire's heart pounded as she pivoted, facing Richard once more.

"God bless you, Richard." Claire's eyes filled with tears as she offered Guy's blessing—the blessings of her parents, *her* blessing on the man who had devastated her world in an instant.

Richard's eyebrows raised as if in surprise.

She smiled, turned, and ambled down the hall to the foyer of the building that used to be her church home, then a place of pain, and … *What is it to me now? These people have been deceived.*

"I can't hold anything against you," Claire said the words out loud, to the walls. To herself.

She looked again at the old church attendance board. The ache was gone—her heart washed clean.

I'm free.

Chapter 32

CLAIRE, JOSEPHINE, AND FERN worked late into the night, finishing the arrangements for the wedding. It would be a beautiful day—no doubt about it.

Oscar popped by as they finished Laurel's bouquet.

"Get out." Fern chastised him as she tried to hide the flowers. "You can't see her flowers."

Oscar's hand flew up to cover his eyes. "I thought I couldn't see her dress. I didn't know it was bad luck to see her bouquet."

"I don't know if it is, but I'm not taking any chances," Fern said. "What do you want?"

"I saw the light on as I drove by, so I thought I'd check and see if you needed anything, that's all. I probably won't sleep much tonight anyway. Honestly, I just want tomorrow to hurry up and get here."

"How sweet." Fern turned him around and pushed him out the door. "Thanks, but no thanks. You've got to rest up for the big day. Tomorrow you're marrying the girl of your dreams."

"And I'm getting the best sister-in-law in the bargain." Oscar opened his truck door. "See you tomorrow."

⁂

Claire and Will arrived at Harley's house at half-past one.

"We've got to be at the church by two," Harley said, beads of sweat sparkling on his brow.

"We're just fixing your tie. We'll be there in plenty of time. It's only three blocks away." Claire chuckled. "Come here, let me see what we're working with." She fiddled with the tie a bit and made a perfect Windsor knot. "Harley, you look so handsome."

"Thanks, Claire."

Millie appeared through the door.

"You are the picture of loveliness," Will declared.

"You're too kind," Millie said, dipping into a curtsy.

"My, oh my, aren't I the lucky one?" Harley reached out his hand. Millie took it, and he twirled her—her lavender chiffon dress billowed.

"All right, you two. We'd better go to the church." Claire took Will's hand. Together, they walked to St. John's Catholic Church.

Claire helped with the final preparations. A tent on the courthouse lawn was filled with tables, each topped with a beautiful bouquet in a weathered vase.

⁂

Harley and the other groomsmen posed for photos.

Between poses, Harley asked Oscar, "How're your feet feelin'? They're not cold, are they?"

"Hot, they're nice and hot, and it's not because of the ninety-degree day, neither." Oscar's smile spanned the width of his face.

⁂

Fern beamed as Laurel and Oscar stood before God, family, and friends in a room streaked with sunlight filtered through one-hundred-year-old stained glass. Beams of blue, red, purple, and brilliant yellow turned the sanctuary of St. John's into a kaleidoscope of happiness. Laurel was beautiful in a strapless, tea-length, white lace dress made from pieces of her mother's high-necked, long-sleeved wedding gown, complete with a long train. Oscar sported a bow tie, clean fingernails, and a trimmed beard. His eyes never left his bride.

The vows were said, rings exchanged, and the celebration began.

The DJ announced, "Please welcome Mr. and Mrs. Oscar Peabody to the dance floor." Guests fanned themselves with paper plates and cheered as Laurel and Oscar made their way through the throng to the dance floor. Mayor Bickerstaff rose, holding his accordion. Laurel stood on one side, Oscar on the other. As the first chords began, he extended his hand, and she floated to him and took it. They waltzed to "Silent Night," the song that started it all.

A smile bloomed on Fern's face. It suited them perfectly, dancing to a Christmas carol in the middle of August. Why not, after all? When the song's last chords faded, Oscar kissed Laurel's mouth, causing Sage to duck and run.

"Ewwwww!" he cried, racing from the tent.

Fern threw her head back and laughed, reveling in her son's antics, her sister's happiness, and the fact that she had come through the heartbreaking end of her marriage a stronger and wiser woman.

❧

Ella Mae glanced over the buffet, acknowledging that if any occasion deserved to be perfect, it was this wedding. Laurel asked her to oversee the reception, and she was pleased as punch to do it. Her only contribution was the miniature white cupcakes with chocolate buttercream icing. The buttercream drooped in the heat, but she refused to get worked up.

She added parsley to a platter of chicken wings and tossed parmesan into the vat of macaroni and cheese. It smelled divine, but what it really needed was a sprinkle of smoked paprika. She looked through the box of garnishes. No paprika. She took a deep breath. She was just an overseer, not the cook. *Let it go.*

Folks strolled through for seconds. Ella Mae fussed over the presentation, glancing at the cupcake table. She couldn't help but notice that, droopy buttercream notwithstanding, her cupcakes stole the show—but that was neither here nor there. *I can't help it if I always strive for excellence.*

Claire watched Harley twirl Millie to the middle of the dance floor. They swayed to and fro, his arms around her waist, her head resting on his barrel chest despite the fact it wasn't a slow dance.

"What do you think of those two?" Claire squeezed Will's hand.

"I think Harley's found himself a sweetheart."

She smiled. She thought of the rough, leathery man she'd met a year ago. The man she watched now was a new Harley— a changed man. He was who he wanted to be and who she had grown to believe he was. "Yeah, he's found a sweetheart."

Bertie watched the dance floor fill to capacity. She and Ramona picked at their food.

"What a beautiful wedding," Bertie said. "Laurel is the most beautiful bride."

"Yes, and Oscar sure is smitten. My goodness, how he looks at her." Ramona fanned herself.

"You want to dance?" Bertie asked.

"Who me?" Ramona giggled.

"Yeah, why not? Guy would want me to have a good time, and you don't need a fella to dance." Her heart beat with excitement at the thought of dancing. How long had it been?

"You are so right. Let's go."

Bertie and Ramona found a bit of space on the dance floor. They danced and twirled each other, giggling all the while.

When the song ended, a slow dance began.

Bertie felt a tap on her shoulder.

"Can I have this dance? My wife is dancing with another man." Will pointed.

She looked across the dance floor to see Sage and Claire dancing a waltz.

"Oh my, you may. Do you mind, Ramona?"

"Not at all."

Bertie took Will's hand, and she giggled as he swung her around. Will was her son now. The events of the last year had endeared him to her heart. He laughed as she stepped on his toes, and she reveled in the comfort of his and Claire's friendship. This day, this dance, this moment of joy was an unexpected blessing.

Ramona sat at the table and took a bite of a cupcake. *Delicious. Ella Mae's outdone herself.* She looked down to see one of her thigh-high stockings around her shin. *Doggone it!* She bent over and hiked it up as discreetly as she could.

"No sense wasting a perfectly good waltz."

Still tugging at her stocking, she looked over to see Josephine's sensible shoes tapping a beat similar but not equal to the song's rhythm.

"I never thought I'd see the day," she said, "*You* want to dance? Don't you think dancing's sinful?"

"If it is, I don't want to know."

Ramona noticed Josephine's eyes. She was content and happy, and the woman wanted to have fun.

The two of them skipped onto the dance floor like schoolgirls at recess.

Chapter 33

HARLEY GLANCED at Millie as they drove to Glenwood.

His stomach fluttered.

They stopped at antique stores along the way. One thing they had in common was the attraction to discarded treasure. Perhaps it spoke to their histories of rejection and struggle—or maybe they just liked junk.

When he invited Millie to visit his daughter, she jumped at the chance to meet Rebecca and Lyle.

"I want my daughter to meet my girl," Harley had said.

The blush on Millie's cheeks told him she liked the idea of being his girl.

How had this happened? When had he let down his guard? Maybe the timing was right. He was ready for a risk, ready to give love another shot.

They met Rebecca and Lyle at the museum for a private tour. As they strolled through each floor, Rebecca shared her knowledge of the area's history. She regaled them with details about each exhibit, from Nez Perce Indian artifacts to mining equipment and methods, as well as local wildlife.

Harley marveled at the young woman with an encyclopedic knowledge of each subject. His heart swelled with pride. What a blessing to know her. What a gift.

When the tour ended, they wandered to the restaurant next door for lunch.

"Millie and I have a lot of Walters Bluff memorabilia between us. We're considering making an official, more formal display to share with Walters Bluff. A little museum of our own."

"I'd love to see what you have and how you preserve it. Where do you plan to show your collection?"

"I'm sellin' the bar, and with some of the proceeds, I'll buy the empty space next door—the old camera shop just closed. It's small and won't be fancy, but it's something. At least some of our history and stories will be preserved for future generations. That's what we're up to." Harley leaned back in his chair and put his arm around Millie's shoulders.

"Why don't you turn the bar into a museum? Make the family legacy into something good, something beautiful?"

"I like how you think, but the space next door would need fewer renovations. A guy contacted me last week about converting the bar into a restaurant. It seems like a good idea. We could use another sit-down restaurant in Walters Bluff besides the diner." Harley smiled.

"I used to love the diner when I was little," Rebecca said. She took a sip of soda. "I'd be happy to help with proper preservation and display. Whatever you need, just holler."

"We're going to organize what we have and decide what to use. We'd love your expertise," Harley said.

They finished lunch and said their goodbyes.

Harley was satisfied with the beginnings of a renewed relationship with his daughter. It was easy—natural.

Harley and Millie drove for several miles in silence.

When they stopped at a red light, Millie took Harley's hand. "What a wonderful day." She sighed.

"It is wonderful," he said. He looked into her eyes. What did he see there?

Kindness. Joy.

Love?

His heart leaped as he leaned over and kissed her.

॰

Claire removed the newspaper wrapped around an old vase.

"What's all this here?" Will straightened his duty belt and filled a water bottle.

"Just going through the antiques we found at the flea market last week." Claire set the relic on the kitchen table.

"I'm glad you're back to doing what you've always enjoyed."

"Me, too." Claire kissed her husband before he headed to the door.

"Enjoy those beat-up vases."

"They're weathered vessels, dear." Claire smiled. *Weathered vessels.* She opened her laptop, and the words flowed.

Chapter 34

CLAIRE LOOKED around the yard. The leaves had turned brilliant yellow, orange, and red almost overnight. She admired the landscape while she sipped coffee. Geese flew overhead, honking a greeting as they skimmed the trees on their way to Adelaide Creek.

She ambled inside to refill her cup and wandered down the hall, looking at pictures. She stopped at a photo of her kids with her parents, taken just a year before their deaths. The journey from that photo to this day was one she couldn't fathom.

How her life had changed.

How her faith had grown—deepened.

Would she change anything? Would she walk the path again? No, not again, but she certainly saw how the Lord had worked in every bit of it.

She topped off her coffee and settled back into a chair on the porch.

"Yoo-hoo," Bertie called.

"Hi, Bertie." Claire watched her friend shuffle through the gate. They hugged, and Claire noted Bertie's puffy eyes. "Are you okay?"

"Oh gracious, this morning's been hard." A tear escaped, following the path of a crease around her perpetually upturned mouth. "I'm starting to clean out Guy's side of the closet. It's too hard to look at all his clothes hanging there." She took in a long breath. "I used to be so frustrated with Guy's persnickety ways. He liked things just so—kept his things so orderly." She dabbed her eyes with a handkerchief. Claire recognized it as one of Guy's. "I miss him. I miss having someone to fuss at." She laughed despite herself. "Sometimes, I think God matches us to our opposite to annoy us—to test us. Now that Guy's gone, it's those annoying details I miss most. That man loved me and put up with all my nagging—he did so much to bring me joy all these years, things I never realized he did. Oh, Claire, pay attention to the little things."

"You two were such a beautiful example to Will and me."

"No." Bertie's voice was firm. "We quibbled too much behind closed doors. Don't think for a minute we had it all figured out. We loved each other, but we drove each other crazy."

"We admired the way you were kind to each other. You doted on him. He bragged on you when you weren't around. Did you know that?" She squeezed her hand.

"I didn't." Bertie's eyes welled again. "I've been writing down things I don't want to forget. I've already filled that journal you gave me. I might start coming to the Grace Writers."

"Oh, we'd love to have you. We can go together if you'd like."

"I'd love that. Listen, I'd like you and Will to come for dinner tonight."

"What time?"

"I'll have the pork chops ready at six."

❧

Claire put her coffee cup in the sink and picked up the newspaper on the coffee table. She turned to the back page.

Dear Wanda,
How is a shy person supposed to make friends? I'm in the sixth grade, and everybody has friends to hang out with, but I'm not included because I'm so quiet. What should I do?
Signed, Friendless.

Dear Friendless,
I used to be shy, too. Here's what I did. I looked around for the kids who weren't talking to anyone. The girl who stands at her locker at lunch, the kid who goes to the library to escape, the one sitting alone at a table in the lunchroom. I sat with them, asked questions, and started a conversation.

Tonight, when you get home, think of some questions you can ask to start a conversation. Memorize them. Find those people and talk to them. I know it's scary, but knowing they are just as uncomfortable makes it a little bit easier, doesn't it? The key to breaking out of your shell is to stop thinking about your shell. Think about other people first. Write to me again and let me know how it works.

Claire smiled. That Wanda was one wise woman.

She put a load of laundry into the dryer and folded the towels, smelling the freshness as she stacked them on the arm of the sofa. She wandered to her closet to collect the rest of the dirty clothes. As she did, her precious carved box caught her eye. With the letter gone, she felt free to enjoy her keepsakes again. Claire sat on the floor and opened it. One by one, she lifted treasures from the box. The diary from her childhood was at the bottom. She chuckled, flipping through the pages, reading excerpts of awkward teenage angst. Then she saw:

Someday, I will be an author.

She drew in a breath. Her love of the written word was here all along. It was fun to write her stories and memories. The Grace Writers encouraged her to keep writing and inspired her to write the more difficult stories. Maybe someday she'd share those, too. And Ramona's book was on the Durham County bestseller list—an inspiration.

She closed the diary and tucked it back into the box. Peace filled her heart as she completed the day's tasks.

&

"You work magic with a pork chop, Bertie." Will put his napkin on his plate. He patted his stomach in satisfaction. "Thank you for a delicious meal."

"Well, there's another reason I invited you over, more than just having company at dinnertime." Bertie seemed excited. "Come with me." She jumped up and started down the hall. "Come on, don't dilly-dally."

"We're coming." Will followed Claire. They tried to keep up as Bertie flew down the hallway. She stopped at the garage door and turned to face them.

"Will, I spoke to my boys, and they agreed with my decision wholeheartedly. You don't get a say."

"What are you talking about, Bertie?" Will wrinkled his nose.

"I want you to have Guy's workshop." The words flew out of her mouth in a gush of excitement.

"Oh, Bertie." Claire began to protest.

"Neither of you gets a say." Bertie was as stern as he'd ever seen her.

"Guy would have wanted you to have it all. He said to me, 'Bertie, I love working with
Will. He has woodworking in his bones.' Well, the boys are car people—cars, cars, cars. They've never been interested in anything without wheels. They were thrilled they wouldn't have to mess with all those tools. And I know you're strapped for space at your place, so you can leave them here and come over anytime you want to." Bertie took in a breath and held up a key. "Here, the key to the side door, a key to your workshop. It will do my heart good to hear the noise of the tools. Honestly, Will, I'd love it if you'd take it."

Will was speechless—his vision blurred by tears. He loved Guy and was blessed to spend so much time with him in his last days. It took a moment before he could speak. "Thank you, Bertie … and thank you, Guy. God bless you both." He scooped Bertie into a hug that lasted as long as it took to compose himself.

Fern's shoulders ached with the weight of the world as she opened The Weathered Vessel. It was strange being in the shop alone. Laurel's quiet demeanor seemed to fade into the background most of the time, but her happy disposition left a void. She was taking time to renovate Oscar's bachelor pad—a ranch house in the middle of a Christmas tree farm and acres of wheat in the country.

Fern sighed. Today, her divorce was on the "dissolutions" list in *The Durham County Herald*. She braced herself for awkward questions. She loved her small town, but with it came a lack of anonymity.

"Good morning." Josephine entered the shop and set her bag on the counter. "How are you? I saw the paper."

"I'm good." She looked at Josephine. The woman's face showed concern. "Sad—but I'm glad it's all over, and I can move on with my new normal."

"I'm sorry for all you've been through. You've handled everything gracefully."

Was that pride in her voice? Is she proud of me?

"Thank you, Jo." Fern smiled as she started a pot of coffee. "I'm glad you still work with me."

"Me, too. What's on the agenda for today?"

Fern took the older woman by the hand and led her to the workroom. She wandered to a tub of roses and breathed in their scent. A smile bloomed on her face. "A few arrangements for the case and an internet order. The usual dusting around the shop and not much else. A light day today."

Fern watched Josephine smile while gathering flowers and greenery. She wondered about the spinster—once crotchety, now … pleasant.

"Josephine, did you ever want to get married?" Fern regretted asking the question as soon as it left her lips.

"Yes, I suppose I did want to be married at one time. Yes, I did think marriage would be nice when I was younger." Josephine seemed to stare right through the bucket of roses.

"Why didn't you?"

"Nobody asked."

☙

Claire and Bertie entered the fellowship room to find the ladies gabbing about the goings-on in Walters Bluff.

"… Harley's feeling pretty good about it," Millie said.

"Did the bar sell?" Claire's heart pounded. This was the last piece of Harley's old life. Could it have sold so quickly?

"Yes. Harley said the man who bought it is moving to town and opening some kind of restaurant." Millie clapped her hands with excitement.

"We could use another restaurant in Walters Bluff. I hope it's Chinese food or pizza. Can you imagine not having to go all the way to Walkersville for pizza?" Joan leaned forward as she spoke, her excitement radiating through the group.

"I'd like a southern barbecue joint. But easy access to fall-off-the-bone ribs would do George in for sure." Ella Mae shook her head. "Scratch that."

"Any restaurant will be welcome. We need variety. Hamburgers and whatever slop the diner's cooking just isn't cuttin' it," Millie said.

"Ella Mae, what did you bring today? Pull that foil off. All this talk of barbecue, Chinese food, and pizza. I'm hungry!" Ramona adjusted her glasses, but they remained crooked on her face.

"I brought cookies—Red Velvet Dreams." Ella Mae removed the foil with a flourish.

"Are they cookies or bars?" Claire asked with a wink.

Ella Mae heaved a sigh. She squinted her eyes at Claire, but her mouth was turned up in a happy grin. "Technically, bars. Good catch."

"We have to look out for each other." Claire smiled at the woman she had grown to love so much.

"I've gained five pounds, and I blame you," Rita said, taking two. "Why must you tempt us so?"

"No one's forcing you to take two," snapped Josephine. "But I understand why you would."

"Saves me the trouble of reaching again." Rita's bracelets jingled as she laughed.

"Try being me." Ella Mae placed her hands on her generous bosom. "I have to lick the bowl and taste test everything I bake—quality control, don't you know. Thank the Lord, George likes a woman with meat on her bones."

"Let's get down to business. Bertie has joined us today. Bertie, what do you like to write?" Joan asked.

She smiled. "I've started to write the ponderings of my heart."

"That's just beautiful," whispered Joan.

"How eloquently put," added Rita.

"The prompt was to write about a journey. As you all know, we can write about anything, so who'd like to start? How about …"

"Claire should start," Josephine proposed in a rare outburst. "She brought Bertie, so she can go first."

"Yes, Claire, you share first." Ella Mae's chin jiggled as she nodded her agreement.

"Oh, okay, thank you, Josephine." Claire fished through her notebook for her papers.

"Well, I wrote about a journey."

"Of course you did. You always stick to the prompt." Millie winked at Claire.

"You're right. I do." She took a deep breath and began. "This is called *The Weathered Vessel*."

A journey brought me to Walters Bluff a year ago. I thought I was running *to* freedom. Freedom from my church, freedom from people who'd let me down, freedom from bitterness, freedom from grief. I didn't want to admit it then, but I was really running *away*.

I was hurt, and I'd grown comfortable in the pain of the injustice done to my family. It was somehow satisfying to wallow. But I yearned for something more … peace.

Claire reached into her tote, placing the blue, white, and gold pitcher on the table.

> My parents collected antiques. Weathered old things surrounded me my whole life. I've always thought they were beautiful, but they grew in meaning this year.
>
> I've shared that my parents were killed two years ago, but few of you know the details. A drunk driver killed them. But that's not all. The driver was a deacon from our church.

Several of the ladies drew in a breath.
Joan said, "Oh, gracious."

> I arrived in Walters Bluff with a heavy burden. Anger had chipped away at the surface of my heart, and bitterness hardened it. Then, I joined The Grace Writers. Your welcoming kindness surprised me, and as I began writing stories and sharing them with you, hope edged in.
>
> Still, a great millstone weighed on my heart. I couldn't think of my parents without the seething anger of the story that took them—the story I wasn't able to share.
>
> Then I found this verse: Hebrews 12:13 says, "Make straight paths for your feet so that what is lame may not be put out of joint but rather healed."
>
> Resentment and bitterness are a steep, treacherous path. When Guy passed away, our painful, then graceful, journey together was a beacon that led me to three words:

I forgive you.

Forgiveness is the path to peace and healing. My father said that giving forgiveness determines the quality of our lives, and receiving forgiveness, our destination in death. I know that to be true.

Weathered vessels have stories to tell. We're all broken, scratched, and worn by life and circumstance. I've learned that God doesn't waste our pain. He makes all things beautiful in His time. He patches us together using His brand of Kintsugi. Mending broken vessels with gold—creating beauty and strength in the broken places.

I don't know how this beautiful pitcher broke, but it holds a valuable treasure—a story. We, as weathered vessels, hold stories too—our testimonies of loss and pain, healing and restoration, and forgiveness given and received.

My journey ends—or rather continues—right here, with forgiveness, peace, and The Grace Writers.

Claire looked up from her paper.

Bertie put her hand on hers. "Share the whole story."

"What do you mean?" Claire dabbed at her eyes with a tissue.

"You've got a book to write. Do you need a bolt of lightning?" Josephine's mouth bent into a smile.

Claire looked around the table, taking in the gaze of each woman. "Write my story?" Her heart skipped a beat.

"Yes, do it." Ella Mae's eyes were as big as saucers. "Share all of your stories."

"Oh, I don't know …." Yet Claire's smile grew as she considered the idea.

"I'm all for it, but you must change our names to protect the innocent." Millie giggled.

"That's a great idea," Joan said. "And maybe you could make us younger and skinnier?"

"Oh, for heaven's sake." Josephine folded her arms.

Seven beautiful souls talked and laughed and nibbled on red velvet dream bars. Bertie threw her head back and laughed at something Ella Mae said. Claire hadn't seen her laugh like that in a long time.

I have no idea where to start.

Claire settled back in her chair, listening to the banter of the women she'd grown to love.

Write a book about my journey?

So she did.

Acknowledgments

I've been working on this book for more than a decade—partly because I was learning to write and partly because of fear. This is what I've learned. You're never too old. Just write the story, paint the picture, and do the thing you think you cannot do. Find people who are experts in the craft you seek to master and learn from them, then value critique for the gift that it is.

I want to thank God for saving me and loving me. The thread throughout this book is forgiveness, grace, His timing, and His unexpected plans. He is always at work, and He is so good.

I would like to thank my critique group, The Inklings—beautiful people who encouraged me, critiqued my work, and helped me make this book better. Kyle Pratt, Julie Zander, Bob Hansen, Debby Lee, Joyce Scott, Tammy Clark, James Pratt, Barbara Blakey, Carolyn Bickel, Kristie Kandoll, and Danette Emberlin-Fuhrer.

My writing journey began many years ago with Evergreen Christian Writers, led by Karen Strand and a group of ladies who inspired me and fueled my love of storytelling. It was a quirky group of fun-loving ladies. Thank you for the inspiration!

I'm so thankful for the writing group I led for many years: The Grace Writers (Becca Jansen, Lilla Glass, Allie Keil, Betty Lausch, Tina Wilbur, Tori Johnson, Donna Morse, Pamela Dickey, Virginia Schnabel, Cecelia Terhune, Jessica Wachtman, Katie Mullinax, Janet Best, Lynda Echols, Mikaela Francis, Lori Richardson, and many others who popped in occasionally). The fun we had still brings a smile to my face and joy to my heart. I am so grateful for your inspiration and encouragement to me and to each other.

My developmental editor, Kate Heister. Your expertise made this book so much better. Thank you!

I love my beautiful book cover! Thank you, Kathy Campbell!

Julie McDonald Zander, thank you for your encouragement through the years and for your hard work in helping me publish this book. You're an amazing editor and my favorite "nitpicker!"

Thank you to my many beta readers over the years. Your eagle eyes and encouragement helped me more than you'll know—most especially Donna Morse and Connie Eldridge, who read my manuscript more than once. Your input was so appreciated.

Lora Iftikhar, Brenda Orth, and Mike and Brenda Schmidt. Thank you for checking in and cheering me on. You are the best!

Kathy Knoedler, Tina Wilbur, and Twylla Jones. Although you have passed to glory, you were three of my greatest cheerleaders. I am so grateful to have been your friend.

My dad loved the written word, and read an early version of this book. He believed I could finish it, and I'm grateful he was right. Love you and miss you, Dad.

Thank you, Mom, for your endless encouragement and nudges to "Get this book published before I die!" ☺ I love you!

Thanks to my kids, Christina and Jake, Jacob and Courtney, and Emily, who are the best encouragers and more precious to me than words can express. I appreciate you and love you all very much.

Finally, a big thank you to my husband, Alex. Your faith in and support of this project have meant the world to me. I could not have finished this book without my biggest cheerleader and best friend. I love you.

Heather Morse Alexander

Ella Mae's Scones
(and Heather's too!)

3 cups flour
1¼ tablespoon baking powder
1/3 cup sugar (for sweet scones only)
1 cup cold butter, cut into small cubes (not margarine, REAL butter!)

Mix with a pastry blender until butter is well incorporated with little bits throughout. Or grate the butter into the flour mixture.

1 cup heavy cream (No substitutes!)
1 teaspoon vanilla

Mix until it mostly holds together—it will be crumbly.
Pat into two flat rounds, approx. 1–1½" thick—or make three rounds for smaller scones.
Cut each round into eight pie-shaped pieces.

Bake at 400 degrees on an ungreased cookie sheet for 14–18 minutes (depending on the size of the scones).
Bottom should be nice and brown.

Make 'em fancy!
The following combinations are delicious:

orange peel & freshly squeezed juice
crystalized ginger and vanilla (or lemon zest)

culinary lavender (add vanilla extract or lemon juice)
almond extract and poppy seed
cinnamon, vanilla, and cinnamon chips
maple syrup in place of sugar, bacon
onion, bacon, cheese of choice (omit sugar)
parmesan, rosemary (omit sugar)

Measurements for the above are to taste.

Glaze sweet scones with simple powdered sugar, cream, and juice/extract glaze if desired.

About the Author

HEATHER MORSE ALEXANDER lives in Washington State with her husband of forty years. She has three grown children and is Nana to three precious boys. She enjoys writing, traveling, watercolor painting, beachcombing, baking scones, hosting "cousin camps," and treasure hunting at flea markets and estate sales. She collects old photographs, which often inspire her stories. This is her debut novel.

Visit her blog at heathermorsealexander.com

Subscribe for news, notifications of new posts, deals, and more!

Other books by

Heather Morse Alexander

Children's Picture Books
(written exclusively for her grandsons)
Beckham's Backpack
Kai's Wild Ride

Gift Books
(en)courage(ment) for You
(en)courage(ment) for New Moms
(en)courage(ment) for Those Who Weep

Available through The Grace Writers Shop on Etsy at http://www.etsy.com/TheGraceWritersShop

Made in United States
Orlando, FL
19 November 2025

72742836R00184